WHISPERED MELODIES

LOST CREEK, TEXAS HILL COUNTRY
BOOK FIVE

ALEXA ASTON

OLIVERHEBERBOOKS

Cover art by Dar Albert at Wicked Smart Designs

Published by Oliver-Heber Books

0 9 8 7 6 5 4 3 2 1

PROLOGUE

*T*ucker Young pulled his wife into his arms and gave her a tender kiss. Then he rested his hand against her protruding belly. Josie was over six months along now, and they would be having a boy right around Christmastime. He only wished his dad could be here to meet the baby and get to know his first grandchild.

But Travis Young had passed away suddenly two months ago from a heart attack. At least his dad had known they were having a boy. The couple hadn't settled on a name at that time, but once Tucker lost his dad, Josie had suggested that they name the boy Travis after his father. The suggestion had touched him, and he hoped that a part of his dad would live on in this baby.

"Are you sure you should stay for the show?" he asked. "There'll be a few people smoking, and I don't like you to be around that. It's bad for the baby."

Josie cupped his face with her hands, kissing him

1

lightly. "If someone is smoking nearby, I'll simply get up and move, Tucker. I want to be here tonight for you. You're going to be playing your own songs for this crowd. I want to support you in every way I can. Once the baby comes, I won't be able to come out and see your shows."

Tucker was a songwriter. In fact, that's how he had met Josie. Her older brother had gained a small but loyal following in the country music world, but he hadn't had a breakout song.

Until Tucker wrote him one.

He had contributed three songs to Matt's second album, and all three had charted. Two had cracked the top ten, while one had gone to number one for six weeks. Tucker had been writing songs for several years for minor country acts, as well as performing every now and then in small clubs in and around Austin. Josie had encouraged him, though, to strike out on his own as a performer. Tonight, he was playing at a small but popular club on the outskirts of Austin, hoping the songs he would perform would have the crowd itching to dance—or cry in their beer.

She smoothed his hair lovingly. "I know you wish Travis were here tonight. But he is here—in spirit." Josie rubbed her belly. "And this Travis is going to start moving and grooving when he hears his daddy playing up there."

He regularly sang to her belly, hoping his son would learn to recognize his dad's voice. Josie had read a lot about that and believed it would be the case. She also knew their baby would know her voice because she talked a lot each day in her job as a pre-kindergarten teacher in

Austin. Josie worked with ESL students and loved what she did. She would take her maternity leave after Travis' birth and then return to the classroom.

Tucker wondered whether he really wanted to make it in country music or not. At least as a performer. He had grown up around the industry. His dad had managed several music acts. Travis Young was forever on the road. A manager had to be there with his band, stroking egos, heading off trouble, and making sure all musicians and their equipment made it to the next venue in one piece. It was a life spent on the road, away from home, and Tucker wasn't certain that was what he truly wanted. Maybe he could continue his songwriting and simply play in places in and around Austin. Josie loved her job so much. He couldn't see asking her to leave it. Besides, being on the road was no life for a kid. He knew that better than most.

His mom had died when Tucker was only five years old. She had been a heavy smoker from the time she was fourteen, and it caught up to her. Gloria Young died of lung cancer at only thirty-five, looking like a shell of herself.

That was when he began traveling full time with his dad. They were gone throughout the school year. His dad supposedly home schooled him, but that was a joke. Fortunately, Tucker was a curious kid about a lot of things. He read widely and was an ace in math. He taught himself Spanish by listening to and then conversing with many of the roadies.

A nice chunk of time, though, had been spent in Lost Creek, Texas. His mom's sister, Shelly, lived in the small

Hill Country town with her husband, Shy. They had one boy, Ry, and his cousin was Tucker's favorite person in the world. They had been more like brothers than cousins, and he looked forward to those summer months each year. Staying in one place. Sleeping in one bed. Having meals at regular times. Just being a typical boy, not one who lived out of a suitcase and had no friends.

Thanks to his outstanding math skills, Tucker won a scholarship to the University of Texas in Austin and earned a business degree. Those four years of college had made him feel like a normal person. When he graduated, he didn't join his dad on the road again. Instead, he worked a day job at a bank and wrote songs at night. Josie was urging him to give up his loan officer job and take the plunge into music full time because she believed in his talent. He had told her he would consider it. For now, though, he was hanging onto the job to keep his insurance until after the baby was born.

"Go find yourself a seat out front," he urged his wife. "You know I'll be singing every song for you."

"Here's a kiss for luck," she said, pulling his mouth down to hers.

Once Josie left the tiny dressing room, Tucker went over his set list again. He would only be playing seven songs. He was the warmup act for the country rock band which would follow him. The owner had told him that if he liked what he heard, he might give Tucker a regular gig at the club.

A knock sounded on the door, and it opened, the owner sticking his head in. "You're on."

Picking up his guitar he moved down the narrow hallway and stood to the side of the stage while the owner introduced him.

"You may know the songs, *Another Beer, Dear* and *I Lost My Love Today*. Well, the guy who wrote 'em is here tonight, and he's gonna play you a few songs. Here's Tucker Young!"

He took the stage to a smattering of applause. He wished he had an entire band backing him up, but there was no money for that at this point in his fledging career. He would need to wow the audience with his voice and guitar alone.

Slipping the guitar strap over his head, he clutched the mike. "How's everyone doing tonight?" he called.

A few people answered, but most were chowing down on their burgers and sipping beers, conversing with friends or dates. He knew not to let that affect him.

His gaze connected with Josie's. She nodded encouragingly at him.

Tucker began with an upbeat song, which got the notice of the crowd. By the end of it, many of them were clapping along.

He moved into his second number, another fast song, and by the time the last note sounded, he had the crowd eating out of his hand.

"This next one's a bit slower, but I wrote it for my wife, Josie. Here's to you, honey."

The crowd continued eating, but as he sang and played, looking out over the room, Tucker saw many of them were listening to him. To his lyrics. His music. He felt the power of the connection between him and the people present at the club. Other than Josie, no one had heard this song, and he could see it moved the audience.

Tucker received resounding applause when he finished. He was flush with success now and returned to a fun song with a fast beat about a one-night stand gone wrong. The audience stayed with him for it and the remaining songs.

When he announced his last song, he was pleased to actually hear a few groans. As he finished, the applause was deafening. The sweet rush of adrenaline ran through him as he slipped off the guitar strap, waving to the crowd, saying, "Goodnight!"

The owner was standing just offstage and gave him a pleased smile. "You're really good, Young," the older man praised. "The crowd responded well to your songs. If you're interested, I think we can talk about booking you long-term as a warmup on weekends. Come in early tomorrow night. We can talk terms then."

"Yes, sir," Tucker said enthusiastically, heading back to the small dressing room.

Josie joined him moments later, throwing her arms around him, squealing. "You were amazing!"

He gave her a deep kiss. "I couldn't have done any of this without your support. Your love and encouragement mean the world to me. I love you so much."

Happiness filled her face. "I love you, too, Tucker." She paused. "I'll bet you've worked up a thirst."

"And I'm also starved," he told her. "I was so nervous, I

didn't eat much today. Now, I think I could eat a whole cow."

"Let's get you burger and beer," she said, taking his hand and leading him back to where several people slapped him on the back as he passed, telling him how good he sounded tonight.

"I'd download anything you put up," one guy told him.

They took seats in an empty booth. Tucker rested his guitar next to him. The server came by, and they ordered two cheeseburgers with grilled onions and basket of fries to share. Josie requested water, while he ordered a beer.

After the server left, his wife said, "You really should think about putting up your songs online. Think about acts which got started on social media. Ed Sheeran. Justin Bieber. Shawn Mendes. You don't need a recording contract these days, Tucker. You can make it without the suits."

He had been toying with that very idea. "We'll have to think about that. In the meantime, the owner wants me to come in early tomorrow night. He liked the crowd's response and wants to talk about me playing here regularly. I know this place is on the outskirts of Austin, but I feel like it could really help me get my foot in the door."

Her eyes lit up. "That's fantastic! I'm so proud of you."

He downed his beer and signaled the server for another one. He drank a third when their cheeseburgers arrived.

"Good thing you're driving us home tonight," he said.

His car hadn't started before work that morning, and he'd

had it towed to a garage. The mechanic had told him it was a faulty alternator, and they would work on the car today. He'd gotten a message it was ready to be picked up while they were on their way to the venue tonight. He would have Josie drop him off tomorrow since it was Saturday. It was hard to get around anywhere in Texas unless you had a car.

They asked for the check, but the server told them, "The manager said it's on the house tonight."

"Thank him for us," Tucker said, leaving a generous tip for the server.

He had worked his fair share of jobs during college to supplement his scholarship. Waiting tables had been one of them. He always made sure a server was taken care of.

Once they reached Josie's car, she climbed behind the wheel as he got into the passenger's seat, a nice buzz making him feel a little sleepy now.

His wife said, "I'd like to hope there wouldn't be much traffic on a Friday night at ten o'clock, but it's Austin. There's always traffic."

She maneuvered them through the streets until they hit the two-lane highway leading them back into Austin and headed toward their apartment.

"The girls at school are going to throw me a baby shower next month," she said, happiness radiating from her. "They asked if you wanted to come. I told them I'd check with you to see if you could take the time off."

"Just let me know the day and time. I can get someone at the bank to cover for me. My boss likes me. Hell, she likes you more than me, so I'm sure she'll give me a few hours off so I can attend."

Suddenly, glaring lights blinded them. Josie screamed and tried to turn the wheel, but something slammed into them with such force that Tucker knew they were going to die.

The car spun and then flipped once. Twice. It came to rest upside down in a gulley beside the road.

He could hardly breathe. Realized the airbag had exploded, pressing against him. Tucker tried to push it away. Somehow, he reached into his pocket and retrieved the pocketknife he always carried with him. He jammed it into the airbag, and it deflated.

"Josie!" he hollered, seeing her face buried in her own opened airbag.

Panicking, he worried about the force of the bag exploding. If it had affected the baby.

Once more, he rammed his knife, seeing the airbag deflate. Josie blinked a few times and weakly asked, "What happened?"

"Someone hit us. Hard." He ached all over, especially his leg and head. Tucker figured out they were upside down, but he couldn't think clearly enough to figure out how to right them.

Her eyes fluttered a few times and then shut.

Tucker grabbed her hand. "Josie? Josie? Wake up!"

He could hear people talking outside the car, and a man appeared next to the window.

"We've called 911," the man yelled. "We'll try to get you out."

Noise surrounded him as he clutched his wife's hand, kissing her fingers, urging her to open her eyes.

Tucker must have passed out because the next thing he knew, he was out of the car, being pushed along the ground on a stretcher.

"My wife," he croaked, trying to sit up.

An EMT nudged him back. "We've already gotten her out the vehicle, sir. Just take it easy."

The ride in the ambulance was a blur, as was everything that happened in the ER. His leg ached something terrible, and heard a doctor say it was broken. He kept asking about Josie and the baby, and one doctor assured him that she was being cared for. That she'd been taken into surgery.

"Put us in a room together," he begged.

That was the last thing he recalled.

When he awoke, he was in a hospital room. Quickly, he glanced over and saw the other bed unoccupied.

Immediately, Tucker yelled at the top of his lungs. "Josie! Josie! I want Josie!"

A nurse rushed in, saying, "You need to calm yourself, Mr. Young. I know you're upset, but getting all excited isn't good for you."

"Where the hell is my wife?" he demanded, his head aching.

One of the doctors from before appeared at his bedside. One look at the man's face, and Tucker knew the worst had happened.

"No," he moaned. "No. No. No. No. No."

"I'm sorry, Mr. Young," the physician said. "We did everything we could to save your wife and the baby. The trauma from the accident was simply too much for either to survive."

"I'll kill the sumbitch who did this," he growled. "I'll kill him."

Tucker tried to climb out of the bed, but the doctor and nurse held him down.

"He did that to himself," the doctor shared. "The other driver was drunk. He's dead, Mr. Young."

Anger swelled within Tucker. He screamed then, the pain of losing his beloved Josie and little Travis more than he could take.

As they gave him an injection, he felt himself drifted off to sleep. Tucker wished he would have died with them.

Without Josie and their baby, his life was over.

1

MANHATTAN—OCTOBER

*R*eagan Bradley closed her eyes, breathing deeply in and out.

She was bored. Tired. And unhappy. The trifecta. But mostly unhappy.

At thirty, she was a success on paper. Finance degree from Harvard Business School. Master's degree from Wharton. She'd worked as a Wall Street trader now for almost seven years, known for her ability to spot trends and take calculated risks that paid off. She put in eighty-hour weeks and had zero personal life.

Once, she had been in love. Was set to marry. But Archibald Coleridge the Fourth had died in a mugging a week before their wedding. Gone was his wallet. His Philippe Patek watch. And his life. Knowing Arch, he had argued with his assailant, especially over the watch. It had belonged to his grandfather and was his most prized possession. The police had found the pawnshop where the watch landed and soon after, the man who had stolen it. Stolen a watch—and a life.

Actually, two lives. She counted hers just as gone as Arch's was.

Reagan hadn't taken off any time from work, despite her sympathetic boss begging her to do so. She knew if she had time alone, she might go crazy. So, work had become a balm. A place to lose herself. Then an addiction, as powerful as any drug. Now, it was an anathema. She hated what she did for a living. The frenetic pace. The drive for more and more money. The superficiality of it all.

It hit her that she finally wanted to go home. To Texas. A place she'd run from so many years ago.

She had grown up in Dickinson, a small town southeast of Houston and northwest of Galveston, which was on the Gulf of Mexico. Her father had been an attorney and mayor of the town. Her mother dabbled in charity work and drank. They were snobs, holding themselves above the average Texan. Reagan had been a daddy's girl—even after his death. He'd wanted her to go into law or finance, and so she'd majored in finance more to please him than herself. Her parents had been killed in a small plane crash while on their way to New Orleans, brought down in a heavy rainstorm. Reagan had just graduated from high school the week before their deaths. Her father's law partner had helped her sue the aircraft maker, settling for a high six-figure number which had paid for her two college degrees, with a little change to spare.

Having spent the last twelve years in the Northeast,

she was tired of the long winters and strangers who avoided eye contact on the streets. Suddenly, she yearned for the friendly faces and warmer climate of Texas.

Glancing around, she saw two dozen other fellow employees at work, staring at their computer screens. Searching for the next trend. Ready to make the next sale. Reel in the next commission.

Reagan was tired of her world revolving around money every waking moment. Especially today. The second anniversary of when she'd gotten the call that changed her life.

She stood. Pierce Bradshaw glanced up at her, bringing his chopsticks to his mouth and taking a bite of moo goo gai pan.

Frowning, he asked, "Are you going somewhere?"

"Home."

He laughed. "Home? What's that? Oh, yeah. It's the miniscule apartment I pay an arm and leg for and never see. I stumble in. Go to bed. The only time I'm awake is for a quick shower and shave before heading out the door again."

"Don't you get tired of not having a life?" she asked.

Pierce shrugged. "This is what we signed up for. I plan to retire by the time I'm fifty. Sooner, if my old man kicks the bucket and I inherit."

Frustrated, Reagan said, "But don't you want more?"

He looked at her sympathetically. "Damn," he said softly. "I'd forgotten. Today's the day Arch died. I'm sorry, Reagan. Go home. Have a drink. Have a few of them," he advised.

She didn't want a drink. She didn't want this life anymore. Reagan might not know exactly what she wanted.

But it wasn't this.

Impulsively, she sat again, typing at her computer for a minute. Then she printed out the page and scrawled her signature on it.

Pierce viewed her with curiosity. "What's that?"

"My resignation letter."

Marching to their boss' office, Reagan opened the door and placed the letter on top of the desk. It would be the first thing her boss would see the next morning.

She returned to her desk, opening drawers, rummaging around, and couldn't find a single thing she wanted to keep.

Standing, she slipped into her trench coat and slung her purse over her shoulder. "Bye, Pierce."

"You can't leave," he said, a little too loudly, causing others to glance in her direction.

"Watch me."

Reagan headed toward the door, knowing she was committing professional suicide.

And didn't care.

Punching the elevator button, she waited. Pierce appeared, looking panicked.

"Come on, Reagan. You're just depressed about Arch. Ask for a few days off. Go see a therapist. Get some meds. For depression. Or anti-anxiety. You don't want to do this."

She studied him a long moment. "Actually, I have

wanted to for a long time, Pierce. I just didn't know I wanted to."

"No one will hire you if you walk out like this," he warned. "No notice. You're throwing years of work down the drain. You won't get any kind of severance package. Certainly, none of the higher ups will ever write you a recommendation. In fact, they'll run your name through the mud. Please, Reagan. Stop and think."

The elevator chimed, and she entered it. Turning to face him, she said, "You've been a good friend to me, Pierce. You were a good friend to Arch, too."

Pierce had introduced her to her fiancé. He had been almost as torn up as she had after Arch's death since he and Arch had known each other for so long, even rooming together at Yale.

Reagan pushed the button. As the doors began to close, she whispered, "Goodbye."

Then Pierce was gone.

For the last time, she rode sixty-eight floors down, saying goodnight to the guy at the security desk. She walked two blocks to the subway station and moved swiftly down the stairs, passing through the turnstile. Her train came two minutes later, and she boarded it, finding a seat.

Deliberately, she kept her mind a blank. She couldn't afford to think now on what she had done. Instead, she observed her fellow passengers. A teenager moving his head to the beat of the music he listened to. A mom with a baby stroller. A man in a suit, scrolling through his cell phone. An elderly gentleman with a rolling cart, a loaf of bread sticking out of a sack.

When her stop came, she got up, noticing her legs were a little shaky. She left the station and walked a block to her favorite pizza place, asking for two slices of pepperoni to go. Once in her apartment, she turned on the lights. Poured herself a glass of wine. Sat on the couch. Ate her pizza.

And cried.

Reagan couldn't have identified what she was crying for because it was for so many things. Losing Arch and the life they had planned together. Her parents being gone. Her twenties, too. She felt she had nothing to show for her life. She was too busy to have friends or hobbies. Had no time for volunteer work. Couldn't think of the last time she'd sat down to read a book or watch something on TV. She hadn't gone to a movie in over a year. Life had been wake up, work, come home, go to bed. Rinse and repeat.

That was done. She was ready to flip everything on its head.

She finished one piece of pizza and wrapped the other in foil, placing it in the empty fridge. The pizza would most likely be breakfast tomorrow morning. Draining the wine, she went to her bedroom, stripping off her clothes and for once, leaving everything on the floor. Once she had on pajamas, she returned to the couch and picked up her cell phone.

It was time to call Aunt Jean.

Jean Bradley was what Reagan's mother called a spinster. Reagan preferred to think of her aunt as simply being too independent to be tied permanently to any man. Aunt Jean had been fifteen when her mother died giving birth to Reagan's father after numerous miscarriages, and Jean had raised her brother. She'd worked all kinds of odd jobs once their father passed in order to support them. Managing a bowling alley. Working at a florist shop. Acting as an elementary school secretary. When her little brother graduated from law school, Jean was almost forty and said she longed for a quiet life.

That had led her to Lost Creek, Texas, where she bought a large, rambling house and turned it into a bed and breakfast. The Hill Country was a popular destination for weekend getaways, and Jean Bradley was consistently booked up. She had even added two separate bungalows near the main house and did quite well. Her aunt was Reagan's only living relative, and they had remained close over the years. Her family had visited Lost Creek every summer when school was out, until Aunt Jean and Reagan's mom had some falling out which neither of them elaborated on. The breach had ended summer visits, but Aunt Jean had encouraged Reagan to text her frequently.

She had been too busy to get to Texas while in college and grad school because she went year-round, graduating early from both programs. Her investment firm strongly discouraged taking more than a day or two in a row for vacation, and so Reagan had remained in New York. Aunt Jean had flown up several times to play tourist, with Reagan taking off two days each time, and Jean had also come for Arch's funeral. If there were anyone she wanted to talk to more about what she had just done, it was Jean Bradley.

Touching her aunt's name on her cell, she listened to the phone ringing.

"Hello, Reagan. How are you? I know today is a hard day for you."

Leave it to Aunt Jean to remember Arch died today.

"It's hard," she admitted, tears suddenly streaming down her cheeks. "I loved Arch. I thought we would have a lifetime together."

"On days like today, I understand it's like ripping a bandage off a wound which hasn't fully healed. The anniversary of Arch's death will always hurt, honey. And I know it doesn't feel like it right now because you're in a world of pain, but time will heal you. You won't be as you were before. You'll always bear a scar. But one day it won't hurt as much. You'll remember more of the good than the bad. I believe you'll even find someone else to love, Reagan."

She brushed away the tears. "I don't know if I can open my heart again," she admitted. "I never loved a man before Arch. It seems impossible I could love anyone *but* him."

"Part of that is because you've buried yourself in your work," Aunt Jean said. "I didn't chastise you for that. I knew you needed a refuge. Work has kept you busy. Filled your time. But it can't completely fill the hole in your heart. You need to get back out there. I'm not saying start dating. Just see friends. Meet someone for coffee and go walk in that beautiful Central Park. Take in a play. Meet a friend for lunch or go to a museum. You need to start doing things away from work, Reagan."

She laughed, trying to keep the hysteria from her voice. "Well, I don't have to worry about work as of today. I quit."

Aunt Jean was silent. Then she spoke. "I know you didn't do this lightly. I understand how much your career has meant to you."

"I walked away on the spur of the moment," she revealed. "Typed out a resignation letter an hour ago and set it on my boss' desk. He'll see it first thing tomorrow—and will be shocked."

"Why did you do it?" her aunt pressed gently.

"Because I'm so tired," she acknowledged. "You're right. I don't do anything but work. After Arch's death, work sheltered me from all the ugliness. It kept me sane. Then somehow, it took over. I'd always put in a lot of hours, but I found I was devoting every waking minute to it. Suddenly, it no longer brought me comfort. It had absorbed me. Engulfed me until nothing of me was left."

Reagan began crying, and her aunt murmured comforting words.

"I'm sorry I'm such a mess," she apologized. "I'm just so unhappy." She hesitated. "And I miss Texas."

"Saints be praised!" Aunt Jean declared. "I never thought my sweet girl would admit that. Why don't you come visit me, Reagan? You're welcome to stay as long as you wish. We can talk over what you want to do in the future. Or we don't have to talk about that at all. Just come to Lost Creek. Give yourself time to heal. Then you can decide what you want to do with your life."

"Thank you," she said fervently. "That's exactly what I need. You. And Texas."

"Let me know when you're coming. I'll have a room ready for you."

"I will. It'll be a couple of days. I have a few things I should do here."

She didn't say what, but Reagan planned to shutter her life in New York. When she left for Lost Creek, all loose ends in the city would be tied up.

Because she was never going to live and work in Manhattan again.

She would investigate Houston. Dallas. San Antonio. Those larger cities would provide more opportunities for her career. Then again, she might be done with finance. It might be time to step away and find something entirely new to do. Thanks to investing wisely, she had a decent-sized nest egg and wouldn't need to work right away. She would have to time explore her options.

"I look forward to seeing you, Reagan," Aunt Jean said. "Love you."

"I love you, too," she replied. "Talk soon."

Hanging up, Reagan made a list of what she would need to do in order to leave New York permanently.

And return to the nurturing arms of her aunt—and Lost Creek.

2

───────

Tucker glanced at the city limits sign as they entered Lost Creek. It had been many years since he had visited the town, a refuge to him during his childhood and teenage years.

He had traveled the country in the two years since Josie's death. At least, after his leg came out of its cast. He'd also received a large settlement from Monroe McLemore's wealthy family, money he considered a bribe not to take the case to trial. McLemore had been excessively drunk when he had crossed the line, slamming into Tucker and Josie. The police investigation had concluded McLemore had consumed eight beers and four shots in the two hours before the fatal car crash. The twenty-year-old came from oil money, and his family hadn't wanted Tucker to bring them to trial, especially since their son had been underaged, and they didn't want any scandal regarding the crash.

His attorney had advised Tucker to accept the money, and he had. But he hadn't spent a cent of it. He felt it was dirty money. Blood money. Money which was supposed to take the place of Josie and his unborn son.

The hell it did.

After the tragedy, Tucker had left Austin. Left Texas. He constantly was on the move. He hitchhiked. Took Greyhound buses. Went from town to town. City to city. State to state. All trying to forget the horrors, which played out in nightmares every night. He had seen both the good and bad of the U.S. Wonderful people were everywhere, generous souls who gave him a kind word or hired him for a temporary job. He'd also witnessed the seedier side of things in his travels.

Through his travels, he'd tried to write. He had thought the one constant which remained would be continuing to write songs as he roamed the nation. Instead, it was as if the spigot had dried up. Nothing creative came from him. Not a note. Not a line. The harder he'd tried to pen a song, the more discouraged he became. And yet his gut told him he still had plenty of music inside him.

Now, it was time to settle in one place and try to live again.

Josie would have wanted that for him. She would never have wanted to see him lost. Rootless. Hell, Josie was so kind, she would even want him to fall in love and have the family he'd always desired. Tucker wasn't about to do that. It would feel like a betrayal if he did.

He was painfully lonely, though. Once a month, he pulled up Josie's Instagram account, scrolling through pictures of their life together in happier times. He knew it was punishing to keep looking at the pictures, but he couldn't help himself. Too many times to count, Tucker had read and ignored texts his cousin Ry had sent to him. Hearing from Emerson Frost, though, had been a turning point. He had answered her DM, which had put him in touch with Ry. Tucker had responded to Emerson's message, leaving his cell number and the ball in her court.

Almost immediately, Tucker heard back from Ry and Emerson. They had just gotten married a few hours earlier. The talk had been a good one. Not long, but satisfying. The couple had convinced him to come to see them in Lost Creek. Ry hadn't pressured him, saying it could be a temporary visit. It would be up to Tucker to decide if he wanted to stay or move on, continuing to be a vagabond.

If he'd ever had a home, it would be Lost Creek. He had spent every summer in the small town from the time he was five until he turned eighteen. Just looking at the passing scenery now caused a lump to form in his throat. He had missed his cousin. His Aunt Shelly and Uncle Shy. If he had to curb his wanderlust and settle down, it might as well be in Lost Creek where he had family.

With the settlement from the McLemores, he wouldn't have to work right away. As it was, he had been living off previous savings, not just from his loan officer job he'd worked at diligently for years, but the modest royalties he received on the songs he had written before his wife's death. While on the road those two years, he'd also taken on temporary jobs. Busing tables. Harvesting farm produce. Even being an extra in a movie production.

He couldn't stomach the idea of going back to an eight-to-five job at a bank. Tucker decided if he could find peace within himself, the music might return to him. He desperately wanted it to because he wanted to try and make it as a songwriter. No desire was left in him to perform, but the last two years had given him a wealth of material to draw from. He was eager unlock those experiences, putting everything he'd been through in a song. If he were able to get something down on paper, he figured a few people in country music might still take his calls.

"Is it Tuesday?" he asked Pete, the elderly gentleman who had stopped and picked him up as he was hitchhiking out of Austin. Pete was headed to Boerne, which was about half an hour south of Lost Creek, and had been happy to give Tucker a ride and have some company for most of his trip.

"Yup, it's Tuesday," Pete said, turning onto the town square.

Tucker's eyes roamed the square, seeing familiar shops. The Bake House. The hardware store. The barbershop. He also saw a few new places, including Java Junction. He could definitely use a cup of coffee.

Pete slowed the truck and pulled into an empty spot by the gazebo.

He offered the older man his hand. "Thanks for taking a chance and picking up a stranger, Pete."

"I did my fair share of hitchhiking back in my teens."

Pete grinned. "A hundred years ago. Or at least it seems like it after six kids and fourteen grandkids. Good luck to you, Tucker."

"Thanks. Same to you." He handed Pete some folded bills and said, "Gas money."

Pete waved it away. "Nah. I was headed this way anyway to see the newest grandbaby. Keep your money."

"Take it," he urged. "Even if you pay it forward. Pay for someone's order in a fast-food line or for someone's coffee behind you. I appreciated spending time with you, Pete. Maybe I'll even write a song about you," he joked.

The old man cackled. "I'll be listening for it on the radio, Tucker. Might even ask you for a piece of the pie if it's a hit."

"You got it," he said, opening the passenger door.

Tucker removed his things from the floorboard, slinging his backpack over one shoulder while lifting his duffel bag from the floorboard. "You take care, Pete."

"You, too."

Shutting the door, he gave a wave, and Pete backed from the parking place and drove away.

The clock above the gazebo said it was a quarter till ten. Too early for lunch, but Tucker was starved. He decided to make his way to The Bake House, which had all kinds of sweet delights. He knew from texting with Emerson that she now owned the place but had someone else manage it for her. She mentioned that she baked cakes for some big place where weddings were held. Ry also catered some of those wedding receptions.

It didn't surprise him that his cousin had come home

from the army and was cooking. The Blackwood family had owned a barbeque joint on Main Street for a few generations now, and Tucker assumed Ry had come back to work for his dad. He definitely had a lot of catching up to do with his cousin, who had served in the military overseas for a dozen years, ever since he was a teen. Tucker looked forward to reconnecting with Ry and getting to know Emerson.

He'd actually texted with Emerson more than Ry in the past couple of weeks since that fateful phone call. He could tell she was a genuine person. Nothing artificial about her. They had even spoken on the phone twice without Ry as Tucker had traveled closer and closer to Texas. Emerson had extended the offer for him to stay with them once he arrived in Lost Creek, but they were newlyweds. Tucker recalled how he and Josie behaved in those early months. Couldn't keep their hands off one another. Made love in every room and in every position.

No, Tucker wouldn't infringe upon the privacy the couple needed as they started their marriage. That meant finding a place to stay was his top priority.

He entered The Bake Shop and glanced around, not seeing Emerson. Looking in the display case, he ordered an apple Danish and sausage kolache to go and decided to check out the new Java Junction.

As he entered the coffeehouse, a warm feeling enveloped him as he glanced around. This would be a good place to come to. To sit and relax and let his thoughts meander.

After he stepped up to the counter, the barista asked what he wanted.

"Coffee black," he replied. "I don't go in for the fancy stuff." Holding up his bakery sack, he asked, "Is it okay to eat something from The Bake House while I'm here?"

"It certainly is," the woman replied. "Go have a seat. We'll get your coffee right out to you."

Tucker moved through the large space, seeing a group of older men holding court at a table in the corner, and he supposed they were retired and came to Java Junction each morning to shoot the breeze. Several moms in athleisure wear were saying goodbye to one another and leaving. The only other person at a table was a man close to Tucker's age, wearing wire-frame glasses, typing furiously on his laptop.

He took a seat a couple of tables away from the guy, figuring he might be a writer from his looks. Slipping the backpack from his shoulder, he set it atop the duffel bag at his feet.

A different barista brought his coffee to him, not in a paper cup, but an actual mug. The mug was huge. He set it on the table and with a friendly smile asked, "Passing through?"

"No. I believe I'll be staying."

The man looked puzzled a moment and then his eyes lit up. "You wouldn't happen to be Tucker Young?"

Guardedly, Tucker asked, "Who's asking?"

The man offered his hand. "I'm Dax Tennyson. Ry and Emerson are friends of mine. I'm married to Ivy Hart. I think you know her."

He relaxed, shaking Dax's hand. "Ivy and Harper were like cousins to me. I came to Lost Creek every summer to stay with Aunt Shelly and Uncle Shy. Ry and Todd were thick as thieves, and the three of us had many adventures together. If I didn't have dinner with my aunt and uncle, Ry and I were at the Harts. Ivy and Harper were great girls. Lots of fun."

"Then you must know Ivy is an artist," Dax said, a proud smile on his face. "She just had a big exhibit in New York City last month. She's focusing on painting the landscape of the Hill Country, and New York is gobbling up her paintings like hotcakes." Dax paused. "We're also going to have a baby come March."

By now, Dax had taken a seat across from Tucker.

"Congratulations," Tucker said. "Ivy was always so sweet. She'll make a great mother."

"She's my everything," Dax said fervently.

Tucker's throat constricted. He understands exactly what Dax Tennyson meant.

Clearing his throat, he asked, "What about Harper? She was a real pistol. I definitely could see her going places."

"She's actually returned to Lost Creek after being an event planner in Austin for several years," Dax revealed. "She spearheaded a big project at Lost Creek Vineyards. Built an event center on the property. She now operates Weddings with Hart. Brides are rushing to be married at the winery."

What he had learned from Ry and Emerson now began to fall into place. They hadn't mentioned Harper by name, but it had to be her place where they were catering weddings.

"Harper's married to the chief winemaker at Lost Creek Vineyards," Dax continued. "She and Braden will have their first baby next month. You need to meet Holden."

Dax turned and looked over at his shoulder at the man whose fingers still flew fast over his keyboard. He turned back. "I hate to interrupt Holden when he's on a creative tear. That's Holden Scott. Another friend of ours. He's married to the former Finley Farrow."

"Hmm. The name sounds familiar."

"She's a little younger than Ivy and Harper. You probably met her in passing over the years. Finley and Emerson are close friends. They used to teach together at Lost Creek Elementary. Nowadays, Finley is a photographer. She works a lot of the weddings at the winery, but she's also branched out and is doing individual photography. Family and senior portraits. She's also hooked up with some movie people, thanks to Holden."

"Wait. Holden Scott. He's a famous author. I've seen a movie based on one of his books." As he'd crisscrossed the country, Tucker had frequented movie theaters, losing himself in the stories of other people.

Dax glanced over his shoulder again, and Tucker saw that the writer had now stopped and was closing his laptop.

"Hey, Holden. Come over here. Got someone for you to meet," Dax said.

The writer came and joined them. "Holden Scott." He offered his hand.

"I'm Tucker Young. Ry Blackwood's cousin."

The two men shook, and Holden smiled. "Ry mentioned to us that you were coming to town soon. It's nice to meet you." He glanced to Dax. "Have you invited Tucker to dinner tomorrow night?"

"I hadn't gotten that far yet," Dax said. Looking at Tucker, he said, "Ry and Emerson would've invited you anyway. A group of us meet every Wednesday night for dinner. We're all pretty busy, and it's a time for friends to catch our breath. Enjoy a home-cooked meal. Be a little bit social. It's always held at Harper and Braden's house. A few of us take turns cooking." He chuckled. "Ivy can barely boil water, but she is good about bringing along different wines from Lost Creek Vineyards for our dinners."

"I hope you'll be able to join us," Holden said. "Tomorrow night, Braden is making jambalaya and dirty rice."

He hated to commit to anything. He hadn't carried on long conversations with anyone, much less large groups of people, ever since he'd hit the road. Just random ones with an individual stranger here and there. Still, Tucker knew he needed to get back to what would be his new normal. Living in one place. Making friends. Trying to contribute to a community.

"I'd be happy to come if you have room for me," he told the pair.

"When did you get here?" Holden asked.

Chuckling, Tucker said, "About fifteen minutes ago. I saw The Bake House and couldn't pass by it. And what goes better with a sweet than a cup of coffee? I decided to check out Java Junction."

"So, Ry and Emerson don't even know you're in town yet," Dax said.

"No. I was going to text them once I finished my coffee."

"Then I'll let you do that in peace," Dax said. "I'm off the clock for a few hours and have some things to do. I'll see you tomorrow night, Tucker. Great having you in Lost Creek."

Dax left, and Holden said, "We have something in common. I heard from Ry and Emerson that you're a songwriter. I write novels and am venturing into screenplays, as well. While I love writing at home, Java Junction is a nice change of scenery, especially if you get stuck. It's super busy in the morning. They have a bit of lunch crowd. Then after school, the place is hopping. Coffee is the new addiction of the teenagers in Lost Creek. But if you get tired of where you are and want to write, I suggest coming here during one of those quiet times."

"Thanks for the tip, Holden."

"I need to head home, but it was a pleasure meeting you, Tucker. I look forward to visiting with you more tomorrow night."

Tucker sipped his coffee after Holden left and tackled the kolache first. The sweetness of the roll balanced perfectly with the spicy sausage nestled inside. He finished it and then savored the Danish. He felt good.

Really good. Dax and Holden had been open and friendly. They hadn't pressed him about his past, which he appreciated. He looked forward to catching up with Ivy and Harper again after so many years.

The last time he'd visited Lost Creek had been for Todd Hart's funeral. Todd had been Ry's best friend and was killed during his military service. The body had been brought home for burial. Ivy and Harper had probably been twenty or so at the time. Tucker knew just how fleeting life could be and how death affected a person and a family. Now that he'd committed to returning to Lost Creek, he was eager to renew his friendship with the two women, as well as others here in town.

Anticipation filled him as he texted his cousin and Emerson.

> Made it to Lost Creek. Sitting in Java Junction. Met Dax and Holden. Eager to see you both.

He sent the message and waited. Almost immediately, his phone chimed.

> Just stopped at The Bake House to check on orders. I'm coming your way now.

That came from Emerson. Moments later, his phone dinged again.

> Have Emerson bring you to the truck. Can't wait to see you!

Ry's message puzzled him. He thought they would

have met up at Blackwood BBQ or Aunt Shelly's diner. Tucker wasn't going to worry about it, though. He had made it to Lost Creek. Already met two people whom he hoped would become friends. It would be hard, starting over without Josie, but it was time to put an end to his nomadic lifestyle and make a life for himself.

And if songwriting didn't work out, maybe he could learn the barbeque business.

3

"Tucker!"

He glanced up and saw Emerson heading across the coffeehouse toward him. She was a striking woman, with long, raven hair and gray eyes.

He rose as she reached him, and she flung her arms about him.

"I'm so glad you made it to Lost Creek."

"I'm happy to be here myself," he replied. "Have a seat. Ry said you're supposed to bring me to some truck."

She took a chair next to his. "Ry owns a food truck. He serves lunch from it five days a week, parking various places around town. On Saturdays, he sometimes takes it to different sporting events, mostly at the city ball fields."

"I assume he's serving barbeque."

Her eyes lit up. "He does. Traditional sandwiches made of brisket and pulled pork, but he really was inspired by his time in the military and the R&R's he took to different countries in Asia. He's begun incorporating Asian flavors into his barbeque."

Tucker whistled. "And how is that going over with Uncle Shy? Tigers don't change their stripes."

Emerson grew serious. "I won't sugar coat it. Things were more than strained between them. When Ry returned from the service, he took over the catering arm of Blackwood BBQ. Since you spent summers in Lost Creek, you may be familiar with the Hart family. Harper, one of the daughters, built an event center at their winery, and brides have been flocking to hold their ceremonies there. Since it's the Hill Country, at the top of Harper's recommendations for wedding receptions was Blackwood BBQ."

She paused. "Shy was becoming a little overwhelmed by all the additional business. When Ry came home, Shy turned over the reception catering to his son. Ry began offering everything on the family's menu, plus his own spin on dishes. Couples went wild over what he was serving."

"And then Uncle Shy found out, didn't he?"

Emerson nodded. "It got ugly. *Really* ugly between them. For a time, Shy wouldn't even speak to Ry because he felt so betrayed. Fortunately, he came around just in time for our wedding."

Tucker had observed people all his life, and his gut made he ask, "You were the person who brought them together again, weren't you?"

She flushed. "I did go and see Shy the day before our wedding. Told him how pigheaded he was being."

"Oh, I'll bet he loved that."

"Actually, I think Shy found new respect for me. Because I was sticking up for the man I loved. Ry's always had such great admiration for his dad. The rift between them pained him. I just let Shy know that he was wasting precious time that could never be regained. That being alienated from his only child was foolish." She grinned. "I also made him sample some of Ry's new creations. That did the trick. Shy saw that Ry was still smoking meats the way he'd been taught— the Blackwood way— but his creativity and skills added a new dimension to Blackwood BBQ. In the end, the two made up."

"I know how stubborn Uncle Shy can be," he said. "You are either a witch who placed my uncle under a spell— or a miracle worker."

"Nope. I'm simply plain old Emerson Blackwood." She reached over and placed her hand atop his. "I can't tell you what it means to Ry for you to have come back to Lost Creek. He looks upon you as his brother."

"I feel the same about him. I don't know how much he's told you about me, but I did spend every summer here for years."

She squeezed his hand. "He did tell me that you were in a terrible car accident. That you lost your wife and child."

Tucker steeled himself, not wanting to show any emotion. "Yes. It was a tough time. I really didn't want to be around anyone, much less talk about it."

"I'm sorry I brought it up," she apologized. "I want you

to know how sorry I am for your loss. Losing a loved one hurts."

"You sound as if you know loss yourself, Emerson."

She shrugged. "I didn't have the best childhood, Tucker. My dad was an alcoholic with a mean temper. The two combined got him into trouble. He killed a man. He died in prison."

"Now, I'm the one needing to say I'm sorry."

"I really didn't know him all that well. He never paid much attention to me. Neither did my mom."

"Were you closer to her after he was sent away?"

"No. The gulf widened between us. Mom turned to drugs as an escape. Half the time, I don't think she even knew I was around. Eventually, she relinquished her parental rights, and I went into the foster system. I aged out at eighteen."

He looked at her with growing respect. "You are some woman, Emerson Blackwood. You mentioned on one of our calls that you'd taught elementary school for several years, so that means you put yourself through school. Earned a degree and became a professional. And now you own The Bake House. That's quite accomplished."

"The Bake House was given to me. Ethel Frederick bequeathed it to me in her will. I had worked weekends and summers when I wasn't teaching for her, and she respected my baking skills."

"You mentioned you baked wedding cakes."

She grew enthusiastic. "I'm the exclusive baker for Weddings with Hart. That's Harper's business. I meet with bridal couples and work on the designs and flavors for their wedding and groom's cakes. Harper's business has grown rapidly since she opened it last fall. It certainly keeps me hopping."

Emerson stood. "Enough about me. We need to get going. Ry is dying to see you."

He gathered his duffel and backpack, following her to her car and placing his things on the back seat.

"Where's Ry's food truck today?"

"It's a Tuesday, so he is parked outside where all the town's municipal offices are located. He has a solid clientele from the city workers, police, and firefighters. He's there today and Thursdays, and he parks on the north end of the square Mondays, Wednesdays, and Fridays."

"Do you ever help him?" he asked as she backed out of the parking spot and left the square.

"Sometimes. It depends upon what I have going. Today, I have two specialty cakes I need to bake and decorate. I still do a few special orders for patrons of The Bake House. I've got one to bake for a birthday party tomorrow night, and another welcome home cake for a soldier returning home from the navy. I'm going to drop you off with Ry, and I'm sure he'll put you to work."

She looked at him earnestly. "I hope you've changed your mind, and you'll stay with us."

"No. I don't want to get in your way."

Emerson snorted. "You wouldn't be in our way, Tucker."

He gave her a knowing look. "I was a newlywed once myself."

Her face flamed. "Thank you," she said. "We really

want to have you with us, but I'm glad you understand. Ry's the first man I've loved. He'll be the last. We both are very busy with our businesses, and I do treasure our time alone at home."

"Be thinking about where I might be able to stay short-term," he said, as they turned on the street where the municipal offices were located.

"Hmm. There might be a few people who have a room to rent. The area does have several B&B's. The Hill Country is a weekend destination for a lot of couples and families. They like to do wine tastings. Go antiquing. Tube and fish. Hike. One I think you might like is The Inn on Lost Creek. Its owner is the cutest, feistiest old woman in Lost Creek."

"You wouldn't happen to be talking about Miss Jean?"

"Ah, you remember Jean Bradley."

"The moment you said feisty, thoughts of her came to mind. I knew she had a place just outside of town. We'd ride our bikes by it sometimes. A good fishing hole was located nearby. Ry, Todd, and I would go there in the summers." He paused, thinking. "I believe I'd like that, being just a little out of town and off the beaten path."

"Why don't you have Ry take you by there after lunch finishes?" she suggested.

"Sounds good."

They pulled into a parking lot and saw Ry's food truck at the far end. His cousin was opening the side where customers would line up to order. Tucker saw the name Smokin' Sweethearts scrawled in script along the side of the truck.

"Let me get my things," Tucker said. "If I decide to stay with Miss Jean, I'll already have everything with me. If that doesn't work out, we can turn to Plan B. You can be working on that."

She laughed softly. Her hand moved up and cupped his cheek. "I'm so glad to have finally met you, Tucker. And I'm very happy you'll be staying. Regardless of what you work out with Jean Bradley, come have dinner with us tonight."

"I can do that," he promised.

After claiming his things from the back, he headed toward Ry. The moment his cousin spotted him, they both broke out in huge grins. Ry rushed toward him, and Tucker dropped his gear, embracing his cousin. It felt odd, this human contact with others. First Emerson and now Ry hugging him. He hadn't touched anyone in that way since his last night with Josie.

He looked at Ry. "When did you grow into a man?" he asked. "Last time I saw you, you were eighteen and heading off so Uncle Sam could whip your ass into shape."

His cousin slapped Tucker on the back. "Hey, buddy, I feel the same. You were a teenager the last time we saw one another. Oh, I know we traded a few pictures in texts for a few years, but it's kinda weird, seeing you all grown up." He paused. "What do you think of Emerson?"

"She's great. Absolutely perfect for you, Ry."

Ry grinned from ear to ear. "That's what I told her. Seriously, I feel like my life didn't start until she came into it. That I was simply marking time until Emerson Frost appeared and stole my heart."

"Frost?" he asked, laughing. "She should've kept her last name after marrying you. That's too wild. A cake decorator named Frost."

"She's a Blackwood now, through and through. My parents adore her."

"I got out of her that she stood up to Uncle Shy. That you two had some trouble between you."

A shadow crossed Ry's face. "You know Dad. If it ain't broke, don't fix it. I knew I was destined to return to Lost Creek and smoke meat, but I learned so much in my travels abroad and my time cooking in the army. I had this burning desire to bring what I'd discovered and marry it to the barbeque of my heart. I'll have to let you taste some. Since Emerson deserted me, you're going to be my Number Two during lunch service today. Let's get in the truck, and I'll show you the ropes."

Ry quickly gave Tucker the tour of the food truck, calling it his pride and joy. Tucker sampled a few bites of brisket and pulled pork, the familiar smoked meats melting in his mouth. He'd forgotten just how good Blackwood meats could be. Then he tried a skewer of what Ry called bulgogi, which also had bites of green and red peppers and onions on it.

"That's thinly sliced brisket, though you can use sirloin or ribeye, which can get pretty pricy. I marinate it in a sauce that's half savory and half sweet. It's got soy sauce, a little sesame oil, some brown sugar, mirin, and Asian pear."

"Wow! That's amazing."

"Try this. Got a little kick to it, so watch out."

"That won't bother me," Tucker assured his cousin, slipping the forkful of meat into his mouth.

"It's jeyuk bokkeum, a spicy pork. I put a ton of fresh garlic and ginger in it. My customers who love spicy claim it's their favorite sandwich. I like the fusion of Asian influences into pure Texas barbeque. While I keep brisket and pulled pork on the menu, every week I change out the other two items I serve."

"This is so delicious. Those flavors exploded in my mouth. No wonder your food is in such demand."

"I do a pretty steady lunch trade, then I'm busy on weekends catering events at Lost Creek Winery. Things are going so well that I plan on investing in a second smoker. They don't come cheap, but I'm doing enough business now that it'll pay for itself quickly."

Customers began showing up, and Ry said, "We'll talk more later."

They worked together steadily for a good two-and-a-half hours. Around one-thirty, things finally slowed to a trickle. Only a few other customers dribbled in, and by two, Ry was ready to close down.

"Let me make both of us a sandwich. I'm sure you're starving."

"After inhaling all these amazing aromas, you bet I am. Haven't you heard my belly growling the last hour?"

Ry fixed them sandwiches, and they talked as they ate. Tucker told his cousin about some of the places he had traveled to around the country.

"I've seen forty-nine of the fifty states. Never made it

to Hawaii. Boats don't take hitchhikers there, but I plan to visit those islands someday."

"You dropped off the face of the earth after the accident," Ry said. "I can understand why now. If I lost Emerson, I think I would lose my mind— and my reason for living. I'm glad you're finally back in touch and here in Lost Creek, Tucker. You are staying with us, aren't' you?"

"No. You and your wife need time to yourself. I need the same. Emerson and I talked it over, and she thought staying at The Inn on Lost Creek might be good for me. At least for a while."

"It's quiet there," Ry agreed. "Jean should have something open. Not one of the little cabins. Those book up and stay booked for a good chunk of the spring, summer, and fall. We are moving into winter soon, though. Maybe one will be available."

"What are those?"

"She's got two small cabins which are away from the main house and face each other. Both contain a sitting area. Bedroom. Kitchenette. They offer a little more privacy. You said you met Holden. He stayed in one of them when he came to Lost Creek to work on a screenplay."

"I liked him. Dax, too."

Ry smiled. "They're solid guys, Tucker. They've been good friends to me. So is Braden, Harper's husband. In fact, you need to come to dinner with everyone tomorrow night."

He chuckled. "Already been invited. I hear we're having jambalaya."

"We are. Braden is cooking. He's amazing in the kitchen, which is nice because it's the one thing Harper isn't good at. A big group of us meets every Wednesday night. Have dinner. Catch up. Emerson and I look forward to going every week. Getting back to the Inn on Lost Creek, though, there are rooms inside the B&B you can rent. Let's go visit with Jean Bradley. Hopefully, we can work out something."

They closed up the food truck and drove to the inn, which hadn't changed much at all. Tucker asked, "Do you remember we fished close to here?"

"I haven't been fishing in ages. Maybe now you're back in town, we can do that."

They went up the steps, and he admired the large, inviting porch, which had several rockers, a few tables, and a swing. It would be nice sitting outside. It was far enough away from the road not to hear any traffic noises. The peace and quiet this porch offered would bring him solace.

Jean Bradley answered the door, and he grinned at her. "Remember me, Miss Jean? It's Tucker Young. I'm Ry's cousin."

The woman, who was probably in her seventies by now, laughed. "Of course, I do, Tucker Young. You're all grown up. I've heard a couple of your songs on the radio. Come on in, boys."

They entered a large foyer, and she said, "Put your things down, Tucker. I gather you've come looking for a place to stay."

"Yes, Miss Jean. I think I'll be staying in Lost Creek for

good. I'll need a temporary place to live while I'm deciding exactly what I want to do."

"With colder weather coming, not many of my rooms inside the house are rented out during the week, and only a few on weekends. Right now, I have one long-termer, a guy who's separated from his wife. My cabins are currently booked up. Let's go look at what I can offer you."

He and Ry accompanied her upstairs. She whipped out her phone and said, "Looking at my calendar, I've got two rooms you could choose from for a few weeks or so. I hope you don't have trouble picking between them." Her eyes sparkled at him.

"Are you remembering that time at The Bake House?" he asked.

"That's exactly what I'm referring to. You and Ry and the Hart boy had enough money to buy a cookie each. You kept dithering between the snickerdoodle and the peanut butter one."

He burst out laughing. "And you finally slipped me a dollar and told me to get both. I can't believe you remember that, Miss Jean."

"There's not much I don't remember," she said saucily.

They passed one room, and she said, "Normally, I'd offer you this one. It's my largest available. But my niece from New York is coming to stay with me soon. I'm not certain how long Reagan will be here. All right, boys. Let's have a look at this one."

She showed him one room which was light and airy. It had a chest, nightstand, and full-sized bed. A TV was hanging from the wall, and in the corner was a chair and table. It was a perfect nook to sit and think.

Or write a song.

"It's just basic cable," she told him. "I've got the premium sports package and HBO on the one down in the main room. All my guests are welcome to watch with me. You have to pull for Texas teams, though, else you'll be out on your ear. Especially the Dallas Cowboys. They are my team."

"Got it," he said, hiding a smile.

The second room was about the same size and offered the identical pieces of furniture, but it didn't get quite the same light. He liked light. Too many of the cheap motels he'd stayed in the past two years had been dark and dingy.

"I'd like to rent the first one, Miss Jean," Tucker said.

"You can pay by the week." She named the price and then added, "That includes breakfast seven days a week and dinner Monday through Friday. If you aren't going to be around for dinner, I'd appreciate a heads up when I can get it. I know you young people have plans that change at the last minute, though."

"I know Emerson wants me at the house tonight for dinner, and I've been invited to eat with a bunch of her and Ry's friends tomorrow night. That's all the plans I have at the moment."

She made a note on her phone. "Got it. Usually, I have someone pay a week's rent up front, but I know you, Tucker Young. That won't be necessary."

"Let me pay you for a month now," he said. "Get that out of the way."

Miss Jean took him downstairs. Ry offered to bring Tucker's things upstairs while he paid with his credit card.

She presented him with two keys. "The gold one is to the front door. Lock it behind you when you come and go. The silver one is to your room. I'd lock it, too, just to be on the safe side. I don't guarantee against theft. I'm happy to let you use the washer and dryer, but you'll need your own washing powder and fabric softener. For now, the bathroom across the hall is all yours. Once my Reagan gets here, you'll share it. You'll have to work out when you both want to use it."

"Will do. I look forward to meeting your niece."

Ry appeared. "I put everything on the floor next to the bed. You can unpack for yourself."

Slipping the keys into his pocket, he accepted the credit card she handed him and signed the slip for a month's stay.

"You just keep me informed about your plans," Miss Jean told him. "You get fresh towels daily. I change the sheets once a week. I'll spot clean during the week. Make your bed. Dust. Sweep. That kind of thing."

"You won't need to do that. I'll make my own bed. Whenever you change the sheets, you can clean the rest. Really, I'm a fairly neat person, Miss Jean."

She nodded approvingly. "Glad to hear it. I like low maintenance men."

"I'll take Tuck back with me now, Miss Jean," Ry said. "I'll also drop him off tonight after dinner."

"Then I'll see you later." She walked them to the door. "Bye, now."

They went back to the food truck, and Ry said, "She's a real character."

"I like her."

"Because she bought you more cookies."

"Well, that, too."

As they drove back into town, Tucker felt a peace descend over him. He was back in a familiar place, with family to count on. The inn would be a good place to stay, especially since it wasn't so busy this time of year. He promised himself he would try his hardest to make a new start.

It was what Josie would have wanted.

4

---

ucker finished shaving and rinsed his razor, drying it and returning it into his Dopp kit. He returned to his room and slipped the kit into a drawer. Making his way down the stairs, he entered the large kitchen, where Miss Jean was pouring herself a cup of coffee.

"Good morning," he greeted.

"You a coffee drinker, Tucker?"

"Yes, ma'am," he replied.

She handed him the cup in her hand and got another for herself, saying, "Sugar's on the table. Creamer's in the fridge."

"No, ma'am. I drink it black, like it's meant to be drunk." He took a seat at the kitchen table.

"Are you a finicky eater?" she asked.

"Not a bit. Other than Brussels sprouts, that is. Never found them little suckers to my taste. Whatever you put in front of me, I'm going to eat it, Miss Jean. And appreciate it."

"How do you like your eggs?"

"Any way I can get them. Scrambled. Fried over easy. Poached."

"Good to know. This morning is pancakes and sausage links."

"Is there anything I can do to help?"

"You can keep me company while I'm making breakfast. I like things done a certain way. I like the conversation, but I don't want you in my way."

He chuckled, thinking her a true original.

As she stirred the pancake batter, she said, "Normally when I have a full house, I serve both breakfast and dinner in the dining room. Right now, though, it's just you and Sid Allen. He works a night shift and shows up here at eight o'clock. Eats his breakfast and heads straight to bed."

She clucked her tongue as she poured the batter onto a heated griddle. "I think working that night shift is the biggest problem in his marriage, but that's something he's going to have to figure out on his own."

"I'll be sure to keep quiet, knowing he's asleep during the day," Tucker promised, watching her drop sausage links into a hot skillet.

"Sid's a heavy sleeper," she revealed. "But I appreciate your effort all the same." As she spoke, she turned the links with one hand and flipped the pancakes with the other. "I'm just making conversation, but if you think I'm a nosy old woman, tell me so."

"Will do, Miss Jean," wondering what she was going to ask him. Because he knew it was coming.

"Did you have a nice dinner with Ry and Emerson last night?"

Relief filled him. Tucker had thought she would ask what he'd been doing since she'd last seen him in Lost Creek. He wasn't ready to talk to people about being a widower. Having quit his job and wandered the country. Even if she meant well, he didn't think he could open up to her. Maybe down the road.

But for now, he wanted to protect his memories— and his heart.

"I did. It's been great connecting with Ry again. We haven't seen each other since we were teenagers, but we picked up like no time had passed. Emerson's a wonderful gal. They can finish each other's sentences."

"That's a good sign in a marriage, especially the early months." She smiled. "I'm with you. I think those two are meant for one another."

"They caught me up on things happening in town. Emerson's going to stop by this morning. She's taking me to Lost Creek Vineyards and giving me a tour of the new event center and her kitchen there."

"Emerson may not be a native to Lost Creek, but it's welcomed her, all the same. She was a mighty fine teacher, and I know Mary Miller misses her, as do her students. Ethel Frederick knew what she was doing, though, leaving The Bake House to Emerson. The quality hasn't slipped one bit. In fact, if anything, it's improved."

The innkeeper began stacking pancakes on a plate and asked, "Milk or OJ?"

"Milk with pancakes or French toast, but I'm not opposed to OJ with other items."

As they ate their breakfast, he shared, "Once I've seen the winery, I'm going to borrow Emerson's car and go see Aunt Shelly and Uncle Shy. They were a big part of my life."

"They'll want you to come and stay with them. If you decide to do so, Tucker, it's fine by me."

"No, ma'am, I'm going to like it here just fine. I need a little bit of peace and quiet. I've got a lot to work out. The Inn on Lost Creek suits me."

Tucker was glad she didn't ask him what was on his mind. Jean Bradford was a smart cookie. She could subtly fish for information, but she seemed to have a sixth sense when to steer clear of a topic.

"I have an old truck out back. And when I say old, I mean old. None of them fancy computer systems in it. It hasn't run in a good while. When it wouldn't start, I thought it would cost too much to fix up. Got myself one of those smart SUVs instead. If you are any good with cars and want to tinker with it, you're welcome to do so. If you get it running, you can have it."

He was a decent mechanic. Being on the road all the time as a kid, he had picked up all kinds of skills. If he spent a little time tinkering with her truck, Tucker thought he had a shot at getting it up and running again. Newer vehicles had computer chips and all kinds of bells and whistles. He couldn't do much of anything on them.

Even changing a sparkplug was impossible. But an old truck like Miss Jean's would offer him a challenge.

"I'd like to give it a whirl, Miss Jean. If I do get it running, though, I want to pay you for it."

She cackled. "If you can get it running, Tucker Young, I'll be the one to pay you."

They finished breakfast, and he went outside to sit on the porch and wait for Emerson since his offer to clear the table was smacked down. The old woman was even particular about how dishes were stacked in the sink and rinsed, and she told him to never attempt to load the dishwasher— because he would do it wrong.

The quiet enveloped him as he rocked, and the hint of a melody began whispering in his ear. He stilled, taken unaware, but thrilled that he heard it speaking to him. He took out his phone and hit record, humming the tune into it. Tucker had learned when inspiration struck to get it down because he might not recall the lyrics or the melody that floated through his head once he had time to sit down and write.

Slipping his phone back into his pocket, he stood as Emerson came up the drive. He went to her car and greeted her.

As he got in, she asked, "How did you sleep in a new bed and place?"

"It was all good. Miss Jean is a really nice lady. She made pancakes for me this morning."

They drove to Lost Creek Vineyards, and he saw how massive the vineyards stretched. He couldn't remember coming out here growing up and was impressed by the size of the operation.

The event center appeared, and he whistled low. "This is nice."

"Trey Watson, a friend of Harper's from Austin, is an architect. He designed it," Emerson explained. "Both she and Ivy had input into the creative process. I even got to specify certain things I wanted in the kitchen. I'm grateful for that because it's made my job baking cakes so much easier."

They walked toward the center, and Emerson added, "Harper's business is mostly weddings, thus Weddings with Hart. She does hold a few other events here, however. Special birthdays and anniversary parties. Quinceaneras and Sweet Sixteens. Even a couple of corporate events. But her bread and butter is the wedding trade."

Entering the building, Tucker was impressed with its size. The glass wall on the far end drew him in, and he moved toward it, spellbound. It overlooked an entire section of grapevines.

Emerson joined him. "This is where couples stand during their ceremonies. Isn't this a beautiful backdrop? Ry and I were married here."

She showed him the various dressing rooms and then the half of the building devoted to receptions. The tables were undressed mid-week, but she told him that each reception catered to the bride and groom's specific tastes, down to the tablecloths and centerpieces.

"Harper has four different sets of china for meals.

Elegant. Traditional. Whimsical. Modern. She also has tablecloths in different colors for brides to choose from. Of course, Lost Creek Vineyards' wines are always served to guests. That goes without saying."

"Does Ry meet with clients as you do?" he asked.

She nodded. "He does similar taste testings. He wants to give each couple their dream meal for them and their guests. It's the same with me. I work closely with every couple on their wedding and groom's cakes."

Emerson showed off the kitchen, which to him looked like a baker's dream come true.

"I need to take you by Harper's office and the tasting room. I texted Harper to let her know you'd be at dinner tonight, and she and Ivy are so eager to see you while you're on the property this morning. Let's stop by Harper's office first."

They drove a short distance, and he saw the Weddings with Hart sign outside a one-story building. Entering, Tucker thought the tastefully decorated room reflected Harper's cool elegance. Her greeting was anything but cool, though.

"Tucker!" she cried, leaping to her feet and rushing toward him, hugging him tightly, her belly large and round under her flowing shirt. "How long has it been?"

"Way too long," he acknowledged. "We just came from the event center. Harper, you've done yourself proud."

She beamed. "I was an event planner in Austin for several years, but I felt the pull of Lost Creek calling me home. It helped that my fiancé jilted me the day before the wedding. Or rather, he had the best man tell me things were done between us."

Her words shocked him. Harper was surely the most beautiful, put together woman he could imagine. Why any man would let her go was beyond him. It angered him that the guy hadn't even had the courage to tell her himself that the wedding was off.

"Wipe that frown off your face, Tucker," Harper chastised. "I'm not sad about it at all. Ath Armistead wasn't the man for me. If I had married him and stayed in Austin, I would have been miserable."

Her face softened. "By coming home, I found myself professionally. And personally. Braden is everything I could ever want. He is the most loving husband, and he's going to be a wonderful father to this little boy." She patted her belly.

"I hear the baby's due next month."

"Yes. Everything is looking good. We're going to name him Beau, after Braden's younger brother who passed away. Come see the rest of the office."

Harper showed off her space and spoke enthusiastically about how rapidly her business was growing.

"We're booked up through the rest of this year, and we only have a few openings for next year."

"How are you going to juggle the baby and business?" he asked.

She gave him a patented Harper Hart look. "Really, Tucker?"

He laughed. "If anyone can do both and excel, it's you."

Emerson's cell dinged, and she read the incoming text.

"Ivy has arrived at the tasting room and is ready to see you."

"Good," Harper said. "I've got clients coming in about ten minutes and need to get a few things ready for them."

Harper hugged him once more. "It's great seeing you back in Lost Creek, Tucker. I look forward to seeing you at dinner this evening and introducing you to Braden."

"Thanks for having me. I hear Braden is a terrific cook."

She grinned. "The one thing I'm *not* good at."

They all laughed.

Emerson drove him to the tasting room, and Ivy was just as enthusiastic as her sister had been in greeting him.

"You've been away from Lost Creek too long, Tucker Young," she declared.

He couldn't help but glance at her belly after their hug, and she caught him doing so.

"Yes, I'm pregnant, just like Harper. The baby is coming in mid-March, so I've got lots of time to prepare."

Ivy led him on a tour of the outdoor space, explaining how the tasting room had been expanded from its original size. She took him through the gift shop and then the large tasting room. It had a lengthy bar for guests to sidle up to, as well as scattered tables. Ivy explained the tastings could occur at the bar or these tables, and then people could stay after and sip some of the wines they had purchased.

"Are you a wine drinker?" Ivy asked.

He gave her a sheepish grin. "Not at all. I'm more of a beer and burger kind of guy."

She laughed. "You sound just like Dax when I met him. He was exactly the same, but I brought him over from the dark side. He actually prefers wine to beer now after I've educated him."

"Then if you could make Dax a convert, I'm next in line."

"I'll give you a personal tasting and teach you something about wines," Ivy told him. "I'll bring a couple of bottles tonight that I think you'll like. I'm delighted you're having dinner with us."

They said their goodbyes, and Emerson drove back to the event center, where she had cakes to bake and a couple of client meetings lined up.

"Keep the car the rest of the day. I know we need to see about getting you some transportation so you won't be dependent upon us to get around town."

He explained about Miss Jean having a truck he was going to try and fix up and drive.

"If you need something sooner, we can see about taking you into Boerne and renting something for a while. Or if you want to try and buy something, you can. They've got a few car dealerships there."

Buying a vehicle meant touching the blood money, and Tucker wasn't quite ready to do so. Maybe sometime in the future, but for now, he still wanted nothing to do with the funds.

"After I see my aunt and uncle, I'll bring the car back to the winery."

"I should be through with business around two. Pick me up then or any time after that," Emerson told him.

"Then I can drop you off at The Inn on Lost Creek, and you can have a couple of hours to yourself before Ry and I pick you up for dinner."

She got out of the car, and he replaced her behind the wheel, waving goodbye. Tucker drove into town. He stopped at Lone Star Diner first, having a reunion with Aunt Shelly. She looked so much like his mother had before the cancer ate her up.

"Are you staying with Ry and Emerson? If not, Shy and I are happy to have you with us. You could even have your old room back if you'd like," she said hopefully.

He explained about taking a room at Jean Bradley's B&B, saying he needed a little quiet time. His aunt nodded, understanding immediately. That's what he'd always liked about his Aunt Shelly. She was warm and loving, giving him the attention he needed, always seeming to understand him. Sometimes, before he understood things himself.

After they talked over a cup of coffee, he left the diner and headed to Blackwood BBQ. As he pulled into the parking lot, the familiar smell of smoked meats lingered in the air.

Once inside, Tucker spent an hour with his uncle Shy, catching up on sports. Shy Blackwood lived for three things. His wife. Barbeque. And sports. Not necessarily in that order.

Leaving the restaurant with a brisket sandwich and a couple of sides in a brown bag, he drove back to The Inn on Lost Creek. Using his key to enter the B&B, he went straight to the kitchen, where Miss Jean bustled about, placing a pie in a plastic container and sealing the lid.

"Oh, hello, Tucker."

"What are you up to, Miss Jean? And stop me if I'm being too nosy," he teased.

Laughing, she said, "I'm heading to my monthly book club. Since you already have dinner arranged, I'll stay in town after our book discussion and eat an early dinner with a few friends."

"Will you even have room for dinner after serving that pie to your club's members?"

She snorted. "I'll be lucky to get a piece of it. Those women are like vultures, descending upon any sweet brought to the book club. I'll probably be home around seven-thirty or so."

"I should be home shortly after you," he said. "From what I gather, the folks I'm having dinner with tonight are all early birds. They eat early because they get up before the crack of dawn."

She picked up the container and her purse, which was sitting on the counter. "I'm off. Have a nice time with your friends, Tucker."

After enjoying the lunch Uncle Shy had sent home with him, Tucker went outside to sit on the porch and enjoy the mid-October day. He took a notebook and pencil with him in case any lyrics came to him. While he didn't mind dictating spur of the moment ideas into his phone, he preferred writing down his lyrics and playing with them on paper.

He rocked, his mind hopscotching from one topic to

another. Lost Creek had always felt like home, and he was glad he was officially becoming a resident of the community now. Whether he could make his living as a songwriter, though, remained to be seen.

Close to two, he returned to the winery and collected Emerson. The sweet aroma of cake hung in the air.

"How did your meetings go?" he asked.

"Both couples came in for cake samplings," she told him. "We'd already met previously, so I had an idea of the flavors and icings they might enjoy."

"I might have to get hitched just to come in a sample all your goodies," he joked.

"I'll bake you anything you want, Tucker Young. As it is, I've also created dessert for tonight. I'm the designated dessert bringer each Wednesday night."

She picked up a cake box sitting on the counter. "Here's tonight's delight. And no peeking," she warned.

Emerson dropped him off at the inn, and Tucker retrieved his pen and paper, returning to the porch and hoping for inspiration to strike. He told himself to be patient. Not to force anything. That the music was inside him. That it would come.

And when it did, he would be ready for it.

Lost in his thoughts, a car suddenly pulled up in front of the B&B, startling him. A woman got out, slinging a purse over her shoulder and making her way up the steps. She was about five-four, with caramel-colored hair and warm brown eyes that stirred him in a way he hadn't felt in years.

"Hello," she said. "Are you staying here?"

He rose and offered her his hand. "Tucker Young. Yes, ma'am, I'm a guest at the inn. If you're looking to book a room, though, Miss Jean isn't here right now."

She shook his hand, and Tucker felt an electricity ripple through him. She must have felt it, too, because her eyes widened slightly, and she quickly pulled her hand from his.

"I already should have a room set aside for me," she explained. "I'm Reagan Bradley. My aunt owns The Inn on Lost Creek."

5

___

*T*ucker Young's smile knocked Reagan for a loop. She was already tingling from shaking his hand.

What was happening to her?

She hadn't looked at a man in the two years since Arch's murder. Of course, she had buried herself in work. Still, she felt disloyal to her fiancé's memory as things inside her began stirring. Feelings she had thought lost to her forever with Arch's death.

"Miss Jean told me you were coming, but she said you would arrive sometime tomorrow."

"I was able to wrap things up in New York sooner than I anticipated," she said stiffly, not wanting to like this man.

"I know exactly which room she's put you in. If you'd like, I can help you bring in your luggage so you can get settled."

Thinking of the two heavy suitcases to be brought up

the stairs, Reagan relented. "Yes, I'd appreciate that." She returned to the car she'd rented at the Austin airport, she popped its trunk, removing her carryon, which was stuffed to the brim.

Tucker had followed her, and he lifted the first suitcase from the trunk. Laughing, he asked, "Is there only one dead body in here? Or did you manage to cram in two?"

He set the suitcase on the ground and pulled out the other one. Then with ease, he picked up both and looked at her expectantly. Without a word, she closed the trunk and moved up the stairs, opening the front door for him. Tucker sailed through it and headed toward the staircase. Reagan closed and locked the door behind her and followed him.

She reached the landing. Looking up, she saw he was almost to the top of the stairs, which gave her a chance to admire his backside for a moment. He was long and lean, the faded jeans molded to his legs and ass. While he didn't appear to be bulging with muscles, he carried her heavy pieces of luggage with no problem at all. His hair was a sandy brown, but what had drawn her in were his hazel eyes and winning smile.

And now, his firm ass.

All in all, Tucker Young was quite the appealing package.

She saw him enter a bedroom and caught up to him, seeing him set her suitcases at the foot of the queen-sized bed. She rested her weekender beside her and said, "You handled those with ease."

He shrugged. "Years of helping roadies haul equipment. It was a better workout than lifting at a gym."

"You were a roadie? For concerts?"

"I grew up around them. My dad managed a few country music acts, and I was always on the road with him. I learned a lot about the music industry from the ground up. I can spout stats about arenas across the country. Tell you the best places to eat in cities far and wide. Name hits off the charts for any given year."

"I don't know much about music," she admitted. "Country or otherwise."

He looked puzzled. "Don't you listen to music when you're in the car or at home?"

"Not really. I focused on my studies growing up. I was driven to be the best kid in every class. Music was a distraction if I tried to listen to it while I wrote essays or tried to balance chemical equations. While other girls slapped rock star posters on their bedroom walls, I was reading Pulitzer Prize winning novels and tinkering with science fair projects."

He chuckled. "I was homeschooled myself. If you could call it that. Dad left me on my own a lot, so I pursued whatever I was interested in. I guess you could say that I was first— and last —in my class of one."

"That sounds terribly irresponsible," she said and then stopped, mortified. "I'm sorry. My remark was judgmental. I didn't mean to come off so high-handed."

Tucker smiled lazily at her, and Regan's heart fluttered inside her chest.

"No offense taken. We just come from very different

worlds. Mine was the School of Hard Knocks. I taught myself whatever I wanted to know. Fortunately, I was a kid who wanted to learn about a lot of stuff and explored all kinds of topics. I would fixate on something. Geology. World War II battles. Science fiction. Then I would pursue that topic with a passion until I knew everything about it."

Reagan had never met anyone as interesting as Tucker Young. "Do you still spend most of your time on the road?"

"If you're asking if I still set up for concerts, the answer is no. I gave up that nomadic life when I went to college. Graduated from UT in Austin and went to work in a bank as a loan officer for several years."

He paused, a shadow crossing his face. Instinct told her there was much more to his story, and Reagan found herself interested in discovering what it might be.

Shrugging, he said, "I've done a little traveling the last couple of years. I just arrived in Lost Creek yesterday and think I'm here to stay."

"What's your connection to Lost Creek?" she asked.

"Have you ever eaten at Blackwood BBQ or Lone Star Diner? My uncle owns and runs the barbeque joint, while my aunt does the same with the diner."

"I ate at both, but that was years ago. I haven't visited Lost Creek in almost twenty years. Something went down between my mom and Aunt Jean. I never knew what it was, but we stopped coming to visit."

"Sounds like me. It's been a long time since I've been here."

Reagan thought he would ask her more about what she

had been doing, but he moved toward the door and said, "I'll let you unpack. Your aunt has gone into town for her monthly book club. Since she wasn't expecting you, she's having dinner with a few friends after that. Miss Jean told me she would be home around seven or seven-thirty."

"Thanks for letting me know, Tucker. I won't text her because she'd drop everything and rush home. I know how much she enjoys book club." She paused. "It was nice meeting you, Tucker."

He stopped in the doorway. "We're sharing the bathroom across the hall. If you'll let me know times you need in there, I can work around your schedule."

She felt herself flushing. She hadn't shared a bathroom with a man since Arch would stay over. The intimacy of it threw her a little. Then again, she recalled Aunt Jean's B&B didn't have en suite rooms.

"Let me think about it, and I'll get back to you. Actually, I'm the one who can be flexible and work around you. I don't have any plans at the moment."

"Miss Jean said your visit was open-ended. Are you on a leave of absence from your job in New York, or are you going to work remotely while you're here?"

"I'm done with New York," she said vehemently, seeing the surprise on his face by her tone. "Sorry. I quit my job there. Gave up my apartment. I've decided to move back permanently to Texas."

He looked at her with interest. "So, is Lost Creek a stopover— or your final destination?"

Reagan sighed. "That's what I'm here to figure out," she revealed, which surprised her because she had only just met this man, and she usually didn't open up to strangers. "I'm a financial analyst. If I stay in that field, I'll probably investigate big cities. Dallas and Ft. Worth. San Antonio or Houston. To be honest, I don't think large cities and finance appeal to me much anymore. I'm here to spend time with Aunt Jean and decide what I want to do with the rest of my life. You'd think at thirty I'd already know what I want."

He shook his head. "No, people change careers all the time. Age doesn't have a thing to do with it. I'm thirty-one and find myself at a crossroads, as well, Reagan." He paused, his gaze pinning hers. "Maybe we can use one another as a sounding board and help discover what we're meant to do."

She had the insane urge to throw her arms about him and kiss him. That was the last thing she would act upon, though. Her heart was still bruised from losing Arch. She wasn't interested in being with another man. It somehow seemed disloyal to Arch's memory.

Still, she said, "I could use a friend. I'm in sore need of one of those."

He cocked his head, studying her a moment. "I spent summers in Lost Creek while I was growing up. My cousin Ry and I were like brothers. He recently left the military and came home, marrying the gal who owns The Bake House."

Reagan laughed. "I definitely recall The Bake House. When my folks brought me here to visit Aunt Jean, that was my favorite destination."

"Since Miss Jean already has other plans tonight,

you're going to need to eat dinner. Why don't you come along with me?" he offered. "Ry and Emerson have a group of friends they eat with every Wednesday night. If you're going to be in town a while, they would be some good people to know."

His offer was tempting. She had never really had friends, only acquaintances. Growing up, she was so focused on learning and being the best student in her class, she didn't make friends. Everyone seemed jealous of her looks and intelligence, and a group of mean girls had bullied her for most of her years in school. She had ignored them, but the pressure they put on others kept anyone from attempting to befriend her.

In college, Reagan preferred studying on her own to study groups. She looked at other students as her competition and pretty much remained a loner. The only true friend she had ever made was Arch.

It was time to shake things up.

"If you don't think it would be an imposition, I'd love to tag along and meet your cousin and his wife. And their friends."

"It won't be a problem," Tucker assured her. "I know Harper and Ivy from years back. Their brother Todd was Ry's best friend growing up. I met Ivy's husband yesterday. Dax runs the coffeehouse on the square. He introduced me to Holden Scott while I was there. He's a part of their friend group. I'm sure you've heard of him."

She looked at him blankly. "I... don't have any idea who that is."

"Your job must've kept you really busy. Holden's a

famous writer. He had a bestseller. *Capitol Crimes.* It was made into a big movie."

She bit her lip. "Sorry. I don't read much or go to movies."

"I'm already seeing that I'll be advising you to leave the world of finance, Reagan Bradley. It seems as if you haven't had a life as a financial analyst. We're going to find something good for you to do. Something rewarding. Challenging. And fun."

The idea of fun seemed beyond her. Getting to know a few others her age, however, did appeal to her a great deal.

"What time is dinner tonight?" she asked.

"Ry and Emerson are picking me up at five. Dinner's at five-thirty."

Her jaw dropped, and Tucker started laughing.

"I guess you New Yorkers eat a little bit later. You're back in Texas, now. A lot of these people have jobs that get them up early, and so they like to eat early. Will that be a problem?"

"No. I've only had a bagel and a cup of coffee before my flight this morning."

"I'll let Harper know to set a place for one extra then," he told her. "Be downstairs on the porch at five. I'll leave you to your unpacking,"

"See you then."

After he left, Reagan closed the door, wanting a little privacy because of the thoughts swirling in her head.

As she opened the first suitcase, it struck her how much she had upended her life in just a handful of days.

After her brief conversation with Tucker Young, she realized she hadn't had much of a life at all. She was eager to pick up a book again and actually read it for pleasure. Watch a movie and talk it over with friends. Hike or practice yoga. Although she had thought she would be spending tonight bending Aunt Jean's ear, she realized her absence— and Tucker's invitation —was a blessing in disguise.

She was in the position now to reinvent herself. Reagan could be anyone she wanted to be.

And Lost Creek was hopefully the place for that to happen.

6

$\mathcal{R}$eagan finished unpacking, setting the last of her things in a drawer, deciding she would leave on her black pants and lightweight fuchsia sweater. She realized she had no casual clothes. Life had revolved around work, and she had usually worn black, gray, or navy pants with a matching blazer and dress shirt. Being in Lost Creek, she would need to pick up pairs of jeans and casual tops. All the clothes she'd dragged with her from New York no longer seemed important. They were sophisticated, tailored, and elegant— and useless. Well, maybe not. She still hadn't ruled out looking for a job in a large city.

But the thought of continuing to do what she had done for years held little appeal for her. Instead, Tucker Young's words intrigued her. If she could find a job which used her skills, but was also challenging and fun, she would accept it in a heartbeat. It didn't matter what it paid. She had enough money. Her job had paid extremely well, but she put in so many hours, she never had time to spend any of the money, other than on clothes that made her look professional.

She also wanted to purchase some workout clothes. Living with her aunt Jean, who was a fabulous cook, she would need to add exercise into her daily routine. Her eating habits as a trader and analyst had been terrible. She either skipped meals or ate at odd hours, mostly pizza or Chinese takeout. She was thirty now. It was time to start taking better care of herself.

Since it was a quarter till five, she gathered her purse and a light jacket, heading downstairs. Not seeing Tucker, she walked through the various rooms, memories flooding her of previous visits to the B&B. Although she had never been close to her mother, she had been a daddy's girl. Reagan pictured herself and her father sitting together in an oversized chair, her reading aloud to him.

Wandering into the large dining room, she wondered how many guests Aunt Jean had staying at the inn this time of year. Then she entered the kitchen.

This was her favorite room in the house. When her family had come to visit each summer during her youth, Reagan had been her aunt's helper. It was the only time she had every cooked. They had a housekeeper and cook back in Dickinson, but in Lost Creek, she enjoyed her time in the kitchen. Aunt Jean had put her to work peeling potatoes, washing lettuce, and shelling peas. Her favorite thing had been to knead dough for the bread baked daily. She decided she would ask her aunt to teach her to cook.

Wherever she eventually got a job, she wouldn't have her usual takeout places on speed dial. She wanted to become self-sufficient in Texas.

Leaving the kitchen, she made her way outside, locking the door behind her. Tucker sat in the same rocker he had been in when she arrived.

"Take a seat," he suggested, and she sat in the rocker next to him. "Get everything put away?"

"I did. It seems as if my New York wardrobe is a bit fancy for Lost Creek. I need jeans. Flannel shirts. T-shirts."

"I wouldn't get rid of anything just yet," he advised. "You might decide you still want to work in some capacity in the business world. The best thing you can do is take the much-needed time off if you're in a position financially to do so. Even if you decide to consult and do a lot of your work from your home base, you'll want nice clothes for business meetings or conventions you attend. You could keep your favorite pieces and sell the others by consignment to help buy some new clothes."

"I'm good for now," she replied, not wishing to discuss the huge nest egg she had grown through investing. "I don't want to dive back into a new job. I plan to take your advice, though. I may take a month or more and relish the peace and quiet of Lost Creek. How about you? What are your plans?"

He grew thoughtful, and that urge to press her lips against his sensual ones overwhelmed her again. Reagan looked away, staring out at the woods a short distance from the house.

"I'm in a similar position to you," he began. "I worked my bank job for several years. Did a little songwriting on the side."

"Really?" she asked, curious about this aspect of his life. "Were they country songs? Did you write any hits?"

"A few. After I quit my day job a couple of years ago, I traveled the U.S. extensively."

"Looking for ideas to write about?" she asked.

Tucker shrugged, and Reagan said, "I'm sorry. That's a very personal question, and we've only just met."

"No, it's fine." He swallowed. "I lost my wife in a car accident a little over two years ago," he shared. "I felt tremendous guilt surviving when she died. I also miss her more than I can ever say. Josie was the love of my life."

Her own throat constricted with emotion. She could see the pain etched on Tucker's face and knew she had found a kindred spirit.

"I was banged up in the crash. I even missed her funeral because I was still in the hospital. Once I got out and got the cast off my leg, I couldn't go back to the life I'd led before. I saw Josie at every turn. So, I quit the bank. Sold our house and everything in it. I just took off. No destination in mind."

"What did you do?" she asked softly.

"I hitchhiked. Stopped in places far and wide. Some were little holes in the wall with only a few hundred people in them. Others were big cities I tried to lose myself in."

His gaze met hers. "I'll always love Josie until my dying day, but she would want me to start living again. I've wallowed in misery long enough. When Emerson contacted me, I felt it was a sign. She and Ry had just gotten married, and they wanted me to come to Lost Creek. For a visit— or to stay." He paused. "I think I'm going to stay."

"After your time on the road, I'm sure freedom means a lot to you. Will you try to pick up songwriting again?"

"That's the plan. I wrote some decent tunes a few years ago. I'd like to try and resurrect that part of me again. It'll be tough, though. Josie was always my barometer, listening to what I had written. Giving me feedback."

"No one will ever take her place, Tucker, but I'm happy to listen to any of your songs. You know I know nothing about music, but I'm ready to hear you play."

He nodded to himself, lost in his thoughts for a moment. She kept silent, letting him mull it over.

"I believe I'll take you up on that offer, Reagan Bradley. You'll be more critical. That'll push me. If you like a song, then other people will, too. If I don't make it as a song-writer, though, I still plan on remaining in Lost Creek. After my youth spent traveling from town to town, this is the closest to home I've ever known."

She wanted to tell him they were kindred spirits. That she had also lost someone she loved. Reagan tried to, but the words seemed stick in her throat.

Then Tucker said, "Here's our ride."

Glancing up, she saw a car coming up the path. She smiled brightly, trying to push aside all the sorrow which welled up within her.

The vehicle came to a stop, and the passenger door

opened. A woman with clear gray eyes and raven hair gave her a welcoming smile. She offered her hand.

"You must be Reagan, Jean's niece. I'm Emerson Blackwood. I'm so glad you could join us for dinner this evening."

A warmth filled her at the friendly greeting. "Thank you so much, Emerson. I was a little reluctant to come."

"It's nice to have you in Lost Creek. Your aunt is a stalwart in the community. Everyone respects her opinions." Emerson giggled. "And Jean Bradley has a lot of them."

"She's definitely does and she's feisty in defending those opinions," Reagan agreed.

Emerson turned to Tucker. "Why don't you ride in the front? You need the legroom like Ry. Just watch the dessert sitting on the floorboard when you get in. Reagan and I can sit in the back."

Tucker opened the rear door, and she climbed into the back seat. Emerson walked around to the other side and then joined her.

The driver turned. Although he had dark hair and blue eyes to Tucker's sandy brown hair and hazel eyes, she could see a resemblance in their facial features, marking them as cousins.

"It's good to meet you, Reagan. I'm Ry Blackwood."

"I have eaten at your family's barbeque place. It was a long time ago. My parents and I used to visit Aunt Jean when I was really young. I haven't been back to Lost Creek in a good number of years, though."

"Well, we're glad you've come for a visit and hope you will stay a while."

They drove to where dinner was being held, Emerson giving Reagan a rundown of who would be there.

"We always gather on Wednesdays and have dinner with this particular group of friends," she explained. "We eat at Braden and Harper's house because they have the largest dining table of the group. Braden works for the Hart family and is their head winemaker. He's gaining quite a reputation in the Hill Country, especially for his blends. Harper owns a business on the winery grounds, and she holds many weddings and other events at the venue there. They're expecting their first baby next month."

"That may change the dynamics of your group dinners," Reagan pointed out.

"I hope not," Emerson replied. "Harper doesn't do any of the cooking. Braden is the cook in their family. He and Finley Scott trade off weeks. They try out all kinds of new, fun recipes on us."

"Tell me about Finley," she encouraged.

Emerson smiled. "Fin was my roommate in college. After graduation, we both took jobs at Lost Creek Elementary and taught for six years. I wound up inheriting The Bake House and left teaching, while Fin stepped away from the classroom to pursue photography full-time. She'd already been doing it as a side gig, photographing weddings for Weddings with Hart and also family and senior portraits of residents in the area. Fin's also involved a little bit in the movie business, thanks to Holden, her husband."

"I hear he's a writer," Reagan said, glad she had a good memory for names and faces.

"If you haven't read either book Holden has written, you should. They'll keep you on the edge of your seat. His first book was made into a movie. The director of that film, Wolf Ramirez, and his wife Ana, started their own production company. They optioned Holden's second book and filmed it this summer near Lost Creek. Holden wrote the screenplay for the film, while Finley took stills during production. She's also worked on some of the ad campaign. *Hill Country Homicide* comes out at the end next month, around the same time Holden's third book releases."

"Then I really need to catch up on my reading," she joked.

"I've told Reagan she should watch *Capitol Crimes*," Tucker added. "It's a thriller, with a ticking time bomb plot."

"Don't forget about Ivy and Dax," Ry reminded his wife.

Emerson turned back to Reagan. "Ivy is Harper's sister, and she is becoming a painter of note. Ivy paints landscapes of the Hill Country, and she had a big show at a famous Manhattan gallery last month. Every painting sold, and she's really making her mark in the art world."

"I'd love to see some of her paintings. The Hill Country really speaks to my heart. I was brought up in Dickinson, which is close to Galveston. While I like being around the water, I prefer the rugged beauty of the Hill Country to the ocean."

"Ivy also serves as the manager of Lost Creek Vineyard's tasting room," Emerson continued. "Something tells me that she's going to have to give that up. Right now, she paints morning and then works at the tasting room afternoons and some weekends."

"You think she'll want to pursue art full-time?" Reagan asked.

Emerson chuckled. "She's also going to have a baby. A girl. She's arriving in March. I think painting and a baby will trump the tasting room."

By now, they had pulled up in front of a beautiful, two-story house.

"We're here," Ry announced.

"I'll grab the dessert for you," Tucker said.

"What did you bring?" she asked as they got out of the car.

Ry answered her question. "Emerson is the one who always provides dessert for us. It's a surprise each time." He grinned. "Though most people hope for chocolate on a regular basis."

Emerson told Reagan, "I try to do a chocolate dessert every other time to appease the chocoholics in the group. Tonight's dessert is different, though."

Ry slipped an arm about his wife's waist as they walked to the front door. "Whatever it is, it'll be a success."

He gave Emerson a sweet kiss, and Reagan felt a pang of sadness. She hadn't kissed anyone in two years. Hadn't even had a date.

And yet for some odd reason, all she could think about was kissing Tucker Young.

They rang the doorbell, and a man with dark brown hair and eyes the color of melted chocolate opened it.

"Hey, everyone," he said, ushering them in.

As she passed, he said, "I'm Dax Tennyson, Ivy's husband. I heard you were joining us tonight. Good to have you in Lost Creek, Reagan."

"It's nice to be here."

"Stop by Java Junction on the square soon," Dax told her. "First cup of coffee is on the house."

A woman her height with blond hair and arresting aquamarine eyes came toward her. "I'm Finley Scott. I would love to meet you for that cup of coffee, Reagan. Look at your calendar and see when is a good time."

She chuckled. "Any time is good for me, Finley. I'm here in Lost Creek to visit Aunt Jean and relax."

Finley pulled out her phone. "How about Friday morning? Nine? Ten?"

Reagan slipped her own phone from her purse. "Whichever is good for you."

Another pretty brunette with hazel eyes joined them. "Let's make it nine," she suggested. "That way, I can tag along. Hi, Reagan. I'm Ivy Tennyson."

"I hear you're a painter. Congratulations. I hear you're having a little girl next year."

Ivy's hands went to her belly. "Thank you. We're going to be parents in March. Dax will be the most amazing father. Here, let me take your purse and jacket."

Ivy hung both on a coat rack and slipped her arm through Reagan's. "Come into the kitchen and meet everyone else."

They entered a large kitchen, where a tall man with California blond, good looks stirred something on the stove. Another man with wire-framed glasses, dark hair, and green eyes talked with him. They both turned as everyone entered.

Ivy introduced her to Holden, the writer, and Braden, the winemaker.

"I hear that you cook quite a bit for this group, Braden."

"Cooking is always something I've enjoyed doing," he said. "Holden here is fast becoming a good cook himself. Finley and I are teaching him the way around a kitchen. We're about ready to add him into the Wednesday night cooking rotation. If I cook a week, then Finley the next, and then Holden pulls a turn, it would help out, especially with the baby coming."

"I heard you'll be parents soon. Congratulations," Reagan said, watching Braden beam with pride.

"You'll have to get Harper to show you the nursery. Honey," he called. "Reagan and Tucker are here."

While Tucker began talking with the two men, she saw a heavily pregnant woman enter the kitchen. Harper Clark was a true beauty like her sister, even though they looked quite different from one another in height, eye, and hair coloring. Harper was probably five-eight, with long auburn hair and sparkling blue eyes.

"Oh, I'm so glad you could join us," Harper said. "And Tucker, too. Tuck was a good friend of my brother, Todd. We lost Todd several years ago, but it's nice to have Ry and now, Tucker, back in town again."

"Show Reagan Beau's nursery," Braden prompted over his shoulder.

"Come along, Reagan," Harper said.

They passed a homey-looking great room and went up the stairs, stopping at a door. Stepping inside, Harper turned on the light. Reagan followed.

"Oh, this is darling!" she exclaimed.

The walls were a soft cream, with a huge tree rising behind the crib. A monkey hung from a branch, while a giraffe munched from its leaves. The mural also had a zebra and a lion perched on a branch, sleeping in the sun. The changing table was in a soft green, reminiscent of the leaves, and a rocker sat in the corner. On another wall was painted the name *Beau.*

"Ivy and Finley did everything. All I had to do was choose the colors. My sister painted the mural you see. Finley chose all the furniture and decorated."

"It's a very welcoming place, Harper. I'm sure your little boy will love it."

"Let's head back downstairs. Dinner is about ready."

They returned to the kitchen, where Holden said, "It's always family style, Reagan. Everything is on the island, and you help yourself."

"Except for drinks," Dax interjected. "Do you like wine, Reagan? There's also iced tea and sparkling water."

As she started around the island, where she saw two large pots of jambalaya, as well as a black-eyed pea salad and hush puppies, Reagan said, "I'll try some wine. To be honest, I don't know much about it. My parents were wine snobs. Actually, they were snobs about everything. I went in the opposite direction and have never really drunk wine because of them."

"Tucker has said the same thing," Ivy said, ladling jambalaya into a bowl. "He's a beer guy. I've offered to walk him through a tasting and teach him a little about reds, whites, and blends. He and I just decided to do that tomorrow. The tasting room closes at five-thirty. If you don't mind, Tucker, you could share the tasting."

"Fine with me," Tucker said, using tongs to place golden hush puppies on his plate.

"As long as you're coming to the winery, you might as well get the fifty-cent tour," Braden said. "I can show you the vineyards and the lab where the magic happens."

"And I'd be happy to show off my kitchen and the event center," Emerson interjected.

"My office better be on this world tour," Harper joked.

They moved into the dining room with their plates and bowls of jambalaya. Dax and Holden went around the table, filling wine glasses, with Finley coming behind with a pitcher of iced tea.

"Ivy brought a zinfandel and a shiraz," Dax explained when he reached her. "I'm going to give you a little of each."

"Thank you," she said, watching the wine being poured into the glasses before her, as Holden added from the bottle he also carried. "What pretty colors."

"Oh, you'll learn all about color in your tasting," Dax teased. "Ivy had to educate me from the ground up. I find I really enjoy wine now." He grinned at Braden. "Especially Lost Creek Vineyards selections."

She was pleasantly surprised how well she fit into the conversation at the table. The others asked her a few questions about herself, nothing intrusive. In turn, she found out more about what they all did for a living and some of the volunteer work they did for the community.

The guys cleared the table, while Emerson brought out the dessert she had baked.

"I've made for you an autumn cheesecake. On top of the cheesecake is a mix of Graham crackers, pecans, and cinnamon, topped with a mixture of cream cheese and cinnamon sugar-coated apples. The crust is pure Graham crackers, though."

"It's beautiful," Finley declared. "And I'll bet there won't be any left."

She was right.

When it was time to go, Reagan thanked Braden and Harper for having her, and Harper said, "I hope you'll become a regular for Wednesday dinners. Maybe we'll convince you to stay in Lost Creek."

Braden asked Emerson, "What time do you think you'll bring Reagan to the winery tomorrow?"

"I've got two cakes to bake." Emerson looked at her. "Would you mind me doing that? I can show you around the event center while they're in the oven. When they're done, I'll take them out to cool, and we can go see either Braden or Harper."

"Work me into your schedule," she replied.

They set a time. She and Tucker accompanied Ry and Emerson to their car. Since Tucker hadn't seen the vineyards, they decided that Reagan would spend time with

Emerson and Harper and then meet up with Tucker and Braden. Afterward, they could head to the tasting room for their private session with Ivy.

They said their goodnights to Ry and Emerson, and Tucker accompanied her to the porch. Reagan already had out her key and opened the door.

"I'm going to find Aunt Jean," she said. "Thanks again for thinking to ask me to come to dinner tonight. Your friends are really nice."

"I really only knew Ry, Ivy, and Harper before I got here, and I hadn't seen any of them in years. I did talk with Emerson a few times while I made my way to Texas. But the others are all new to me, too. You're right. They're a great group of people. Very welcoming."

"I agree. I didn't sense any awkwardness at all, like there can be when you're meeting new people. I never felt left out, either."

"They were good about including us," Tucker agreed. "Goodnight, Reagan. I'll see you tomorrow."

"Goodnight," she said softly, watching him head up the stairs.

The evening had turned out well. Better than she had expected.

And at some point, Reagan would share her story with Tucker.

7

*R*eagan did a quick sweep through the first floor of the house, not finding Aunt Jean in any of the common rooms. She headed toward her aunt's bedroom, located at the rear of the house, hoping she was home from her dinner with friends.

As she raised a hand to knock on Aunt Jean's bedroom door, it opened, startling both women.

"For land's sake!" her aunt exclaimed. Then her features softened. "Oh, Reagan. You're here."

She found herself enfolded in a warm embrace, one which comforted her. She drew strength from it, as well. Aunt Jean had always had a calming effect on her.

Pulling away, her aunt studied her. "You're prettier than ever, Reagan. And you're early!"

"I hope you don't mind the surprise. I finished up what needed to be done in New York and was able to catch an earlier flight."

Aunt Jean pulled Reagan toward her again for another, long hug. "I'm delighted you made it. I was just going to the kitchen to make myself a cup of tea. Would you like one?"

"That— and a long talk," she said, feeling her troubles slide from her shoulders now that she was in the presence of no-nonsense, feisty Jean Bradley.

Reagan followed her aunt to the kitchen, heading to the tea caddy to select a flavor. The tea caddy had fascinated her when she was younger. She used to read through all the different packets, marveling at the variety of flavors. Her aunt didn't tolerate caffeine, and so most of the caddy held various herbal flavors, along with a few decaffeinated Earl Grey and green teas.

Choosing a ginger turmeric, she asked, "What would you like? Chamomile to help you sleep tonight?"

"Yes, dear. There's a new chamomile with honey vanilla that I'm partial to. I'll take that."

She located the packet and pulled it out as her aunt filled two large mugs with water and placed them in the microwave.

"Have a seat," Aunt Jean told her.

She wondered if this would be a good time for them to talk and asked, "Who are your guests this week?"

"Weekdays start slowing this time of year. You know that. Weekends are still busy as always, though. Right now, only two guests are with me. I have Sid Allen upstairs in the last room at the end of the hall. Poor fellow is separated from his wife. Works nights. Most weekends, too. I hope he can sort things out. He keeps to himself pretty much. See him at breakfast when he gets off his shift. Sleeps all day. Eats his dinner at six and then heads out again."

Aunt Jean opened the cookie jar. "Want anything sweet to nibble on?"

"No. I'm full from dinner."

Her aunt removed two cookies and placed them on a paper napkin, setting it on the table and taking a seat. "Did you eat on your way to Lost Creek?"

"No. Tucker Young was here when I arrived. He told me you were in town at your book club and then having dinner with friends."

"Dang it, Reagan. You should've called me," her aunt chided. "I would've rushed home right away."

She laughed. "That's exactly what I didn't want. There was no reason for you to come home and miss time with your friends, especially since I'm going to be here a while."

Aunt Jean beamed. "I'm so glad to hear that, honey. What did you think of Tucker?"

"I like him," she responded. "He was kind enough to invite me to dinner with a group of friends. It's a weekly gathering."

"Oh, I know all about that. It's held at Braden and Harper Clark's house. She used to be Harper Hart."

Reagan grinned. "Of course, you do. You know everything that goes on in Lost Creek," she teased.

"You bet I do. It's a lovely group of young people. They're all around your age."

"They were very welcoming to me. I fit right in. It was as if I'd known them for years."

Her aunt nodded knowingly. "You couldn't do better."

The microwave beeped, and she said, "I'll get it."

Retrieving the mugs, she brought them to the table. Both women tore open their tea packets and dipped their tea bags into the scalding water several times, then let it steep.

"Emerson Blackwood is picking me up tomorrow. She's going to show me the event center and the kitchen she bakes in at Lost Creek Winery. Harper wants me to stop in and see her office. Braden is going to give Tucker and me a tour of the grapevines and tell us about the process of making wine. Then Ivy is going to do a private wine tasting for us."

"My, it seems as if you've got a full day planned."

Enthusiastically, she added, "Dax wants me to stop by Java Junction. Finley Scott made a coffee date with me, and Ivy is also going to join us for that." Hesitating, she said, "I've never felt so welcomed. I've never really had friends, Aunt Jean. You know that."

Her aunt placed a hand over Reagan's. "I do, my little love. But I think your life is going to take a turn here in Lost Creek."

They sipped their tea in amiable silence for a few minutes before her aunt asked, "Do you know how long you'll be here? I'm not trying to run you off, now. Don't get the wrong idea."

"I don't have any plans," she admitted. "For the first time in my life, I'm not working toward a goal." She swallowed. "Or working to survive."

Tears filled her eyes, and her aunt squeezed Reagan's

hand. "I know how rough the past two years have been for you. Losing Arch was just horrible."

"To be honest, I numbed myself to everything. I spent ninety or more hours at work each week. Other than the people at my office or the delivery guys who brought me takeout, I didn't talk to anyone else. I buried my head in the sand and hoped work would heal all the hurt I felt inside."

"Did it?" Aunt Jean asked gently.

"It finally hit me that I wasn't living. I was existing. I realized I needed to move on. From my job. From New York. From the emptiness inside." She sighed. "That's why I'm here. I don't want to ever forget Arch, but I'm hoping I can put myself back together and heal."

"You know you can stay as long as you wish, my darling."

Reagan laughed. "You should be careful about extending invitations like that. You might not be able to get rid of me."

"I'd love that," her aunt said, her eyes sparkling. "You told me you quit your job. Will you eventually go back to New York to work?"

"I've cut all ties with New York," she revealed. "The apartment is gone. I burned all professional bridges when I left, so I doubt my old boss would give me any kind of decent recommendation." She shook her head. "I'm thirty. I'm starting fresh. I don't even know if I still want to work in finance."

Her aunt studied her a long moment. "Then you've come to the right place. I arrived in Lost Creek years ago, at a crossroads in my own life. I'd given up everything to raise your father after our parents died. My dreams of college, in particular. I wanted to be a teacher, you know."

That surprised Reagan. "No, I didn't know that. You would've have made for a great teacher, Aunt Jean."

"Maybe. Once your dad was all set, I decided to go somewhere new. Reinvent myself. I was about to be forty and had always lived for him. I was ready to live for myself. I didn't want to go back to school at that age. I would've had to work full-time to put myself through, so it would've taken me until I was probably fifty before I graduated. Instead, I heard about an opportunity here and took a leap of faith."

"You bought the inn."

Aunt Jean laughed. "It wasn't the inn you see today. It was a dilapidated shell, which I got it for a song. Did all the work myself, fixing it up. I taught myself about plumbing and wiring. Sanded the floors. Painted the walls. I opened up the B&B and never looked back. It's been a wonderful place to have over the years. I've met so many interesting people who've stayed here."

"You also have great friends. I remember meeting some of them when I was younger."

"My friends have become my family," her aunt admitted. "Especially after I didn't see you anymore."

"What happened, Aunt Jean? I was twelve when we stopped coming to visit you. It had to be something with Mom. Was it her drinking?"

Her aunt snorted. "Your mom was definitely the root of the estrangement. She always thought she was better than I was. I didn't have her education and came from nothing. She put on airs and thought she was better than everyone around her."

"I wonder how she wound up with Dad then. His background was yours."

"Your daddy took advantage of the education I paid for. He sidled up to the right people and made friends with them. While I was working two, three jobs putting him through school, he spent weekends and holidays with that rich crowd. He taught himself how to speak like them. Imitate their gestures. He could mimic anything. Used to do great impressions of people, famous and otherwise." Aunt Jean paused. "He might not have been born into that world, but he fit into it like a hand fits a glove. I'll hand it to him. He studied hard. Made top grades. That gave him the chance to make a different kind of life for himself."

"I knew we had money. We had a housekeeper and cook. People who cared for the lawn and garden. Our house was the always the biggest and nicest. I had the best clothes. But I was so unhappy."

"I know you were. Believe me, my heart hurt because of that. Because I didn't know how to fix it."

"I always felt so different from my parents," Reagan said, pouring her heart out to her aunt. "Mom was such a snob, and Dad went along with whatever she wanted. Actually, I realize now that they were big fish in a little pond. Dickinson was a small town, but they were at the top of the heap, financially and socially. And still Mom was unhappy. Or I guess she was. Isn't that what drinking is all about?"

Her aunt pondered that statement. "I think she was happy in the beginning. Marrying your dad was a step up for her. Her background wasn't nearly as grand as she let people think it was. She came from working-class parents. Their only child. They sacrificed everything so that she could have whatever she wanted. I hate to say it, honey, but your mom was spoiled rotten. Yes, she got to go to college and pledge the right sorority. She made friends with the up and comers, as well as the wealthy. But her life was empty. I don't think she ever really knew who she was because she was always pretending to be someone else."

Anger filled Reagan. "She had Dad. She had me. I was never enough for her, though. She wanted me to be home-coming queen. The most popular girl in school. She never supported me. Complimented me. Never really seemed to care for me. I guess that's why I became a daddy's girl. He saw me for who I was. I knew he loved me." She paused. "I don't think Mom ever did."

Aunt Jean seemed to choose her words carefully now. "I believe there are people who are incapable of love, Reagan. They only love themselves. Your mom fit smack dab in that category."

"I think she loved Dad."

Her aunt sniffed. "I think she put on a good show about loving your dad, honey. She liked the easy life. The money he made. The opportunities it brought her. The clothes and house and nice cars he provided her with. She could run around and dabble in volunteer work, getting her name slapped on committees and letterheads, not every really doing any of the true work."

"Tell me what happened between the two of you," Reagan urged.

After a long moment, Aunt Jean said, "She tolerated coming here. Your parents even left you with me several times while they jetted off to Cozumel or Fiji or Paris when you were young. As you got older, your dad wanted you included on those trips."

She recalled stretches of happy times when she was young, staying with Aunt Jean in Lost Creek. Those had ended when she was around six or seven, and she started traveling with her parents to exotic places during summer vacations. Her family only came for a week to Lost Creek and then left. After those brief visits, Reagan either went with her parents to cities abroad, or she was left at home with the housekeeper to supervise her while her parents traveled on their own.

"You called her out, didn't you?"

"I most certainly did. I told her she was a selfish creature who never should have had a darling girl like you if she was going to ignore you the way she did. Our discussion grew pretty heated. She let it slip that she wished she'd never had you. That she wound up pregnant and had to marry your dad. Bragged about getting her tubes tied the moment you came out of her. Kids hadn't been in her plans. She resented you, Reagan. Was jealous of you. Hated the time your dad spent with you."

Reagan remembered how deliberately indifferent her mother was to her. It caused her to increasingly draw closer to her dad, who always seemed to have time for her.

"So, the blow-up was over me then."

"Yes. Don't feel guilty about it, though. It was coming. I'm surprised we both held our tongues as long as we did. In the long run, she hurt the two of us the most. Your mama knew cutting ties with me would kill me because I wouldn't' be able to see you anymore. Thank goodness your dad had the sense to give you your own phone."

She had thought she received a cell phone because other girls in her class were getting them. Reagan had been overjoyed to have one. Not that she texted with any of her classmates. But the cell had allowed her to stay in close touch with her aunt.

"I'm sorry Mom hurt you so much."

"I'm sorry she hurt you," her aunt apologized. "It's water under the bridge, though. You have a chance to start a new life now, Reagan."

Tears filled her eyes. "I'm desperate to do that. Arch was my whole world. He was the first guy who really paid attention to me. He thought I was beautiful and funny."

"Well, you are," Aunt Jean insisted.

"I never felt like either until Arch. And then he was gone so fast. No warning. Just... dead. I'll admit I was angry with him for a long time. Then I became blue. I know now I should've seen a therapist. Instead, I just delved deeper and deeper into work. It became my salvation. Then the bane of my existence."

"I know you adored Arch, Reagan. You saw a life with him. You were going to create a marriage and then a family with him. Then the rug was pulled out from underneath you."

"That's exactly how it felt," she agreed. "I was on steady ground. I had a plan. And then *boom!* It was gone."

"You're still young. I know you don't want to hear this, but you'll find love again. You've already made steps toward finding friends." Aunt Jean smiled knowingly. "I have a feeling you're going to discover exactly what you want to do with your life. And who you want to do it with."

"I hope so," she said fervently.

They had finished their tea by now, and her aunt said, "I think I'll head on to bed. I'd like to read a while and then watch the news. I'm assuming Tucker showed you which room was yours."

Just the thought of the handsome country songwriter brought a smile to her lips.

"He did. I unpacked before we went to dinner."

They hugged goodnight, and Reagan went to her room. She had talked with more people today than she had in the two years Arch had been gone.

And it felt really good.

As she fell asleep, she hoped Lost Creek would be the answer to her myriad of problems.

8

---

*R*eagan awoke the next morning, surprised that she had slept through the night. Even though she had worked outrageous hours in New York and fell into bed exhausted, she oftentimes had trouble falling asleep. Worse, she would wake up at three or four in the morning and not be able to fall back asleep. Being in Lost Creek with no career worries, however, had gifted her the first night of sound sleep since Arch's untimely death.

She tossed on a robe and went across the hall to the bathroom she and Tucker Young would be sharing. The door was open, and Tucker stood at the sink, shaving. A towel was wrapped around his hips, slung low, and his chest was bare. It was a beautiful, muscular chest, and she fought the urge to reach out and move her palms up and down it.

"Mornin', Reagan," he said in that Texas drawl that caused tingles to run along her spine. "I'm done with the shower and will be finished here in a moment. Hope you don't mind the open door as I shave. I was trying to let the steam escape and cool off things for you."

She watched his long fingers wrapped around the razor, the smooth strokes along his face. Her own cheeks heated, and she forced herself to look away, faking a cough.

By the time she looked up again, he was rinsing his face. His clear, hazel eyes fastened on her, and her stomach did a flip-flop that would have earned a perfect ten in an Olympics gymnastics competition. She was proud that she kept her eyes on his, avoiding letting them slide up and down his magnificent frame.

"Done. Miss Jean brought up a little sign for us to use."

He indicated the door behind him. Hanging from the nail was a sign that said *OCCUPIED*. Tucker flipped it over. *AVAILABLE* was on the reverse side.

"With neither of us having a schedule, I hope this system will work for us now," he told her. "If you have somewhere to be, I'm happy to give it up to you so you can get ready. See you at breakfast."

She hurried across the hall and gathered up something to wear for the day and her travel kit that contained her makeup and toiletries. After showering, she dressed and brushed her teeth, only applying a coat of mascara and some lipstick. She'd noticed all the women last night wore minimal makeup, and she didn't want to be accused of bringing fancy New York ways with her. It was a relief not to do full makeup for once. She brushed her hair and then placed it into a ponytail, feeling lighthearted and free.

Going downstairs, she heard voices and followed them, seeing her aunt and Tucker seated in the dining room.

"I've set out the morning buffet, Reagan," Aunt Jean said. "This morning is scrambled eggs, bacon, and toast. I remember you always loved sourdough bread."

"Still do," she said, though she couldn't recall the last time she'd eaten it. Bagels were her go-to breakfast.

"I'll pop a couple of pieces in the toaster for you while you fix yourself a plate," her aunt said. "Juice?"

"Do you still have cranberry?" she asked, recalling it was a special treat.

"I do. Coffee?"

"Yes. A splash of cream and sugar," she replied.

Tucker rose. "Fill your plate. I'll grab coffee for you." He followed her aunt into the kitchen, giving Reagan another nice view of his broad shoulders and firm ass. And now that she'd seen the top half of him without clothes, she couldn't stop thinking about it.

Or what the bottom half would look like.

She went to the buffet and was seated by the time Tucker returned. He set a coffee cup in front of her.

"Looks perfect," she said.

"I never add anything to mine, so I was guessing what a splash of both meant," he said, grinning at her lazily.

Now, her heart was thumping. Reagan feared he'd see her shirt moving. What was it about this man that made her go weak in the knees? Other than having an incredible body, gorgeous smile, and sparkling eyes, that is. And he was kind and friendly on top of that. She hadn't crushed this hard on anyone since Pete Prater moved to Dickinson in eighth grade. Pete had taken every girl's breath away, with his good looks and sweet smile. He'd only spent a year in town before his parents moved again, and Reagan had continued to spin fantasies about him until she left for college.

But even a grown-up Pete would pale in comparison to Tucker Young.

He returned to his breakfast, and she picked up a piece of bacon. Biting into it, she said, "Perfect."

"Glad you like it," Aunt Jean said, coming through the door with a small plate. Atop it rested two golden slices of toast. She sat the plate on the table, and Reagan reached for the crock of butter.

As she spread the butter on the bread, she said, "You always had real butter. That, and whole milk. I remember thinking they were the most wonderful tasting things I'd ever had." Turning to Tucker, she added, "My mother was constantly on a diet. We only had skim milk and some weird butter substitute. Coming to Lost Creek was like heaven. Aunt Jean was such a great cook."

Glancing to her aunt, she said, "Speaking of cooking, I'd really like it if you'd teach me how to cook."

Her aunt looked pleased. "What do you want to learn? How to fry a chicken? Make buttermilk biscuits?"

"Everything you can teach me. I don't know how to do anything except heat up a can of soup in the microwave, and I haven't done that in a long time."

Tucker frowned. "How did you eat? Did you have a roommate who cooked for the two of you?"

Laughing, Reagan shook her head. "It's called takeout, cowboy. More than half of my cell's contact list is all the takeout places within three blocks of my apartment."

He frowned. "Even I can cook a few things. I can mash potatoes. Mix a meatloaf. Grill just about any meat you give me."

"New York is different. Here, you drive to a grocery store. Load your basket with a couple of weeks' worth of food. Drive home and unload it. In Manhattan, you stop in a market and only buy what you can carry, whether you're walking home or walking to a subway station and then carrying the bag or two home from there. It's easier to simply order dinner and have it delivered to you. For the most part, I lived on Chinese takeout and pizza deliveries."

Tucker chuckled. "That sounds pretty boring, Reagan. Even when I was traveling with bands, we'd stop in at greasy spoons to eat."

"That's why I'd like to learn how to cook," she said. "I want to become self-sufficient. It's a different way of life down here. I want to learn how and fit in."

"I'm happy to teach you any and everything," her aunt said. "You're a smart girl. You'll pick things up fast."

"I might want to horn in on a few of those lessons, Miss Jean," Tucker announced. "If I stay in Lost Creek, I'll eventually need to find a place to live. I can't show up at Ry and Emerson's every night and sponge off them." He paused, his gaze meeting Reagan's. "Would you mind sharing those lessons?"

"I'm happy to have you along for the ride," she told him.

"You'll probably be the best at every dish, but I don't mind coming in number two each time. Long as I learn to feed myself."

A man appeared in the doorway. He looked to be just under six feet, with nondescript brown hair and eyes. He glanced about, seeming startled that people were in the dining room.

"Come in, Sid," Aunt Jean encouraged. "This is Sid Allen. Sid, my niece Reagan Bradley. My other guest is Tucker Young. He's the nephew of Shy and Shelly Blackwood."

Sid came in and took a seat. "My wife works at Lone Star Diner. She says Shelly is a terrific boss."

Tucker nodded encouragingly. "Aunt Shelly is a really nice lady. Glad to hear your wife likes working for her."

Her aunt rose. "I'll get your coffee and juice, Sid. Grab a plate and get yourself some breakfast."

Sid didn't talk much during the meal, eating quickly and excusing himself while the other three drank a second cup of coffee and relaxed.

"Is Sid shy?" Reagan asked. "Or does he just not like talking to people?"

"Probably a little of both," Aunt Jean said. "He's a quiet tenant. Sleeps most of the day. What time will Emerson pick you up?"

"Eleven," she replied. "Then Tucker and I will be at the winery until after we do our tasting with Ivy."

"The tasting room closes at five-thirty," Tucker volunteered. "So, we'll probably get out of there after an hour or so. I know you serve dinner at six."

"I can keep it warm for you two," Aunt Jean said.

He glanced to Reagan. "I was thinking maybe we might stop and eat at my uncle's place afterward. Then Uncle Shy could give us a ride back here."

"Barbeque sounds good to me," she said, wanting to spend more time in Tucker's company. "We can have Emerson drop us at the inn, though. That way, we can take my car to dinner and not inconvenience anyone else."

Her aunt nodded approvingly. "Then I won't be expecting you for dinner. I hope you have fun today."

"We'll clear the dishes," Tucker said, rising. "But you can rinse and put them in the dishwasher, Miss Jean."

Once the dishes were in the sink, he asked Reagan, "Would you like to stretch your legs a bit? Emerson won't be here for a good while."

"I'd love to," she agreed. "Let me grab a jacket. I'll meet you in the foyer."

When she returned downstairs, he had on a jean jacket and a cowboy hat.

"Ready, cowboy?"

That slow, lazy smile appeared again, taking her breath. "You called me *cowboy* before, and I wasn't even wearing my hat."

Reagan shrugged. "You just looked like one to me. I think it'll be my nickname for you."

"Then I'm gonna need a nickname for you," he said, his eyes dancing mischievously.

Tucker opened the door. She went through it and

descended the steps. The cool of the morning hit her, but the warm sunshine spread over her, too, making Reagan think this was a perfect day.

With a perfect guy.

"Caramel," Tucker said, scampering down the steps in his worn cowboy boots.

"What?"

"Your nickname. Your hair is like caramel. The sun hitting it shows all kinds of shades of golds and browns, all tumbled together. Besides, I like caramels. One of the roadies used to carry some in his pockets. He'd give me one every now and then. Not because I was good or helped unload things or carried stuff around for him. Just because. He told me a caramel is a treat, and you never know when to expect one."

Tucker paused, studying her. "I think meeting you has been a treat, Reagan. I feel I've already made some new friends since I got to Lost Creek, and I'm counting you as one of them. Remember, you're going to be my sounding board. And I'll be yours."

A warm glow filled her. She liked this man. Liked his looks and openness. But Reagan told herself not to rush anything. Or expect anything. She'd been disappointed too many times by others. She would be wary until she got to know him better.

"Let's walk, Caramel."

She fell into step beside him. It was faster than a stroll but not an all-out, race walk pace. Just something in-between. They walked along a path that took them into the woods behind the B&B. Eventually, they reached the water, and Tucker slowed.

"Along here is where we used to fish. Ry, Todd, and me."

He led her down to a large rock and offered her his hand. She took it, feeling both a sense of comfort and a thrill at the same time, sensations she never would have married together.

They both eased down until they were seated atop the rock. The sky had not a cloud in it. The river running beside them moved swiftly. In the distance, she figured there was a drop-off because she heard a swooshing sound of water.

"Harper mentioned last night that Todd had died a few years ago."

Tucker nodded, a grim look on his face. "He and Ry were closer than brothers. Had been since before they could walk and talk. I joined them each summer. We did everything a boy growing up in a small town might do. Got into a little mischief, but mostly it was riding bikes. Fishing. Swimming. Playing board games. Hanging out."

"You came every summer?"

"From the time I was five."

Reagan waited, certain something was coming.

"My mom and Aunt Shelly were sisters. Aunt Shelly was the good one of the pair. Did what her parents said to do. Brought home good grades. Never caused anyone a minute of trouble. My mom was the opposite. A year younger and a hellion from the time she was born. Hated being compared with her sister by all the teachers in school. Mom began smoking a pack a day when she was ten. Drank. Ran around. Dabbled in drugs but never got sucked into that pit."

He paused again, and she patiently waited. It seemed his story came out in small bits. She was eager to hear it, but she would never rush him.

"Mom moved to Austin before the ink dried on her diploma. It was a fun, freaky place, and she loved every minute of it. She followed certain bands, and that's how she came to meet my dad. She'd find a way backstage after a band played at a local club and would party with them some. Dad was always around, watching his investment, making sure no one got too drunk or too high. They got to talking, and sparks flew. Next thing you know, they were married."

Tucker reached for a few small stones sitting on the ground and flicked his wrist, sending them skimming across the water one at a time.

"Did she travel with him?" Reagan asked. Tucker had mentioned being on the road with his dad, but he had never opened up about his mom until now.

"For a while. Then she got bored. Nothing held her attention for long. Not even me," he said quietly.

She heard the hurt in his voice. Instinctively, she covered his hand with hers.

"A doctor told her she couldn't have kids. Then all of a sudden, after being married five years, she got pregnant. Had awful sickness around the clock the entire nine months. Then I popped out." He hesitated. "Let's just put it this way. Dad was more maternal than Mom, if that makes any sense."

"I get that," she said, lifting her hand.

He caught it, though, his fingers entwining with hers, pulling it back down. "Bad mom?" he asked.

"Haughty. Disdainful. Detached. Those are the first things that come to mind. My mother was a snob. Thought she was better than everyone around her. My dad was an attorney and made buckets of money. Not just from clients. He had a feel for investing. Mom dabbled in volunteer work and gossiped ferociously. Our house had to have the best of everything. She wore designer clothes. Had enough jewelry to fund a Third World nation for years. And I was her greatest disappointment."

His thumb stroked hers. "How so?"

"I never really fit in with others at school. I kept apart. Always had my nose in a book. She wanted me to be popular. Rule the school. That kind of thing. When it was obvious I never would, she lost any interest in me. Around me, she was always cold. Aloof. Disinterested. It drove me to be closer to my dad. We talked all the time. He traveled for business, though. They traveled the world together when I was young. Later, as I grew older, Dad insisted I go along on their trips in the summer. I've seen Paris. Milan. Tokyo. Dubai. London. Mom would sulk most of the trip. She'd go off and have spa treatments. Shop. Dad and I would visit castles and museums and tourist attractions such as Tokyo Tower or the London Eye."

"Did things get better between the two of you after you became an adult?" he asked.

"My parents died in a plane crash shortly after I graduated from high school," she said quietly. "After all these years I still really miss my dad."

"I'm sorry." His gaze met hers. "I lost my mom when I was five. Cancer. All those smokes finally caught up to her. Dad had said the road was no place for a baby or toddler, so he'd made sure she stayed home with me. Do you know I can't ever remember a time she read to me or played with me? As far as she was concerned, I was a lump that had to be attended to. Fed every now and then, but she left me to myself.

"She was beautiful, though. Until the cancer hit. Even now, though I was so young, I can remember the change that came over her. How she stopped eating and became skin and bones. The chemo caused her hair to fall out. She just gave up on life. Refused to go to any treatments. And then she was gone."

"I'm so sorry, Tucker," Reagan murmured.

"It's okay. Really. I traveled with Dad during the months kids were in school. He was a nice guy. Did the best he could with a small child. Summers, Aunt Shelly convinced him to let me come to Lost Creek. I had my own room. Uncle Shy bought me a bike. I had three meals a day with my family and was nagged to wash behind my ears. For those summer months, I slept in the same bed every night— unless we were camping —and I felt like a normal kid."

Tucker sighed. "Maybe I romanticized Lost Creek, but this place always has felt like home. Even if I've been gone a really long time from it."

"Sounding board speaking here," she said. "This is the

place you were happiest. I know you're suffering because you lost Josie and feel guilty you survived the crash. But I think Lost Creek could be the place you might heal, Tucker."

His gaze pinned her. "Sounds to me as if you have also had some nice times here yourself. Maybe this is the place you need to wind up, as well."

Tucker's free hand caught her chin. Slowly, he moved his head toward her, his lips coming closer. Her heart sped up. Her mouth grew dry.

Then he gave her a soft, sweet kiss.

It wasn't a lover's kiss. It didn't have the passion and fire of that. It was more a kiss of friendship. Of two lost souls coming together as friends. Two people who had experienced hardships in life and by sharing some of their burdens, found those burdens begin to lift.

He broke the kiss, his lips hovering just above hers.

"I hope that wasn't too forward."

"It wasn't," she told him.

Tucker moved away, releasing her hand. "I want you as a friend, Reagan, but I'm feeling an attraction to you." He smiled wryly. "And it's confusing the hell out of me."

9

ucker couldn't believe he had kissed Reagan Bradley. He'd felt an attraction to her from the time they first met, yet guilt flooded him because it seemed as if his feelings toward Reagan made him disloyal to Josie. Yet Josie would be the first to encourage Tucker to ease up on himself and find love with someone else.

Truthfully, he was frightened to do so. If he did, he might begin to lose the memories he had of his wonderful wife.

"We can look past the kiss," Reagan assured him, interrupting his thoughts. "I know we've spoken about being friends. I told you I could use one. The truth is that I lost someone close to me. Just like you did."

His gaze met hers, and Tucker saw pain reflected in her eyes.

"I want to be your friend because we're what Aunt Jean might call kindred spirits," she continued.

"Mind explaining?" he asked. "I've pretty much bared my soul to you."

She swallowed. "I know. I wanted to tell you. When you told me about Josie. But… it's hard, Tucker. You, above all people, should know that."

Taking a deep breath, Reagan said, "I was engaged. To Archibald Coleridge. The fourth man to bear such a pompous name."

Tucker chuckled. "Yeah. It does sound pretty pretentious."

"Arch wasn't like that at all," she shared. "He was funny. The smartest person I'd ever met. An attorney. Not the slick type that comes to mind, but one who is caring and passionate about his clients and seeing justice occur." She paused, a wistful look crossing her face. "He made me laugh. He drew me out of my shell and made me try things I never would have done in a thousand years."

Reagan fell silent, lost in her memories. Tucker knew enough about grief to keep quiet and let her ride it out.

"He was killed a week before our wedding took place."

Her words hit him out of the blue. Just like Josie had been snatched from him in an instant, Reagan's fiancé had also left her life abruptly. While he didn't know how—and wouldn't ask —Tucker knew the suddenness of the event had scarred her as deeply as Josie's death had affected him.

"I'm sorry," he said quietly.

"I appreciate hearing that." She licked her lips, drawing his attention to them.

He wanted to kiss her. Badly.

And that would be the worst thing to do. For both of them. Tucker forced his thoughts away from that and focused his attention on what Reagan would reveal next.

"I keep thinking if he'd been sick and then died, I would have had time to adjust to the idea of him being gone," she said, frustration in her voice. "I didn't know when I said goodbye to him that it was the final time I'd see him. How could I know it was our last kiss? I kept going over and over things in my head. For months. Would I have done or said anything differently? Squeezed more out of those moments?"

She was right. At least he'd been with Josie when the truck slammed into them. Despite being helpless and not having a way to save his wife, they had been together when tragedy struck.

Tucker still hadn't touched Reagan. He wanted to, but now he knew she'd probably feel disloyal to Arch if he did so.

Instead, he asked, "What happened?" He wanted to be her friend now because if anyone looked like they could use one, it was Reagan Bradley.

Suddenly, storm clouds appeared in her brown eyes, darkening them almost to black.

"He was murdered." Anger spilled from her. "Arch was mugged. From what the police put together, it was a junkie who needed money for a quick fix. It wasn't enough to rob Arch. No, the bastard had to take his life."

Tears spilled down her cheeks. Without thinking, Tucker leaned over, his hands framing her face, his thumbs wiping them away.

"You're okay," he said gently, letting his hands fall, wishing he could take her in his arms and hold her. "It's okay to be mad. Frustrated. It's a part of it," he assured her.

"Yes, I'm mad. And the thing is, I'm just as mad at Arch as I am the guy they caught. It's hard to admit that. Even two years later, these feelings will suddenly bubble up inside me, upsetting me all over again."

He nodded. "I can see that. I was furious at the guy who smashed into us. Wanted to kill him on the spot. But I also had a little anger directed at Josie. I was pissed that she had died. That she had left me behind to face life without her."

Reagan shook her head. "Mine is petty anger," she revealed. "Yes, I was glad they caught the guy who murdered Arch. He was found guilty and sent to prison. But I also know how stubborn Arch could be. He attached importance to material things sometimes. Not only did the robber take Arch's wallet, he also stole his watch. It was a family watch, handed down from generation to generation."

Suddenly, she pushed to her feet and was off the rock, pacing.

"I can hear him now. He would never have been parted from that stupid watch. I don't care if it was in his family for years. I know Arch's refusal to hand it over was what made the guy kill him. Or maybe they tussled over it, and Arch was accidentally killed. The thing is, Tucker, I've stayed mad at Arch for the last two years. He left me. *Left* me. We were supposed to be married. Start a brand-new life together. Be with each other for fifty years or more. Have kids. Grandkids. Travel. Work. Then retire together. And he's gone from me forever, all because he refused to give up some watch. If he had, he would still be alive. I wouldn't be here at Aunt Jean's in Texas. I'd be married. I'd be with my best friend and the man I thought I'd love until my dying day."

She sniffed. "It's like I can't move on. I'm stuck. I can't go forward or backward."

Tucker slid off the rock. This time he acted on his intuition, bringing his arms around her and pulling her to him. She clung to him, her face buried against his chest. He could feel the hot tears through his flannel shirt.

"Cry it out," he urged.

After a few minutes, she pulled away from him, wiping her eyes with her sleeve. "I'm sorry."

"I'm not. I understand you a lot better now, Reagan. I hope you also understand me. We both lost the most important person in the world to us. Their deaths changed the trajectory of our lives."

"I want the anger to subside," Reagan said. "I want to be whole again and not feel like half of me is gone and can never be replaced."

"I think sharing what we've gone through with one another is a start," Tucker said firmly. "Being in a different place will also help. We can clear our heads. Get out of the rut we've been stuck in. Find something worthwhile to do." He hesitated. "And maybe someday, we'll even open our hearts to love again."

"I hope so," she said sincerely.

"Let's head back," he suggested.

He didn't take her hand, but he knew something had changed between them. They were going to be more than friends. Whether or not love grew between them was something far down the road. But they had opened up to each other and shared the darkest parts of their souls with one another. He thought it had to help jumpstart their healing.

They reached the inn, and Reagan paused before opening the front door.

"I really trust you, Tucker. I can't say I feel that way about anyone other than Aunt Jean. But I do feel as if some of my burden has been lifted by sharing my story with you."

"I feel the same," he seconded. "And now we're in Lost Creek, we have a chance for a new start. That includes making friends."

"I already like everyone who was at dinner last night. They were very welcoming."

"Last night was a good start for us." He placed his hands on her shoulders. "Let's promise to take one day at a time, Caramel."

She smiled, a smile that tugged on his heart. "Agreed, Cowboy."

They entered the house, and he glanced at the grandfather clock which stood in the foyer. "Emerson should be here in about forty-five minutes."

"I'm going to blow my nose and wash my face," she said. "I hope by the time Emerson arrives that I look human again."

"See you then."

Tucker watched her head up the stairs before turning around and heading back to the porch, which was rapidly becoming his thinking spot.

It startled him when Miss Jean said, "Reagan's in a world of hurt."

He faced the innkeeper. "She's not the only one. But I think we can help one another, Miss Jean."

"I hope that's the case."

As he returned to his favorite rocker, Tucker was determined to bounce back from Josie's death.

And resolved that he would help Reagan Bradley do the same.

EMERSON PICKED THEM UP FROM THE B&B. SHE DROPPED Tucker off to spend time with Braden, and then she drove straight to the events center. Reagan was impressed at the size of the facility and the professional kitchen Emerson used in her baking.

"I bake all the cakes for weddings and other events held here at the venue. I also stop by The Bake House and pick up any requests for special orders. I usually bake those cakes here, as well. I can keep an eye on them while I get other work done."

She showed Reagan her office and then called up her website.

"You are incredibly creative," Reagan praised. "I've never seen designs such as these."

"I can do anything in a traditional style, but I also like to experiment. I have each couple come in for a meeting, and we talk about them. Their personalities. Their lifestyles. What they enjoy doing together. I gather that information and then use it in designing the wedding and groom's cakes. At that time, I also have them give me ideas of the flavors they both enjoy. We also look at various styles of icing. Then they return a second time."

"I assume they taste samples then?" she asked.

"Yes. I bake small cakes, much like individual pizzas you can order. We slice into them so they can taste and compare. Most couples decide what they want served at their reception at that point. A few are still hesitant to commit, so I have them take the samples home with them. I encourage them to allow those close to them to taste and give their opinions." Emerson paused. "I remind them, though, that in the end it's their choice. They can solicit input from others, but they should choose what will make them happiest."

Emerson then showed Reagan where Ry set up when he was catering events.

"He has a smoker behind the event center, as well as one in town. That one he uses to stock his food truck, which he takes around Lost Creek for lunch every weekday and also out on Saturdays. The smoker at the winery is used exclusively for events at this venue."

"That sounds like a lot of work," she remarked.

"Ry has never shied away from hard work. He was in the military for a dozen years, and the discipline instilled in him has carried over to his civilian life."

"I would have thought his dad would've catered events here since he has a large restaurant."

Emerson laughed. "Oh, Shy used to. But that's a story for another day. For now, Ry does about eighty percent of the catering for Weddings with Hart. I'm even learning my way around a smoker. The business is really growing. Though I pinch hit every now and then, it's getting to the point where he's going to need to hire some help, or else he'll be drowning."

"Maybe Tucker would be interested," Reagan said, knowing her new friend would have to find a way to support himself while he tried to reignite his songwriting career.

"Ry and I talked about that very thing," Emerson shared. "We don't want to rush Tucker or put any unneeded pressure on him. Tucker did help out with a lunch service the day he arrived. Ry said his cousin picked up quickly on things. If Tucker wants a job, Ry is ready to offer it to him."

"Would you mind if I mention that to him?" she asked. "We've become friends in a short period. We've had... some similar experiences. It's really helped us to bond with one another."

"Please do," Emerson encouraged. "But don't make him feel obligated. I know that's a fine line to dance upon."

"I'll be diplomatic," she guaranteed. "Besides, if Tucker doesn't want to help out, who knows? I might for a little while."

"Really? That would be terrific. Do you have a background in food service?"

Not ready to go into her past history, Reagan merely said, "I was in finance. But I catch on quickly. I'm taking some time off while I'm in Lost Creek. Deciding my next career move. I'd be happy to help out on a temporary basis if Ry needs my help."

Emerson put some cakes on to bake, walking Reagan through the various steps as she mixed the batter and placed it into baking pans of various sizes. While those baked, she received a tour of the event center, from the rooms where the bride and groom got ready with their attendants to the storage room. It housed various sets of china, tablecloths, glassware, silverware, and a variety of centerpieces.

Reagan loved where weddings took place, with a couple standing before a glass wall that looked out over the Lost Creek vineyards. It made for a spectacular setting. She also saw where the receptions occurred and where Dax set up, either as a DJ or with his band, the Lone Star Rebels.

By then, it was time to take out the cakes and place them on racks to cool. Emerson said she usually baked Saturday wedding and groom's cakes on Thursdays and iced and decorated them on Fridays. Friday cakes mirrored that schedule but were a day earlier. The center was also starting to hold a few events on Sunday afternoons though Emerson said Harper hadn't put any Sundays on the calendar from next week through the end of the year.

"Because of the baby," Emerson explained. "Harper will be on maternity leave. She wanted a break on

Sundays for the weeks leading up to the delivery and the weeks after."

"Who will take over for her when the time comes?" Reagan asked, curious about how things would continue to run.

"Oh, she has two amazing assistants, Paula and Dayna. Things will be fine. They've been with Harper from the beginning. She also has people who come in to bartend and clean up."

Emerson's cell sounded. She pulled it out and read the text message.

"Harper has some open time now for you to come see her office. I'll drop you there and then come back here to finish up some work."

Reagan was impressed with how organized Harper was. As her new friend led her through the offices and conference room, she voiced that opinion.

"Thank you. I've always been more than a little Type A," Harper admitted. "To me, it just makes sense having everything in a fashion so it's easy to find. Even as a kid, I put everything back in its place." She laughed. "Ivy, on the other hand, reminded me of Pig-Pen from the Peanuts comics when we were growing up. Her stuff was everywhere. She was a swirling mess."

"I guess it was her artist's temperament," Reagan said.

"Maybe. She's changed a lot. Got her act together in college. Then she worked in a Houston art gallery for several years as its assistant manager. She was the manager except in name only. Did all her boss's work, while he took the credit. She asked me for a few tips on

ALEXA ASTON

how to organize things at work. I provided them. Now, you should see her studio. Ivy is as disciplined as Ry or me."

"I'm eager to see her work."

They returned to Harper's office, where Reagan asked dozens of questions. Harper was willing to share how she managed the office and was patient explaining everything to Reagan.

"No one has ever taken this much an interest in what I do or how I do it," Harper said. "You've asked me more questions than my assistants."

"I hope I didn't come off as too nosy," she apologized.

"Not at all. In fact, I might have a proposition for you. While I'm on maternity leave, Paula and Dayna could probably use another set of hands. Would you be willing to work for Weddings with Hart for a few weeks? I don't know what your plans are or how long you'll be in Lost Creek, but I already like you a lot, Reagan. It would be terrific to have you here temporarily."

"When would you need me?" she asked, intrigued by the idea.

Harper rubbed her belly. "Well, it will depend upon when Beau decides to make his arrival in the world. Actually, if I had you here, I might take off a week before my due date. Just put my feet up and relax."

"Could you really do that?" she asked. "I'm sensing we're pretty much alike when it comes to work."

Harper laughed. "I can't recall when I've ever done that. I'm due November fifteenth. I plan to take off the

130

rest of the year and then come back in January. That would keep you here through the holidays."

The thought appealed to her greatly. She had nowhere to go and would love to spend Thanksgiving and Christmas with Aunt Jean. Plus, it would be something fun and interesting to keep her busy while she decided what she wanted to do for a living.

"I'll do it," she said. "And mind you, I'm never impulsive. But this just feels right."

"I hear you," Harper said, hugging her. "Thank you so much, Reagan. I'm relieved to know you'll be here to help out. I'm a worrier by nature, and as much as I cannot wait to meet Beau, I have worried about Weddings with Hart, my first baby. Let me think about how I'm going to divvy up duties. Paula will nominally be in charge. She knows to run most decisions by me, though. Give me a couple of days, then we can all meet, and I'll go over who will be responsible for what."

Harper consulted her calendar. "How does Monday look for you?"

Reagan grinned. "Wide open."

"Then let's meet here at my office at ten Monday morning. I'll have coffee and pick up some pastries from The Bake House." Harper glanced at her watch. "Oh, we need to get you over to Braden. He wants to show you all about the winemaking process before you and Tucker go for your tasting with Ivy."

Harper texted Braden, who said he and Tucker would be over in the golf cart to pick up Reagan.

"Braden had us buy a cart a few months ago. I thought it was a silly idea at first, but it's really come in handy."

Reagan looked forward to the rest of the day. Of becoming a part of Weddings with Hart, if only for a limited time.

And what she really couldn't wait was to see Tucker Young again and share her news that she would be staying in Lost Creek until the new year.

10

$\mathcal{T}$ucker walked around the rows of grapevines with Braden, half-listening to what the winemaker said.

Because his thoughts were centered on Reagan Bradley.

He didn't know what to do about the feelings stirring within him about her. Feelings he never expected to experience again. An attraction which wanted to suddenly consume him. Yes, he had kissed her impulsively and admitted he was drawn to her. He had deliberately kept the kiss friendly and gentle, though. All the while, raging desire rushed through him for the former New Yorker. Thank goodness he'd been able to control himself.

"Earth to Tucker," he heard.

Turning, he saw Braden Clark grinning at him.

"You zoned out on me, Tucker. Is wine that boring? Or is it because of a woman? I'm assuming it's Reagan."

He winced. "Am I being that obvious?"

Braden shrugged. "I just caught you looking at her last night at the table. There was something in that look which let me know you were interested in her."

"I can't be!" he said vehemently. "I'm in love with my wife."

Braden's eyebrows shot up, and Tucker knew he needed to explain.

Calming himself, he said, "I'm a widower. Never even used that word before to describe myself. Josie and I were hit by a drunk driver a couple of years ago. I survived. She didn't," he said flatly.

Sympathy sprang to Braden's eyes, and he placed a hand on Tucker's shoulder, squeezing gently. "I'm sorry to hear that, Tucker. Losing someone you love so unexpectedly hurts."

"I never thought I would be interested in another woman. I took off once my body healed from the crash. I've wandered this country restlessly ever since, never staying in one place for too long. I'm not sure why I came back to Lost Creek, only that I knew I needed something from this place."

Nodding understandingly, Braden said, "You're not the only one who's come to Lost Creek searching. Needing to heal. The same is true for me. Dax and Holden. Even natives such as Harper and Ivy and your cousin Ry have returned to their roots. Because they know this town has something to offer that other places don't."

Braden paused. "I was homeless before I came here, Tucker. My family had a thriving wine business in California, and I was engaged to be married to a woman I loved. Everything I thought my life was going to be vanished in the blink of an eye. My dad went to jail. The family lost our winery and all our money. My fiancée jilted me, embarrassed by the whole situation. Lost Creek was my last chance— and it became my salvation."

Tucker was surprised by Braden's story. "It's hard to think of you anywhere but this place. With Harper. The two of you look like you're meant to be together."

Braden smiled. "We are. Harper herself was also engaged to a real jerk in Austin. Both of us being dumped by our partners altered the course of our lives. They changed again when we met one another. I love the life I've built here in Lost Creek with Harper. I can't wait for our baby to come into the world and for us to be parents to him."

Looking at Tucker thoughtfully, Braden said, "It sounds like you're in need of some healing yourself. I think Lost Creek is where that can happen. Other than a visit with her aunt, I'm not sure why Reagan is here. I think we all knew not to push her last night. She seems like a terrific lady, though, and she fit right in with our group. Same as you did, Tucker. Who knows? Maybe you and Reagan will remain in Lost Creek and find a path with one another."

It wasn't his place to share her story, so all Tucker said was, "Reagan has been on an emotional rollercoaster herself, same as me. I don't know if she'll make Lost Creek her permanent home or not."

"Don't close any doors," Braden advised. "If Reagan

isn't the one for you, she may be the one right now who you need. Fate might have brought the two of you together in Lost Creek, even if it's only for a short time. You still love your wife. That'll never change. But I've discovered hearts are a funny thing. They're big enough and can be filled with more love without losing what you feel for anyone else."

He took those words to heart. Maybe he still could love Josie and make peace with that as he moved forward and tried to begin the next chapter in his life.

Possibly one with Reagan Bradley.

"You've got my attention now, Braden," Tucker promised. "Let's get back to our tour."

Braden took him through the vast fields, explaining about the vines and why they grew so well in the Texas Hill Country. Without lecturing, his new friend made the talk interesting. Tucker learned a lot about how the vines were protected when the temperatures dropped and the times of year the different varieties of grapes were harvested.

They went into a large building, where Braden explained the process of creating a wine from start to finish. He saw the tank room, where grapes were destemmed and crushed, along with the tall tanks where the liquid was first stored and fermentation began. Braden also took him to the barrel room, where a quarter of the barrels were new ones from France and Chile, and the remaining barrels were recycled for a time.

Entering Braden's office, Tucker saw records kept on each crop of red and white grapes produced at Lost Creek

Vineyards, meticulous notes that made him realize how vast and complicated producing wines actually was.

"I do samplings each day of various barrels," Braden told him. "I know you're doing a tasting with Ivy soon, but let me have you test a few with me now."

They did so, and Braden shared different tidbits about the small samples so Tucker had an idea what to look for as he tasted the wines.

Glancing at his watch, Braden said, "Let me text Harper. Reagan should be with her by now, and we can go pick her up and bring her back here for a mini-tour."

Soon, the two men were riding in a golf cart across the property, headed toward Harper's office. Reagan joined them in the cart, and Braden drove them back to the rows of grapevines. Tucker accompanied Reagan and Braden on the much quicker tour, glad he had received the full-blown explanations from Braden about the business.

Reagan had several questions about the barrels used to store the wines, and Braden went into detail, discussing American and European oaks.

"In Eastern Europe, especially Romania, they cut the wood and allow it to sit outside for two to three years in the elements before they toast it. They pull off the weathering and cut the wood around a frame hoop. Sand it and drill a hole to tap into for tasting the wines stored in them over time."

"Where in the U.S. do wine barrels come from?" she wanted to know.

"Mostly Kansas and Missouri," the winemaker told her. "American oak barrels are about seven hundred dollars each, where French ones cost about eleven hundred a barrel. French oak gives a wine a smoother, softer taste. They're good for a merlot." He laughed. "Cabs, on the other hand, are tough. Any barrel will do for them. And once we're done with a barrel, we recycle them. Old barrels have been used to make the benches, tables, and chairs you see scattered about the winery, especially outdoors at the tasting room, so watch for that when you go there."

"You're incredibly knowledgeable, Braden," Reagan praised. "Thanks so much for taking me around and sharing with me what goes into producing wines."

"Let me get you over to the tasting room," Braden said. "It's a little after four-thirty now. Not many customers show up so late in the day this time of year during the week. Ivy might be ready for you now."

They climbed into the golf cart again, and Braden dropped them off at the tasting room. Ivy greeted them and since no clients were in sight, she quickly showed Reagan around. Tucker perused the gift shop while they did so, seeing the variety of clever merchandise which bore the Lost Creek Vineyards label.

Ivy had them stand at the long, sleek bar for their tasting.

"Since neither of you happen to be wine drinkers, let me tell you a little bit about what we produce here at Lost Creek Vineyards."

Ivy launched into a fascinating explanation of the difference between white and red wines, telling them that most novices preferred whites to begin with.

"Whites run from the sweet to the dry, but they are lighter in body. Some have almost a buttery taste to them, and it's easier to discern the floral notes in a white. Reds, on the other hand, are full-bodied. When we start in a minute, I'll tell you some of the flavors to look for, such as plums, apples, or vanilla. I'll see if you can pick up any others."

She provided bottles of water for them to cleanse their palate between samplings and also pulled out a tray.

"These are some various cheeses. Wines pair with different types of food. You may have heard that whites are for fish and chicken dishes, while reds lean toward pairing well with beef. We'll nibble a little from this tray as we go along. These cheeses will enhance the flavors of the wines."

Before they took a single sip, Ivy explained what to look for in a wine, including how to hold it against a napkin to check for color and how to swirl and sniff deeply before sampling. She also told them why she would pour different wines into various shaped wineglasses and finished up with telling them during the tasting, they shouldn't swallow immediately. Instead, they needed to allow their taste buds to absorb the wine and let its flavors explode in their mouth before swallowing.

"This is fascinating," Reagan said. "I never knew how complex wine really was. I told you my parents were well-to-do, and they drank the best wines available. I'm sure neither of them had any idea about all this background regarding wines or what makes one wine better than the next."

They started with several whites, sampling everything from a Chardonnay to a Sauvignon Blanc. They finished with a Riesling, which was much too sweet for Tucker's taste buds, and the face he made caused both women to laugh.

"Let's move on to reds," Ivy said, and they sampled a Pinot Noir, Merlot, and Cabernet Sauvignon.

"I already lean toward the reds," he told them. "I like how mellow and rich they are."

Reagan chuckled. "I'm the opposite. I'm really drawn to the whites we sampled, especially the Moscato and Sauvignon Blanc."

"We also need to try a few blends and get your opinions regarding those," Ivy said. "After Braden was here for several months, Dad asked him to take over as the chief winemaker for the Lost Creek Vineyards label. We've always been a family operation, with Dad creating the wines and doing the marketing, while Mom handled all the bookkeeping, insurance, and taxes. Dad wanted to step away from the actual making of the wines, however, and focus his time on marketing and growing our label's footprint. Braden has continued to make our reds and whites, but he is really moving us more into blends."

Ivy explained to them the ratio of various blends, and Reagan said, "If I would've had a teacher like you in school, you would have been my favorite, Ivy. I feel I'm learning so much in such a short amount of time."

Ivy laughed. "I could talk about wines all day. I do miss being able to sip one, though." She patted her belly fondly. "It's a good thing I know enough about the process and taste so that I'm still able to manage the tasting room and conduct tastings with customers who are eager to learn more about wine."

They tried a couple of blends, and Reagan said, "I think these are my favorite. They seem to bring the best of both worlds together."

"I do like them," Tucker added. "Not that I'll give up beer anytime soon, but I have a greater appreciation now of all the hard work which goes into making a wine. I discovered a few tonight that I'd actually choose to drink again. Over beer."

"I'm always bringing different wines to Wednesday dinners," Ivy said. "I check with whoever is cooking the meal that week and then choose bottles accordingly." She looked at them hopefully. "You two better join us again. Finley will be preparing a Mediterranean feast this coming Wednesday."

Reagan shook her head. "It was lovely to be invited this week, but I don't expect an invitation every week. Tucker's different. He's from here. Well, sort of."

"No, Reagan," Ivy protested. "We want you to come. For as long as you're in Lost Creek. You don't have to give me an answer now." Then she grinned. "Finley and I will tag team and simply wear you down at coffee tomorrow."

Laughter bubbled up from Reagan, and Tucker thought he'd never heard a sweeter sound. He pushed aside the thought, telling himself he'd come back to it later and decipher what it meant.

"I'm looking forward to coffee in the morning with the

two of you," Reagan said. "And to seeing your art at some point if you're willing to allow me a glimpse."

"My studio is above the hardware store on the square. It used to be an apartment Mayor Bennett leased out, but I've taken over the space for my painting. Why don't you stop by about eight-thirty before we're due at Java Junction? You can see my work then."

"Is that too early?" Reagan asked.

Ivy replied, "I'm an early bird. There are times I get to the studio at six and paint several hours before I leave to come here for my shift at eleven-thirty."

"I don't want to inconvenience you. Or interrupt your painting time," Reagan said.

"I finished something new yesterday," Ivy said. "All I'll be doing tomorrow morning is sketching, trying to figure out the next subject I'll paint. You won't be interrupting anything, and I won't even have brushes to clean before we head to Java Junction."

"Then I'll park on the square and meet you there," Reagan promised.

"Em texted and asked if I could drop you two back at the B&B," Ivy said. "Give me a couple of minutes to clean up, and I'll be ready to go."

"Anything we can do to help?" Tucker asked.

"Thanks for the offer, but it won't take me long."

He and Reagan walked through the rest of the tasting room, viewing the different awards Lost Creek Vineyards wines had received over the years.

"This is really laid out nicely," Reagan commented.

"Ivy told me the original tasting room was much

smaller, but the architect who worked on the event center designed a new tasting room to her specifications."

"From what I gather, the Hill Country is a popular weekend destination for wine tasting and antiquing. Aunt Jean usually books up most weekends, especially the two cottages on the property."

"Are you still up for dinner at Blackwood BBQ?" he asked.

Her gaze met his. "I am. I can't wait to eat some Texas barbeque again. It's been too long. It will also give us time to talk more."

Tucker nodded. "Yes. It's something I know we need to do. There are things I need to say to you, Reagan."

11

*I*vy dropped them at The Inn at Lost Creek, saying she would see Reagan in the morning at her studio. They got out of the car, and Reagan pointed to her rental.

"Let's go straight to dinner," she suggested.

"Sounds good to me. Even though we nibbled on some cheese at the tasting, I'm always ready for barbeque," Tucker said.

Driving back into town, Reagan headed down Main Street, where many of Lost Creek's stores and restaurants were located. She turned into the parking lot of Blackwood BBQ, and they got out of the car.

Tucker came to meet her. "First thing? Wait for me to help you out of the car. I know you've been a fancy, do things yourself New Yorker for a long time, but you're back in Texas now, Reagan."

She liked hearing that. She remembered her dad

always opening the car door for her mom whenever they went places.

They walked through the parking lot, and Reagan saw the smokers lined along the side of the property. The delicious aroma of smoked meats wafted through the air.

As they entered the restaurant, she saw that it was a self-service place. Tucker handed her a tray and wrapped napkin containing silverware, and she put it down and began sliding it along the track.

"Tucker!" a man called jovially. "You didn't tell me you were coming in for dinner tonight. Glad I stuck around."

"I'll forward my entire social calendar to you, Uncle Shy," he said, and she saw the mischievous glint in his eyes. "This here is Reagan Bradley. My uncle, Shy Blackwood, Reagan."

The restaurant owner beamed at her. "You have to be Jean Bradley's Reagan," he said. "Miss Jean is mighty proud of you. Heard you were coming to stay with her. You work in New York, I think?"

"I have for many years, Mr. Blackwood, but I've decided to move back to Texas."

"The little lady has good sense," he declared. "And it's Shy. Mr. Blackwood was my daddy, and he's been gone a good many years now. What can I get for you, Reagan?"

She hesitated, looking at the numerous cuts of meat. "I'm not quite sure."

"I'll order for us, Uncle Shy," Tucker said, taking charge. "We're going to share some so that Reagan can taste most of what's on the menu. She'll do the two-meat plate. Sliced brisket and smoked sausage."

"You got it," Shy said, and he went to work. His hands moved quickly as he sliced the beef and sausage.

Reagan said, "If they had an Olympics for carving and slicing meat, you'd be the USA's gold medalist, Shy."

He laughed heartily, a pleased look on his face. "You better watch this one, Tuck."

"Oh, I plan to keep an eye on her."

She glanced at him and caught the appreciative look in his eye. Her stomach erupted, butterflies fluttering madly.

"I'll do the three-meat," Tucker continued. "Give me ham, turkey, and more of the sliced brisket. We'll also take a couple of those jalapeño poppers."

As Shy got to work, she asked Tucker, "What are those?"

"Sweetest thing you'll ever put in your mouth that isn't dessert. It's a jumbo-sized shrimp, wrapped in bacon, with just a bit of jalapeño to give it a nice kick. You'll like it. I promise."

She knew she would like it. Reagan also knew how much she already liked this man. More than was wise. Her head told her to slam on the brakes, but her heart was opening up more with the passing of each minute in Tucker Young's company.

Shy handed over their plates and said, "Make sure you get some of the coleslaw, Reagan. It's tasty."

"I will, Shy. And this isn't the last you'll see of me."

He looked from her to Tucker and back again. "No, I expect it isn't." To Tucker, he added, "Shelly wants you to come to dinner. Bring Reagan here with you. How 'bout Sunday night at six?"

"That's good for me," Tucker said, looking to her.

Reagan nodded. "I'd be happy to come for dinner and meet your wife, Shy."

"Good deal. See you then."

They pushed their trays down the line, Tucker picking up a few sides as they went.

"This is a lot of food," she said, eyeing everything on their trays.

"I'll polish off whatever you can't finish."

He insisted on paying for the two of them, and they carried their trays to a corner booth.

"I'll be back. Want to get an extra plate," Tucker said.

When he returned, he set it between them. "This'll be the communal plate. I'm going to give you some of what I got." He paused, his gaze penetrating. "I know eating off someone's plate can be pretty intimate, and I don't want to rush anything."

She appreciated his candor as he placed a slice of the ham and turkey on it for her. He also spooned a couple of bites of each side onto the plate for her.

"Let me give you one of these sausage links," she said, spearing it and passing it to him. Then Reagan poured barbeque sauce over her brisket and dove in.

She chewed thoughtfully for a moment, savoring the rich, smoky taste of the brisket. "Your uncle sure knows his barbeque."

"Uncle Shy learned everything from his dad and grandfather. Barbequing is in the Blackwood genes."

Thinking to what she had heard earlier today from Emerson, she said, "I know you want to write music, but you probably need to come up with a way to put food on the table. According to Emerson, Ry's business is booming. He really could use a hand. She helps out sometimes, but she's busy with her baking and supervising at The Bake House."

"I think I'll approach Ry and see if we can work out something," Tucker said thoughtfully. "I helped him the other day on his food truck, and we proved to be a darn good team."

They talked about different things in Lost Creek as they ate dinner, but Reagan was aware the entire time of the more serious things that should be discussed. When they finished eating, Tucker set down his fork.

"We need to talk about what happened before," he said bluntly. "About that kiss."

"I thought it was a very sweet one," she said. "It made me feel special, Tucker, and I haven't felt that way in a very long time."

"I held back," he admitted. "I've just gained you as a friend, Reagan, and I don't want to lose your friendship. I think because of what we've both experienced, we understand one another better than most people do. It's created an instant bond between us because we lost someone we loved so quickly and unexpectedly."

She nodded encouragingly, wondering where he was going with this.

"I've been existing for the past couple of years since Josie's death," he shared. "It's like I didn't want to face the fact that she was gone. It's why I took off. Everything in our house reminded me of her. Even the faint scent of perfume on her pillowcase. I had to get as far away as I could before I went crazy." He paused. "Or killed myself."

She gasped.

He took a sip of his iced tea. "It took Emerson reaching out to me to realize I can't run anymore. I'm too tired. I've got to face the fact that Josie's dead. She's gone. She's never coming back."

"You'll always have your memories of her," Reagan said, wanting to comfort him, understanding exactly where he was coming from. "You'll love Josie forever. That will never change. I get it, though. You may have restlessly roamed the country, trying to escape your pain. I pushed aside my grief and buried myself in my work. My life was the same as yours. I merely existed. Put one foot in front of the other. Kept making the next deal. The next trade. I worked practically every waking hour, falling into bed late at night, trying never to think about what had happened."

She swallowed. "I put my life on hold because the life I'd pictured with Arch would never come to pass. I still love him. I still grieve for what we could have had and never got to experience. Arch was so full of life, Tucker. He would be angry at me for sticking my head in the sand and letting life pass me by. I guess I've come to Lost Creek to find myself once again. To figure out who I really am without Arch. And to move forward with this new me. The me that's left."

He nodded solemnly. "I get that. Josie was a real firecracker. She would be pissed because I'm still moping around two years later."

Tucker reached and took her hand. A calm descended upon Reagan. It was as if this man now anchored her after she'd been adrift for so long. She needed to be open to the possibilities that lay ahead.

"I want to be your friend, Reagan. I think I want to be more than that, too. It isn't something I want to rush into, though."

"I agree. I think we'll be dealing with a lot of emotions. Some similar. Some different. I think the most important thing is for us to be honest with one another. Communication is going to be key in whatever we do."

Tucker nodded in agreement. "I've never been one to talk things out in the past. Josie used to get frustrated with me about that. Maybe that's one lesson she tried to teach me that I'll finally take to heart now. We do need to talk every step of the way. If we're comfortable with something, we keep going. If one of us needs to put the brakes on, we do."

His gaze met hers, and Reagan felt as if Tucker could see down to her very soul, a place she'd only allowed Arch to venture.

"This may be a temporary thing, Reagan," he added. "We may explore the attraction between us and decide it's best to leave things as being friends. You might figure out that you want to leave Lost Creek, and I would support your decision." He hesitated. "What I'm willing to say is that I'm open to whatever possibilities lie ahead. Temporary— or permanent."

He squeezed her hand.

"I'll admit I haven't looked at or even thought about

another man since Arch." She smiled. "That changed the moment I pulled up at the inn and saw you rocking on the porch. You're quite the looker, Cowboy," she teased, trying to lighten the mood some.

His hand tightened around hers. "Let me just say one thing, Caramel. The next time I kiss you— *if* there's a next time —it's not going to be some friendly little peck on the lips. Your toes are going to curl."

The electricity crackled between them, and Reagan knew despite the conversation they'd just had about taking things slowly, the inevitable was going to happen between them.

She was going to kiss Tucker Young. Make love with Tucker Young.

Reagan didn't know if it would be a one and done and they would move on, or if it would be the start of a new relationship.

He released her hand. "So, I guess we're going to call this our first date. Are you up for a second one?"

Grinning at him, she said, "I believe I am. You have anything in mind?"

He pointed to the wall, which was peppered with flyers. "On the way in, we passed a poster of the football team's schedule. The Lost Creek Lions have a home game tomorrow night. How about you and I go cheer them on? Nothing like a Friday night football game date."

A nervous giggle erupted from her, and Tucker gave her a questioning look. "What? You don't want to go to a high school game?"

"I may have been born and bred in Texas, but I've

never attended a football game in my life. I've never even watched one on TV. I don't know the first thing about it."

"Sacrilege!" he proclaimed facetiously. "How could you make it through school without going to game? Football is life."

The old Reagan popped out suddenly, the one which was shy and unsure of herself. She had fought for years to keep that Reagan in a box and had succeeded in doing so during her professional days in New York.

"I was a big dork in high school, Tucker. The worst kind. Not even a band geek. I never had a date in high school or college. Friday nights, you could find me with my nose stuck in a book."

"Well, that's going to change, Miss Bradley. I'm going to explain the rules of football to you, and knowing how you soak up knowledge quickly, you will become a football expert in no time."

She laughed, hoping this man could bring her out of the dark cave she had lurked in since Arch's death. She had been a hermit for too long.

It was time to live again.

"You'll need to start at the very beginning," Reagan declared.

He gave her a lopsided grin. "This is one thing I know a lot about." Tucker looked at her hungrily. "And I think you'll be a terrific student, Caramel."

12

———————

*R*eagan eased her car into a parking spot halfway between the hardware store and Java Junction. As she got out, she thought that she would need to purchase her own vehicle now that she was going to live in Texas. Renting was expensive. Not that she couldn't afford it, but she'd rather buy or lease something to her own taste instead of the rental she'd taken when she landed in Austin. She would need to think about when she could return the car to Austin and find something permanent and jotted a note on her phone's to-do list as she approached the hardware store.

Ivy had told her there was a set of stairs in back, and she went to the side of the building to take them, knocking on the door.

It opened, and Ivy gave her a warm embrace, as if she were family. It still surprised Reagan how friendly people

155

were in Lost Creek and that she already had a growing group of friends after being here such a short while.

"Come in," Ivy said. "I'm so glad you could stop by this morning."

Entering the studio, she caught the faint scent of paint and turpentine in the air. Reagan gazed about the room, seeing a few finished canvasses resting on easels and was immediately drawn to one, in particular.

"Oh, my!" she exclaimed, moving toward it. "This is stunning, Ivy."

Her friend joined her as they viewed the painting together and said, "This is Lost Creek Rock. It's not as famous as Enchanted Rock, a well-known rock formation in the Hill Country, but I've been drawn to it time and again over the years. I've painted it from many different angles."

"It's incredible."

Reagan began moving about the room, looking at the other completed works of art.

"You've really captured the essence of the Texas Hill Country," she praised. "I always loved coming here when I was growing up. Not only to see Aunt Jean, but to experience the beauty and wonder of this area."

"I feel privileged to have grown up here," Ivy said. "Apparently, the land speaks to others, too. I recently had a showing of my art in New York, and I'm proud to say that every painting sold."

"I can see why. You're very talented, Ivy. Your paintings show great skill, but they also have heart. Have you ever thought about painting full-time?"

"That's the plan," Ivy revealed. "Dax and I have talked about it at length. I worked in an art gallery in Houston after I graduated from college and then came back to Lost Creek last year. My parents' tasting room manager was retiring. Since I knew so much about wines, it made sense for me to step into that role. The hours the tasting room is open helped me work painting into my schedule again on a regular basis. I hadn't had any time to paint during my Houston years. I'd forgotten how much it feeds my soul. With the baby coming, however, something has to give."

"Who'll take over the tasting room?"

"That hasn't been decided yet, but I'm leaning toward Melanie. She's one of two sisters who works at the tasting room. While both Melanie and Sarah are knowledgeable about wines and good with people, Melanie has a really good head for numbers. Whoever operates the tasting room has to always make certain enough of the different wines are stocked. I also oversee the gift shop, and that responsibility will be part of the manager's job, as well. I've already talked to Mom and Dad about it, and they agree Melanie would be a great choice. I think I'll approach her soon and make the offer."

"What if she doesn't take it?"

Ivy chuckled. "That's the best reason I should talk to her sooner rather than later. If she doesn't want the position, I'll have to go to Plan B. I do want to pursue my art full-time, as well as motherhood." She stroked her small bump. "And I want to leave the tasting room in capable hands."

"You said you were going to start something new. Have you decided what you'll paint next? "Reagan asked.

"Come sit and look at a few of the sketches I've been working on."

They adjourned to a dilapidated couch which had seen better days, and Ivy picked up a sketchbook, turning the pages to show Reagan different drawings.

"Finley and I go out and meander around the area for inspiration. In fact, I have a few of her photographs I can show you."

Ivy handed the sketchbook to Reagan and retrieved a folder.

Passing it to Reagan, she said, "Fin not only takes pictures of people, she also photographs the Texas countryside."

Opening the folder, she looked at a series of a dozen photos. All were in black and white, showing the stark beauty and majesty of the Hill Country.

"I had no idea Finley was so talented."

"I think Fin is only scratching the surface of her creativity," Ivy shared. "She had a small exhibition of her landscape photography at our local library. In fact, that's how Holden found her."

Ivy explained how Holden had stepped into the public library when he first arrived in town and had been taken with the work of the photographer— and then the photographer herself.

"Speaking of Finley, we better head over to Java Junction," Ivy reminded.

They walked the short distance to the coffeehouse, which was about half full at the moment.

As they joined the back of the line, Ivy said, "The old geezers hold court in the back there every morning. They gather for coffee and gossip. If you ever want to know what's happening in Lost Creek, just ask them. They have their hand on the pulse of the community."

They moved up in line, and Reagan saw a sign which said *Goodies for purchase from The Bake House.*

"These are from Emerson's bakery?" she asked.

Ivy nodded. "When Dax first opened Java Junction, he was taken with how delicious the pastries and rolls were at The Bake House. He arranged with Ethel Frederick, the original owner, to provide Java Junction with an assortment of baked goods each morning. It's convenient for people who come in for a cup of coffee and want to linger, like the soccer moms over there. Or even those who grab something on the go because they don't have to stop at both places. The Bake House still makes money. Em continued the arrangement once she took over."

"I already ate breakfast at Aunt Jean's this morning, but everything on that tray looks too good to pass up."

"I love everything on display, but I can never pass up a sausage kolache."

"What's that?"

"It's a spiced sausage link wrapped in a heavenly pillow of yeasty roll," Ivy explained. "Let's each get one."

They reached the front of the line, where Dax and another barista worked.

Dax grinned at them. "I know my lovely wife wants a cup of herbal tea to drink. What can I get for you, Reagan?"

She glanced up at the menu and back to Dax. "I think I'll go with a hazelnut latte. And a sausage kolache for both of us."

"Go have a seat, ladies. I'll bring your order to you shortly."

They sat at a table near the window. Moments later, Finley joined them, giving each of them a hug.

"I'm so glad you had time to have coffee with us, Reagan," Finley said.

Chuckling, she said, "This was the only thing on my calendar. Well, until Tucker asked me to go to tonight's high school football game."

The other two women exchanged a glance.

"I'm glad you're joining in on community activities," Finley said. "There's nothing like going to a high school game. I try to hit up a few football, volleyball, basketball, and baseball games when I can. I have former students playing all those sports."

"How long did you teach?" she asked.

"Both Em and I taught six years. We were at Lost Creek Elementary, so many of our former students are hitting middle and high school. It's fun to be able to watch them play different sports and see how they've matured since grade school."

"I've never attended a high school game before. I know zero about football. Tucker said he'd teach me all I need to know."

"I'm glad you've hit it off so well with him," Finley said. "Tucker seems like a great guy."

"He came around summers to our house with Ry," Ivy said. "Ry was our brother's best friend. Harper and I have always looked upon Ry as another brother and Tucker as extended family. I really hope Tucker decides to stay in Lost Creek." She looked hopefully at Reagan. "I hope you'll be staying, too."

"I haven't made up my mind yet," she shared. "I did quit my job in finance in New York, though. If I return to the business world in that capacity, I'll need to relocate to a larger city, such as Dallas or Houston. If I find something else to do, though, I may very well stay in Lost Creek. Aunt Jean is the only family I have left, and I really love being near her."

"I second career changes," Finley said. "Though Em and I got our degrees in education and really enjoyed our time in the classroom, when new opportunities arose for each of us, we jumped on them. Em is flourishing as a baker."

"I've seen some of her cake designs. She's really creative," Reagan said. "I also saw some of your black and white photographs of the Hill Country. They blew me away, Finley."

"Thank you. I began taking senior portraits as a side endeavor. Education doesn't pay its teachers enough, and photography proved to be lucrative. Plus, I enjoyed shooting subjects. I'm happy I've been able to move into doing it full time. I take all kinds of portraits. Photograph most of the Weddings with Hart clients, both their bridal portraits and the ceremonies and receptions. I've also done some work on a movie for Wolf and Ana Ramirez. They formed WEBA, their own production company, and shot Holden's second book this summer, *Hill Country Homicide.*"

Finley brightened. "Wait a minute. I have something for you, Reagan." She leaned down and unzipped her large tote, removing two hardback books.

Passing them to Reagan, she said, "Holden sent these along since you hadn't read either of them."

"That was so generous of him." She opened the cover of one and saw it was autographed by the author. "I'll thank him when I see him. I haven't been able to read for pleasure in forever, and I'm looking forward to reading both and seeing the movie of *Capitol Crimes.*"

"Maybe you'd like to come to the world premiere of *Hill Country Homicide,*" Finley said excitedly. "It's in three weeks. It'll open in Austin. Everyone but Harper and Braden are coming. She'll be close to her due date and doesn't want to ride in a car that long to Austin and back, much less be that far away from her OB. First babies don't always come when they're expected."

Ivy laughed. "Unless they're my sister's baby, that is. You know how organized she is. Harper will probably instruct the baby down to the second regarding what time to come out."

All three women laughed, and Finley said, "Seriously, Reagan. I hope you'll come with us to Austin. Ry and Emerson will be there. It's one of the rare weekends Ry doesn't have to cater a Saturday night wedding. Dax and

Ivy are also coming. We'd be happy for you and Tucker to come as our guests, as well."

She felt a blush rising on her cheeks. "We're not... a couple."

Finley smiled. "Not yet. Or at least not that you're willing to admit. Holden and I talked about it after dinner. It just seems the two of you belong together. I hope you'll give Tucker a chance. Going to a football game sounds like a fun date. In the meantime, I'll text you the info about the premiere."

"I'll tell you now that I'll go," Reagan said. "I think it would be exciting to attend a premiere. Besides, the only plans I have right now are to help out Harper once the baby comes."

"You mean you'll be working for Weddings with Hart?" Ivy asked excitedly.

"Yes. Harper and I talked for a long time yesterday. We really do have a lot in common. We're both very organized, detail-oriented, disciplined individuals. While Paula is going to take charge of the operation, I said I'd be happy to pitch in and help wherever I might be needed. I'm supposed to go to the wedding being held Saturday night. I'll be shadowing Harper and watching everything to give me a better idea of what goes on, including behind the scenes."

"Harper will be so relieved to have you on board," Finley said enthusiastically. "She has a tendency to micromanage. I worried about her taking time off when the baby comes."

"Beau is her priority," Ivy said firmly. "No matter how

dedicated Harper is to her business, Beau and Braden will always come first." Looking to Reagan, Ivy added, "I know she wants to take her maternity leave through the end of the year. At least you'll be with us in Lost Creek for that long."

"Hopefully by then, I'll have figured out what I want to do," she said. "In the meantime, I'm going to enjoy some downtime." She held up the copy of *Capitol Crimes*. "This is the first thing I plan to do when I get back to Aunt Jean's. Kick back with a cup of hot tea and begin Holden's book."

She looked at the book jacket's picture of Holden.

Finley glanced down. "Isn't he handsome? It still amazes me that he can come up with all this murder and mayhem since he's such a regular guy."

"I look forward to reading about murder and mayhem," Reagan said, laughing. "I'm also eager to see the movie version of each book and compare them."

"I've seen the new film twice," Finley confided. "It's terrific. You'll be on the edge of your seat. Jack Calder is incredible in it."

When she looked at Finley blankly, Finley noted, "You don't know who Jack Calder is, do you? I guess you don't hit the movies much."

"That was the old Reagan," she said, her voice brimming with confidence. "The new Reagan is going to read books. Go to movies. Take time and enjoy coffee with her friends."

Holden suddenly appeared. He bent and kissed his wife's cheek. "I see you got the book copies, Reagan."

"Yes, thank you so much, Holden. That was really thoughtful of you."

"If intrigue and murder aren't up your alley, I'll understand. Maybe you'll like next year's book and movie release better."

His words piqued her curiosity. "What is it about?"

Holden pulled up a chair to join them. "It's a personal book. About Mr. Hamilton, the school janitor who befriended me when I was a boy. I was a lonely kid, Reagan. My home life sucked. Alcoholic dad. Mom working so much she was never home. Mr. Hamilton took me under his wing and helped me become the man I am today. He taught me everything important about life which I needed to know. I'm forever in his debt."

His words touched Reagan. "I came from a privileged background, but I was a lonely child, too. I never had friends growing up. Aunt Jean was the closest thing I had to a friend."

Finley reached and took Reagan's hand, squeezing it. "You have friends here in Lost Creek, Reagan," she said fervently. "We'll be here for you. Whenever you need us."

Ivy took her other hand. "It seems already as if I've known you forever, Reagan. Harper, Finley, and I were drawn back to Lost Creek. Even though we grew up here, we were searching for something."

Holden spoke up. "Then there are those of us who came to Lost Creek hoping to find ourselves and our purpose in life. If that's the journey you're on, Reagan, you've come to the right place. You'll find all the support you need here in Lost Creek."

Tears misted her eyes. "I've had a rough couple of years," she admitted. "I walked away from an incredibly lucrative job because I wasn't happy. I hope, like the rest of you, that I can find my purpose in life. And happiness."

13

Tucker spread out the dominos he borrowed from Miss Jean, placing some face up to represent one football team and others face down to play the role of the other.

"This side is one team," he explained to Reagan. "This side is the other. We'll call them the Blanks and the Dots."

"Okay," she said carefully, taking in the two lines facing one another as he scattered other dominos around.

"Football has a simple concept, but it can become incredibly complex," he began. "Basically, you want to get the ball over the goal line. That's a touchdown and worth six points. If you get close but can't quite get it across the goal line, you can kick a field goal. That's good for three points if the kicker makes it."

He finished setting up the dominos. "A team gets four tries to make it ten yards down the field. They can run the ball or pass it. If they accomplish that small goal and make it those ten yards or more, they get another four tries to do so again."

"Another ten yards?"

Tucker nodded. "If they fail to gain ten yards, they have to turn the ball over to the other team. Most of the times if they don't make it in three tries, they kick it way down the field on the fourth attempt. Or fourth down. That's called a punt."

Reagan studied the dominos. "Okay. Four tries. Ten yards. Kick it away if you can't make those ten yards."

"The tries are called downs. First down. Second down. Like that. The team wanting to move the ball huddles up and talks about the play they'll run. Then they come to the line where the ball is. It's called the line of scrimmage, where things get started." He swept his hand along one line of dominos. "This is the Blanks' offensive line. The Dots across from them are the defensive line. The lines can change and have a different number of players on them, but we'll stick with basics for now."

Pointing to a domino, he said, "This is the Blanks' quarterback. Think of him as the president of the team. He makes all the calls on the field. He's the man in charge of making sure the ball moves in the right direction and his team scores."

Tucker indicated another Blank domino. "This is a running back. They come in different varieties and are called different names, but his job basically is to run the ball as fast and far as he can when he gets the call. These two on each end? They're the wide receivers. They run down the field and try to catch the ball thrown by the quarterback."

"This guy." She touched a domino.

"Right. They've already talked about the play in the huddle, so every Blank knows the play they'll run. The wide receivers run their routes. Not always a straight line. Sometimes, they'll zig and zag around, but they know where they're supposed to be if the ball is coming to them and will be there when the ball is thrown to them. At least that's the idea."

"What if they aren't supposed to catch the ball?" she asked. "What do they do then?"

"They're sneaky. They pretend the ball is going to be thrown to them. Try to make the guys guarding them think it's coming their way."

Understanding lit her eyes. "Oh, so they draw attention away from who really is getting the ball, so he'll get farther."

"Yes!" Tucker said enthusiastically.

"Who are these players?" she asked.

"They're a part of the Dots' defense. They try to figure out what the play will be." He indicated three dominos. "These are the linebackers." He pointed to a few more. "These are the defensive backs. They have all kinds of names. Strong safety. Free safety. Don't worry about that now. Just remember they'll be covering the wide receivers, trying to keep them from catching the ball. In fact, they'll try to catch it themselves. If they do, that's called an interception."

"Could they run it the other way if they catch it?"

He grinned. "You're catching on, Caramel. Yes, they can run all the way toward their goal line and try to score themselves. It's a big deal if the defense can take the ball away from the other team and score."

Tucker went over a few kinds of plays with her. Straight up the middle runs. End arounds. Fakes. When he saw how quickly she was learning, he even added in how a tight end functioned as a swing man, both blocking and receiving.

She tucked a lock of hair behind her ear. "This is a lot to learn, but I'm fascinated."

"It's a game a strategy. Try to outthink your opponent. Spot a weak player. A wide receiver might go back to the huddle and tell the quarterback of something he's noticed about the guy guarding him while he's running his routes. The quarterback will try to take advantage of any weakness."

"How does he decide whether to run or pass?"

"Good question. Most quarterbacks don't. The CEO is the coach, who stands on the sidelines and watches the game. In high school, the head coach almost always calls all the plays. He'll send a player in with the play to call in the huddle as another player comes out of the game. You can only have eleven men on the field for your side at any given time. In college and the pros, sometimes the coach calls the plays, and other times the offensive head coach will call them. Usually, a team has a coach up in the press box, watching the game with that height advantage. He can see all kinds of things from that position, things where players on the field or coaches on the sidelines might be hard to spot. He can relay what he's seeing, and the Blanks can take advantage of whatever he recommends."

"Whew. It *is* starting to get complicated."

"Most every team knows they have only three plays to make those ten yards. Remember we talked about if you don't get a first down after three plays, you almost always punt the ball to the other team."

"Go over why again. You said they have four tries to make a first down."

"Pretend each end of the dining room table is the goal line for the two teams. Let's say the Blanks are here. Football fields are a hundred yards in length. If they're at their own thirty-yard line and don't make a first down, they have to turn the ball over to the Dots."

She brightened. "And the Dots would be close enough that their chances of scoring are better since they're so close. Even if they couldn't make a first down because the Blanks dug deep and wouldn't give up any yardage, they could kick a field goal."

He beamed at her. "You are catching on fast."

"So, if they kick it down the field— punt it —what happens?"

"The punt returner tries to run it back as far as he can. Sometimes, though, he can see the other team is moving fast toward him. He might wave and call for a fair catch. That means he catches it and doesn't move. No one from the other team can hit him. Play will start at that spot."

"But if he does catch it and sees daylight, he can run down the field and try to score."

"Exactly."

Tucker wanted to kiss her as a reward. Badly. Hell, he didn't need an excuse to kiss her. He just wanted to. Desperately. But his head told him he needed to give both of them time and space. Even the thought of kissing someone besides Josie was a little hard to wrap his head around, which was adding to his confusion. Reagan had to feel the same way since she hadn't looked at a guy since Arch.

Yet this woman was starting to fill more and more of his thoughts.

"I think you have enough background now, Reagan," Tucker said, pushing his growing feelings aside. "Seeing a game live is really going to help cement what you've learned."

Miss Jean entered the dining room and asked, "How is the football lesson taking?"

"Your niece knows enough to follow the game tonight, but not enough to make her dangerous," he replied.

Jean Bradley cackled. "Football is in the blood of most every Texan, Reagan. Your daddy shortchanged you when he didn't teach you the ins and outs of the game. I'm glad Tucker's taken it upon himself to help you figure it out."

"He also said we'd eat at the game tonight, Aunt Jean. Ry's food truck will be there until the barbeque runs out."

"Then you better get yourself a jacket and head over to the stadium," Miss Jean told them.

As they got into Reagan's car, Tucker said, "I tinkered some with your aunt's truck today. Used the tools she had handy, but I think I'm going to need to swing by and borrow a few from Uncle Shy's friend who owns the auto garage on South Main."

"I'd be happy to give you a ride there tomorrow," Reagan said.

"I'd appreciate that."

On their way into town, she said, "I'm going to want to turn this rental car in soon. Staying in Texas, I'll need to have my own transportation. I'll have to drive to the Austin airport to return this rental. There should be several dealerships there where I can look for a car. I think I'll ask Harper since she lived in Austin for several years."

"Do you know what kind of car you want?"

"Anything that isn't puce colored."

He died laughing— since this was the exact color of the car she drove now. "You aren't fond of puce? Why, I thought it was every woman's favorite color."

"Changing the subject, we got an invitation today."

"We?" he asked, looking at her curiously.

"Not exactly *we* as a couple. We as in Finley invited two people that just happened to be us. In two weekends, Holden's new movie will have its world premiere in Austin. There'll be some big to-do. Finley told me Dax and Ivy were going. Ry and Emerson, too."

'I've never been to a fancy film premiere. Then again, Austin isn't quite a Hollywood red carpet event kind of place. It's actually a fun, laid-back town, for the most part. Liberal as all get-out in a mostly conservative state, but it has some terrific places to eat and a lot of interesting stores and bars where you can listen to good music."

"Is Austin where you and Josie lived?" she asked quietly.

Tucker nodded. "I can probably recommend a car dealership to you. We both bought vehicles there. After the wreck, the insurance company paid for the car, which was totaled. I sold my truck back to the same dealership and hit the road."

"If it's going to bring back sad memories for you, Tucker, you don't need to attend the movie premiere. I'll even stay home with you."

"No way. I know we don't know Holden very well, but I think it's important to go and support him on his big night. Dax told me that Holden wrote the screenplay from his own novel. Supposedly, that's a huge deal because it's a different kind of writing. Kind of like an Olympic sprinter in the one-hundred-meter race changing horses midstream and becoming a marathon runner."

"Holden gave me copies of both his books. I started *Capitol Crimes* when I got home today. I read for four hours nonstop. I'll be able to finish it tomorrow since I have just a little bit to go."

"Then we need to stream the movie together. With the book's details so fresh in your mind, you can make a good comparison between the two. Personally, I usually prefer the book to the movie version of it."

They reached the stadium and though it was only five-thirty, the parking lot was more than half full for a seven o'clock kick.

"It looks like there'll be a nice turnout for this game."

"It's a big rival of Lost Creek. That— and Ry's barbeque truck —have probably pulled in the crowd."

Reagan parked, and they headed toward the food truck. Tucker said, "You'll see a couple of familiar items on Ry's menu. Sliced beef. Chopped beef. Those kinds of sandwiches. But Ry served in the military overseas. He picked up some interesting food knowledge along the way. He's infused some barbeque dishes with an Asian flair. From what I gather, those new creations have become pretty popular, both around town with people who patronize the food truck and with Harper's clients at the winery."

"Is that why Ry does the catering for the event center and not Shy?"

Tucker nodded. "Aunt Shelly gave me the lowdown when I arrived in Lost Creek. Things were pretty strained between Uncle Shy and Ry, and it was all about Ry wanting to change things up a bit. Uncle Shy is all about tradition and things not changing. Thanks to Emerson, though, she helped them patch things up. The catering end was becoming a little too much for Uncle Shy to handle, so he's turned it over to Ry."

By now, they joined the long line which stood in front of Ry's food truck. Tucker saw both Ry and Emerson getting orders out as fast as possible. Watching his cousin and wife work, he decided he was ready to speak to Ry about working in the barbeque business alongside him. Ry had mentioned wanting to invest in a new smoker because of his growing business. Tucker thought it was time to touch some of the blood money and turn it into something useful.

They reached the front, and Reagan said, "Take care of us, Ry. I'm sure I'll like whatever you give us to eat. My treat," she said in Tucker's direction.

"Coming right up," Ry said with a smile.

"I'll get you two banana puddings," Emerson added. "It's Ry's grandmother's recipe. To die for."

"Looks like a big crowd has turned out for the game," Tucker said as Ry wrapped their food in brown paper. "Think I need to talk to you about a few things, Cuz."

"I'm all ears," Ry said. "Text me when you want to get together."

"Are you working a wedding tomorrow night at the winery?" he asked.

His cousin laughed. "I most definitely am. A big one. I hear that Reagan is going to be shadowing Harper."

That was news to him. "How about I stop by the kitchen and help you get meals out tomorrow night?" he suggested. "We can talk afterward."

"It's a date," Ry said, handing over their food.

He turned and saw Emerson had already given Reagan their desserts, and so they set off to find a place to eat.

"Why don't we head back and sit on the hood of my car?" Reagan said.

"Good idea. I don't see anywhere open except the ground."

They took their dinner back to her rental and climbed atop the hood, stretching out their legs.

As they opened their food, he saw Ry had given each of

them a sandwich and long stick speared with smoked meat and vegetables.

"I hear you'll be at the event center tomorrow night."

She brightened. "I'm going to follow Harper around to see all she does during a wedding and reception. She's going on maternity leave come mid-November and will be out for six weeks. We had a long talk yesterday, and we found out how alike we are in so many ways. Just our approach to life and business. Anyway, her two assistants will be stepping in to fill her shoes while she's away, but Harper said she could use another set of hands."

"That's where you come in, I suppose."

"I'm going to see how things go tomorrow night. Get there a few hours before the wedding and learn about the pre-ceremony activities, then stay after for the reception, as well. I meet with Harper, Paula, and Dayna Monday morning at ten. Harper is going to have a plan outlined by then, so each of us can see what our responsibilities will be in her absence. Of course, I know it involves more than just working the wedding itself. There'll also be clients to meet with. That kind of thing. I probably won't be involved in much of that since I'm new to the operation, but I'd like to sit in on some of those meetings to see what they're like."

"That'll keep you in Lost Creek for the next couple of months," he noted, happy to hear she'd be sticking around.

"It will. If there aren't any complications, Harper will return at the beginning of the new year in January. By then, I hope to have figured out what I want to do.

Working for Weddings with Hart won't take up all my time."

Tucker hoped it didn't.

Because he planned to spend a lot of time with her himself.

"I'm going to be at the wedding tomorrow, too. I'm helping Ry with the catering. We'll talk afterward about me joining him in the food truck."

"That's terrific, Tucker. Like me, that won't be full-time, though. It should give you plenty of time to work on your songwriting."

She had a bit of barbeque sauce in the corner of her mouth, and he wanted to lick it away. The only thing that stopped him from doing so were all the people passing by in the parking lot.

Instead, he took the pad of his thumb and wiped it away, causing her to blush profusely. He wanted to lick his thumb but dabbed it on a napkin instead.

"I think you look presentable enough to go to the game now, Caramel. What do you say?"

Her eyes lit with mischief. "I say we eat our banana pudding first and then go inside the stadium."

14

Tucker climbed behind the wheel of the truck he had been working on. Reagan had taken him to the garage that morning, where the owner had agreed to lend him the tools he needed. They had talked about the truck's repair needs for a few minutes, and then Reagan had returned him to the inn, where he'd been working ever since.

Inserting the key, he turned it and heard the truck trying to start. He tried again, and the engine turned over this time. Relief swept through him as he backed it out of the barn. He decided to take it for a spin. Leaving it running, he quickly gathered the borrowed tools and placed them in a bag, setting it on the front seat.

First, he drove into Lost Creek, dropping the bag with one of the mechanics, thanking him for the loan. Then he cruised out of town and along the road for half an hour, making certain the truck was running properly at various speeds. It gave him a chance to see some of the surrounding area and drink in its beauty. He decided before the weather turned too cold, he would ask Reagan if she might like to go on a picnic with him.

Ever since he had met her, the melodies locked within him seemed to be freeing themselves. He'd left his phone on record the entire time he worked on the truck's engine, humming different melodies that came to him. Tomorrow, he'd listen again to the recording and start putting pencil to paper in order to capture these tunes. What he needed, though, was a new guitar. He'd sold his before he hit the road, and now he was sorely in need of one.

He felt he was on the verge of a creative explosion. If he could get half a dozen songs written, with lyrics put to the melodies, he would consider giving Matt a call. Tucker hadn't spoken to Josie's brother since her death. It wasn't for lack of trying on Matt's part. His brother-in-law had left voicemails and periodically texted Tucker over the past two years. The breakdown had been on Tucker's end. He knew Matt was hurting as he was, but Tucker had crawled inside his pain and avoided contact with anyone who'd reached out to him. Maybe if Matt and he could make some new music together, it would help ease their sorrow and bring them close again.

He returned to The Inn at Lost Creek and parked in front of the B&B. Going inside, he ran into Miss Jean.

"I apologize for being a filthy mess, Miss Jean, but I have the truck running. I took it out for a ride, and everything seems to be in good working order. I'll still take it in to be inspected and see if there's anything I missed that needs to be done."

The innkeeper smiled at him. "I knew you'd be able to fix it, Tucker. I had so much faith in you that I even looked online to see how to transfer the title to you. I'll make sure my lawyer, Merilee Swan, gets you the release of lien. All you'll do then is take the signed title and an application you can download to the local county tax office. Show everything to them, and all it'll cost you will be the required fees and taxes. I'll even go with you to make certain everything is handled smoothly."

"I appreciate that, Miss Jean. I'm happy to pay whatever is owed, but you need to let me give you something for the truck. It might be old, but it's in good condition."

"Nonsense, Tucker. I won't hear of it. I love what I'm driving now. That truck was just sitting in the barn, taking up space. You're in need of transportation. The truck is your reward for getting it running again and out of my hair."

"You're very generous. Thank you so much. I need to go and get cleaned up now. You haven't happened to see Reagan, have you?"

"You just missed her. She finished reading Holden's book and then left for Lost Creek Vineyards. She told me Harper wanted her there three hours before the ceremony began. I guess there's a lot of fuss to getting married nowadays."

"I better shower and head over to the venue myself. Ry asked me to be there two hours before the ceremony started."

"Are you going to be working with your cousin doing catering?" she asked.

"That's the plan. I'm hoping I can work out the details with Ry tonight."

In the shower, Tucker began humming another melody, relieved that the dam had finally broken and that his creativity had returned. And not just the creativity. The *desire* to write songs again. Songwriting had been the last thing he would've touched these past two years. Returning to Texas and Lost Creek, though, had made a huge difference.

In part, he knew it was due to meeting Reagan and having her in his life. Josie had always been a muse to him. Without her, Tucker felt his talent dry up. Now, though, he was finally able to think of his wife without all the bitterness and a heavy burden of grief pressing against him, suffocating him. He was trying his best to take Reagan's advice and remember the good in his relationship with Josie.

He only hoped he might have a second chance at life.

And love. With Reagan Bradley.

Maybe it was foolish, thinking about something like that. He'd only met Reagan, but there was something about her that spoke to his soul. It could be that they had undergone a similar experience, losing a loved one by tragedy. But they had more than that in common. For the first time in a long time, Tucker could feel himself coming alive. It was if he had been frozen in time after Josie's death and lived through a long, cruel winter in hibernation, numb to everything. Spring had finally come, melting the ice he'd been encased in. He wondered if Reagan was experiencing anything remotely similar.

He dressed in a clean shirt and pair of jeans and left for the venue, parking behind the event center when he arrived. Tucker passed the smoker, smelling the rich aroma coming from it, and entered the back door.

As he stepped into the kitchen, he saw Emerson rolling a cake.

"Here, I'll get that for you," he told her.

Stepping up to the cake cart, Tucker gazed at it in wonder. "This is what you do?" he asked. "In my mind, I just saw a round, white cake with *Best Wishes* in script and a couple's name scrawled atop it."

He gazed at the five tiers, looking up and down, seeing the intricate flowers and design within the icing itself. "It's a damn work of art, Emerson."

"Thank you, Tucker," she said, looking pleased. "I really feel as if I'm coming into my own as a cake baker. I have such fun meeting with the engaged couples and designing their cakes. Here, let me show you where this goes."

He followed her, rolling the cake along, to a designated area for the cake cutting during the reception. A chocolate groom's cake was already in place.

"I see this groom is a baseball nut by the looks of this cake. And a Texas Rangers' fan."

"Grooms get pushed to the side a lot of times during wedding planning," Emerson said. "Their cake is the one time they get all the attention and can shine. I try to incorporate not only the flavors they enjoy but any hobby or interest they might have."

Harper and Reagan joined them, with Harper saying, "You should have seen last week's cake, Tucker. The groom was a spelunker, and Em created magic. His cake looked like a cave, with stalactites hanging from the ceiling of it and pools of water within it. It was the most remarkable thing I've ever seen."

Emerson blushed, and Tucker thought just how lucky his cousin was to have her as his wife.

"How are you ladies coming along?" he asked, seeing Reagan was dressed in a white blouse and slim black pants which looked good on her. Really good. Her hair was swept away from her face, in a knot at her nape. All he wanted to do was spin her around and brush his lips against the soft skin of that nape.

"Harper has already showed me so much," Reagan enthused. "The bridal party has arrived, and we've got them on schedule. The ladies are their having hair and makeup done. The guys are watching a football game, drinking beer and eating some snacks."

"Reagan really knows how to pay attention to detail," Harper said. "In fact, she's already made a few suggestions to me that I intend to implement. We were just checking in here to see how things were progressing. We'll see you later."

"I need to check with Ry in the kitchen," Emerson said as the two women left.

When they returned, Ry was at the stovetop, where eight gas burners were, stirring a huge pot of beans.

"Glad you could make it, Tuck," Ry said. "I'm not going to ask you to do a lot tonight. Just watch what

Emerson and I do and if you can join in and help, that's fine."

Ry took him through the kitchen, showing Tucker various things, including the walk-in fridge where huge bowls of potato salad and coleslaw for tonight's guests were stored.

"Emerson's got several dishes of macaroni and cheese which she'll put on to bake soon. This bride said all she really needed as a side was mac and cheese, but we talked her into adding a few other things."

"What's on tonight's menu?' he inquired.

"We're going with a combo plate," Ry explained. "Some brides like to offer guests a choice, but this one wanted some of each entrée to be served. The first is galbi, which features fall-off-the-bone beef short ribs smothered in a sauce that's a mix of both sweet and savory. The other is a spicy marinated pork butt."

"How many guests are coming this evening?"

"Close to two hundred, counting the wedding party," Ry responded. "We've done weddings as small as twenty guests and some more than ten times that. Harper really has a steady business going. Smokin' Sweethearts caters about eighty percent of the receptions."

"I heard Uncle Shy had turned the catering arm over to you, so it's not actually Blackwood BBQ that does the catering. I saw the Smokin' Sweethearts name on the food truck. Is that the name of your business?"

"Yup. I'm on my own. The food truck is solely my operation, as is catering events for Weddings with Hart." Ry paused, rubbing his chin in thought. "I never wanted to compete with Dad. We had a bit of a falling out over dishes I wanted to serve that weren't traditional menu items for Blackwood BBQ. We were only able to patch things up thanks to Emerson. Dad gave me the go-ahead to do my own thing. Blackwood BBQ in town is enough for him."

"I hear you're going to Austin for Holden's movie premiere."

Ry squeezed more honey into the beans, stirring and tasting them. "We are. Thank goodness, it's a rare Saturday night I don't have a booking here. The local steakhouse is taking care of catering dinner that night. Of course, Emerson will already have the cakes baked and decorated. Harper will manage the displays for her."

"Reagan and I have been invited to attend the premiere, too."

"That's great. Holden is a terrific guy. He's really fit into Lost Creek well. You'll enjoy meeting the people who put the film together. Wolf Ramirez directed *Capitol Crimes* for one of the big studios, but he was ready to start his own production company and go indie. He liked Holden's second book and had enjoyed working with him before, so they agreed for it to be the first film released by WEBA Productions. Ana, Wolf's wife, is the producer of the film. She's really a sweetheart and keeps Wolf on his toes."

Dax stuck his head in the kitchen and gave a wave. "Hey. Just thought I'd say hi before I started setting up."

Tucker looked to his cousin. "I need to talk to Dax about something. Be right back."

He followed Dax and asked, "I see you have some band equipment here."

"I DJ weddings here fairly often. Other times, when a bride and groom want live entertainment, my band plays. We're called the Lone Star Rebels and do a mix of country and rock, with a few ballads thrown in."

"I used to write songs on the side, apart from my day job at a bank," Tucker revealed. "Have you ever heard of *Another Beer, Dear?*"

Dax broke out in a grin. "I sure have. That was you?"

He nodded and named a couple of other songs he'd written for Matt.

"I write all my own stuff," Dax shared. "While the band covers a lot of popular songs, every now and then we'll play one I've written. Maybe we could write something together," he suggested.

"I'll be honest, Dax. I haven't written any song for a few years. I lost my wife pretty suddenly, and the desire to write music simply faded away. It's come back now, though, and I have a crazy thought of trying to make my living that way. What I need, however, is a new guitar. Where can I get one around here?"

"If you're not performing, I have an old guitar you're welcome to have. I have two I use when I play here or at Java Junction. Saturday nights, I have a different local artist come in and play at the coffeehouse. I'd be happy to work you into the schedule. We can look at the calendar. That is, if you're a performer, as well as a songwriter."

"I used to be. Played little roadhouses here and there,

but I haven't sung for a long time. I wouldn't mind the loan of a guitar until I can pick up something for myself."

"I can drop it off to you tomorrow," Dax assured him.

"Thanks. I really appreciate that."

Dax introduced him to the band's drummer, who'd just arrived, and then Tucker returned to the kitchen. He watched closely everything that Ry and Emerson did, helping out when he could, including bringing in the meats which had been smoking outside, allowing them to rest before they were plated.

Reagan appeared in the kitchen. "You can start sending out appetizers in eight minutes."

"Do you serve the guests?" Tucker asked.

"No. Harper's assistants take on that job. They also handle cleanup after the meal. With a big wedding like this, Harper hires a couple of locals to help serve and clean."

Soon, he met Paula and Dayna, the venue's two assistants, and two others who would be serving guests this evening. He learned that Harper also had bartenders on staff who manned the drink stations. Trays of appetizers started flying out of the kitchen, and Ry and Emerson began retrieving other parts of the meal, getting cold sides from the fridge and removing large pans of macaroni and cheese, which had been kept warming in the ovens.

Ry arranged the meats on each plate, with Emerson coming behind him and placing the macaroni on the plate, as well. The cold sides were placed into small bowls with an ice cream scoop. Dishes were put on trays, and there was a constant flow of people coming in and out of the kitchen as guests were served their dinners, as well as glasses of wine and iced tea. He could hear music playing softly, and Ry told him it was a tape Dax used and that the band would beginning playing live once the guests finished eating.

"Most brides prefer to have dinner over and done and some of the dancing to begin before they take a break and do the cake cutting," Emerson explained. "They do the father-daughter dance and continue dancing usually thirty to forty-five minutes. Then there's a break for speeches and cake cutting. At least, that's how tonight's reception is rolling out. Each bride customizes the order to her liking."

After all the plates had gone out, cleanup ensued. Tucker jumped in quickly to help with this. He was no stranger to washing dishes. He had picked up menial jobs during his travels around the country to earn money to get to the next place.

"Our part is over," Ry told him. "Harper's crew will handle washing all the dishes, glasses, and silverware after dinner. You said you wanted to talk. Let's sit."

They moved to a table on the far side of the kitchen, with Emerson joining them. Tucker knew his cousin wouldn't make any decision without her input.

"I've decided I'm staying in Lost Creek," he began. "I'm going to need a way to earn a living, though, and I can't see myself returning to work nine-to-five at a bank. I have a strong desire to pick up songwriting again after being away from it for so long, but that's going to take a while and sure won't pay my bills in the meantime. If you have room for me, Ry, I'd be honored to work for you at Smokin' Sweethearts."

Ry beamed at him. "I was hoping you'd come to that conclusion. Emerson has pitched in, but that's taken time away from her own businesses. I could definitely use you onboard, Tuck. I thought we worked well together in the food truck the other day."

"I'm not the smoke master you are and have a lot to learn about meat, but I'm eager to start."

"Are you interested in working the food truck lunches Monday through Friday?"

"Definitely. And catering receptions like tonight, too, if you need me then."

Ry nodded. "Do you have any interest in learning how to prepare food, beyond smoking meats?"

"I'll do whatever you need me to do, Ry. I just need the work."

"Let's get together tomorrow afternoon. I'll come up with a schedule. Part of it will include tutoring time, teaching you all about smoking. I can also give you some lessons on the sides we prepare and how to put those together."

"This is going to be a big relief, Tucker," Emerson inserted. "It'll free me up. I'm thrilled that you've decided to stay in Lost Creek and that you and Ry will be working together. I also hope that you'll make the time for your songwriting."

"Ideas are starting to float around in my head. I think working with Ry will still give me time to also work on my music."

"Ivy gets up early and paints each morning before she goes into the tasting room," Emerson said. "Maybe you can do some writing before the lunch rush. Or usually, Ry finishes lunch up by two. That would give you some afternoons and evenings to ply your trade."

His cousin stood. "We're off." He offered Tucker his hand, and they shook. "Thanks for wanting to come onboard."

They arranged a time to meet tomorrow afternoon, which would still give him plenty of time to go to his aunt and uncle's for Sunday dinner.

Tucker bid the couple goodnight and opened the kitchen door, standing and listening to Dax and his band play. Dax had a smooth, mellow voice, but he also did a nice job on the harder, faster numbers.

A slow ballad began, and suddenly Reagan stood before him.

"Did you have a busy night?" she asked.

He nodded. "I'm going to be working on the food truck and catering events with Ry."

"I'm so happy for you, Tucker."

He couldn't ignore the urge any longer and pulled her into his arms. Slowly, they began swaying together to the music. Everything about the moment felt right. Her warm body pressed against his. The light scent of her vanilla perfume swirling about them. The quickening of his heart.

Tucker gazed into her eyes. "I told you the next time I kissed you, I would really mean it. Are you ready for that, Caramel?"

15

"Yes," Reagan whispered, a mix of anticipation and fear moving through her.

She only hoped the fear didn't win out.

Arch had been the only man in her life. The only man she had ever made love with. She had always been laser-focused on academics and then her career, not allowing any time for friendships or romance. Arch had been different from everyone else, though. He had broken down the walls she'd built around her, allowing her to relax in his company. Arch had always been gentle with her, from his kisses to his lovemaking.

Tucker Young frightened her a little bit. Maybe more than a little bit— because the feelings that stirred within her whenever she was around him were so different from those she'd had for Arch.

Reagan thought that was a good thing. She wouldn't

compare the two men. She only hoped her lack of experience wouldn't ruin this moment.

Gazing into Tucker's eyes, she saw desire flicker there. Desire for her. He had kissed her once. Gently. Now, though, she expected this kiss would be different. She had no way to prepare herself for what it would be like, though, because his mouth covered hers, and Reagan gave herself over to the sensations rippling through her.

The kiss was passionate from the beginning, nothing gentle about it. His mouth moved on hers, possessing her. Tucker's arms wrapped around her, pinning her to him. She could feel his heart beating rapidly and knew her own thundered just as wildly.

Suddenly, he broke the kiss, confusing her, making her think she did something wrong. He grabbed her hand and pulled her through the kitchen without explanation. Then she realized where he was going as he rushed her into Emerson's tiny office and closed the door behind them.

They were in utter darkness now, but she sensed the heat of his body. He captured her in his arms again, and his mouth came down on hers, hard and demanding. Tucker didn't let up. The kiss was wild, freeing her from any preconceived notions of what a kiss should be. He bit softly into her lower lip, causing Reagan to gasp, as much in surprise as in need. He took the opportunity to sweep his tongue inside her mouth, gliding his tongue along hers.

All kinds of incredible, wonderful sensations began rolling through her at the touch, and their tongues began waging a war between them. Reagan relished the idea that they both would be victors in this battle, though.

She didn't know how long they kissed in the dark. All she knew was the warmth of his body pressed against hers. The beating of their hearts, seemingly synchronizing. The taste of this man, filled with mysteries to be unlocked.

Gradually, she began aware of voices. Tucker must have also heard them because he gentled the kiss and then ended it.

His forehead rested against hers as he said, "I think we need to carry this somewhere else."

"Harper!" she exclaimed. "I'm supposed to be shadowing her now."

He stroked her cheek tenderly. "Then I'll wait for you outside. As long as it takes."

"I'm not sure how long I'll be tied up," she responded, reluctant to leave him but knowing she had other obligations.

"Go take care of business," he said huskily, brushing his lips softly against hers a final time.

Releasing her, Tucker opened the door. Reagan listened and heard the voices closer now, and they quickly stepped from the office. Thank goodness it was down a small hallway, and they couldn't be seen from the kitchen.

He captured her hand and raised it to his lips, tenderly kissing her knuckles. "I'll see you outside."

She waited, letting him leave the kitchen, hoping she could compose herself before she saw anyone else. Reagan took three deep breaths, expelling each slowly, feeling her heartbeat returning to normal. She entered the kitchen, seeing Dayna moving across it, along with another of the workers bringing dishes in.

"There you are," Dayna said. "Harper was looking for you."

"I'll go check in with her and then be back to help you," she promised, putting on a bright smile.

Reagan moved from the kitchen, her eyes sweeping across the large room. She spied Harper, Braden by her side, and made her way toward the couple. As she approached them, Braden winked at her, and she felt a blush spilling across her cheeks.

"Things will wrap up soon," Harper told her. "The only thing left to do is wash and dry all the dishes. We will come in the next day and strike the tables and linens. Move things back to storage and launder all the table-cloths and napkins before redressing the tables and reset-ting them again later in the week for the next wedding."

Harper paused, studying her a moment. "I really appreciate you coming tonight, Reagan. Do you still think this might be something you will want to do while I'm on maternity leave?"

"Absolutely," she assured Harper.

"You don't have to worry about cleaning up. Dax has given me the signal. They'll play a final, slow number. The bride and groom will then depart, and the guests will follow shortly afterward. Why don't you call it a night?"

She started to protest, but Braden said, "Follow the boss' orders, Reagan. It's just easier to do it that way. In fact, I'm taking Harper home now and getting her off her feet. Paula and Dayna can handle the wrap-up."

A thrill shot through her, knowing Tucker was waiting for her.

"Then I guess I'll see you Monday morning in the office."

Excusing herself, Reagan went through the kitchen, where Paula said, "We've got this under control. I hope you've decided to work temporarily at Weddings with Hart."

"I definitely want to do so. I'll see you at the meeting Monday morning."

When she went out the back door and headed toward her car, her heart sped up. She saw Tucker leaning against it, looking sexy. All she could think of was his hot mouth on hers.

"Hey," she said, approaching him.

"Are you already done?" he asked.

"Everything's almost over. A last dance and then the send-off for the couple. Harper sent me home. She said the others could handle the cleanup."

He stepped toward her, causing her heart to race as he slipped his arms around her. "Then I hope we can continue what we started earlier."

She nodded, suddenly feeling incredibly shy.

His fingers lifted her chin so they were looking at one another. "Are you sure that's what you want, Reagan?" he asked huskily.

"Yes," she said softly.

He gave her a lopsided grin. "Good. Because I'm not done with you yet."

His words caused hot desire to shoot through her. Fishing her keys from her pocket, she said, "Meet you at the inn?"

"No. I think we should go somewhere else. Follow me."

Tucker opened the driver's door for her, and Reagan slid behind the wheel. He got into his truck, and she followed him from the winery. Instead of going back to town, he veered off before they reached Lost Creek, and she wondered where they were going.

A few minutes later, he turned down a road, and she read the sign they passed.

Lost Creek Lake.

She had never been to the lake before. Neither of her parents enjoyed the water although they had built a pool in their back yard. Her mother had called it a status symbol, and she had never dipped a toe into it.

Reagan, on the other hand, found she enjoyed being in the water and taught herself to swim. She had spent many hours in that pool, passing the time with her imaginary friends. She hadn't been swimming, though, in many years and wondered if Tucker had skinny dipping in mind on this cool evening.

He turned into an empty parking lot, and she did the same, easing her car into a spot next to him. They both got out of their vehicles.

Threading his fingers through hers, he said, "I thought we might take a romantic stroll along the water."

"Let me get my jacket," she said, returning to her car and slipping into it before rejoining him.

He took her hand again, and they walked down a gravel road until they reached the lake. No one was on it this time of night. It was as if they had the entire lake to themselves.

They moved leisurely along the shore, no words necessary. It was enough simply to be with this man. Holding his hand. Knowing they were on the brink of a new phase in their relationship.

When they reached a set of picnic tables, Tucker led them to one, sitting and then pulling her into his lap.

"I've always thought you were beautiful, Reagan, but never more so than now, by moonlight."

He kissed her softly, and her arms went around his neck instinctively. The kiss started easy, a level of comfort between them now. It soon heated up, though, and it surprised her when she moved to take the lead. Obviously, that didn't bother Tucker. She liked that about him.

Who was she kidding?

She liked everything about him.

They kissed for a long time. Sometimes, the passion erupted in waves, and she felt they were consumed by them. At other times, it gentled, and she responded to the changes.

Finally, he ended the kiss, and Reagan rested her temple against his, content merely being close to him.

She couldn't have guessed how long they sat that way, but eventually he said, "We should get back to the inn."

Reagan started to climb from his lap, but his arms

tightened about her and he stood, bringing her with him. He gave her a long, slow, delicious kiss before setting her on her feet again. Slipping an arm about her, they strolled along the shoreline again and returned to their vehicles.

When they arrived at The Inn on Lost Creek, they both parked and moved up the porch steps together. He gave her a lazy smile.

"I think I'm going to get a song out of this. What happened between us tonight."

"I hope you do," she said encouragingly. "I'd love to hear your take on what occurred tonight." She grinned. "Especially if it is set to music."

His hands framed her face, and he gazed down at her. "Something did happen between us tonight. Something that let me know I have a chance to live again. To feel alive."

"I agree," she said quietly. "I don't know if this will last between us, Tucker, but I'm ready to explore whatever comes our way."

"I was hoping you'd say that, Caramel. Because I wanted to ask if you would be my girl."

Frowning, she asked, "What does that even mean?"

He smiled. "Let me explain it to the New Yorker since you've obviously been away from Texas too long. Being my girl means we're exclusive. We don't see anyone else. We take it day-by-day and see where it goes. And we decide together if it goes farther physically and emotionally than it did tonight."

She leaned up and kissed him softly. "Then my answer is yes, Tucker Young. I'll be happy to be your girl."

$\mathcal{T}$he past two weeks had flown by. Where he once had wondered if he would ever pen a song's music and lyrics again, the floodgates had opened. Melodies and words poured from him, faster than ever before. His confidence soared. He'd regained the pep in his step.

And it was all due to Reagan Bradley.

They were both settling into life in Lost Creek. He was working weekdays with Ry on the food truck, serving lunch, and had become familiar with many of the customers, several of whom were repeats throughout the week. A good number of teaching sessions had occurred, with his cousin tutoring Tucker on the art of smoking meats. He'd learned all about how exposing various cuts of meat to low, indirect heat for ten or more hours allowed the smoke to literally change the composition of the meat, turning it into a fine delicacy. Tucker could now babysit a brisket for twelve hours, making certain the outside was blackened, while the inside results were melt-in-your-mouth beef. He understood the reasons behind switching up the wood from hickory to maple to mesquite and the best cuts of meat, pork, chicken, and fish to use in smoking. Now, after practice, he had a feel for how long a smoked item should be rested, as well.

Barbequing was part science, part art— and part becoming one with what you smoked.

He'd also worked three different weddings with Ry. Emerson had been on hand that first time in case she was needed, but Tucker and Ry found their groove and went with the flow. Their camaraderie, whether in the truck or the event center's kitchen, was easy and yet efficient.

After a week, he'd approached Ry about investing in Smokin' Sweethearts, explaining he had money from a settlement he hadn't touched. Ry had protested at first, but Tucker gently kept up the pressure for a couple of days, offering good reasons why his cousin should accept the financial offer. Tucker said he wanted the money to go toward something good, and he couldn't think of anything better than assisting Ry's business to blossom. Since business was booming, they wouldn't be able to drive and pick up the new smoker they'd ordered as Ry had when he'd first begun his business. Tucker didn't mind paying the shipping fees. The additional smoker would arrive some-time next week, and it would join the one at the winery. Satisfaction filled him, knowing some of the blood money would go to a good cause and make things easier for Ry.

Reagan had been busy herself, meeting with Harper

and her staff as they hammered out a plan for when Harper went into labor and took several weeks off to be with her baby boy. Even though Reagan was new to the wedding event business, she was enthusiastic about it, contributing new ideas which Harper had taken to. Tucker thought from the sound of it that Reagan should be put in charge of things, but he understood why Harper chose to allow one of her assistants who'd been with Weddings with Hart from the start to oversee things in her absence.

She'd also had daily cooking lessons with her aunt. For the past several nights, dinner at the inn had been prepared by Reagan under Miss Jean's watchful eye. As she did everything, Reagan had gone all-in on cooking and excelled at every dish she had made, from lasagna to meatloaf to fried chicken.

Despite being busy, he'd managed to spend plenty of time in Reagan's company. The more he was around her, the more he knew he wanted her in his life permanently. Tucker wasn't ready to make that kind of declaration, though. He wanted to give Reagan as much time as she needed to come to the same realization. This second chance for them both was a tricky thing. Both had loved and lost. He still loved Josie and always would. But he understood while she would always be in his heart and be a part of him, he needed Reagan, too.

When he wasn't working with Ry or spending time with Reagan, Tucker was writing songs at a pace unfamiliar to him. In the past, he had tinkered with a melody for a few weeks before ever committing anything to paper. After that, he still tweaked it a while before it was set in stone. Then he worked on the lyrics to match the tune.

This time, things had flip-flopped. The words were first coming to him. He scrawled them in notebooks. Recorded them on his phone. Spoke them aloud in the shower, aiming for the right rhythm and rhyme. Country song lovers loved a good rhyme. It was a different way to work, though. He now took those verses and choruses and built a melody around them. Some came from the music that had first come to him when he ventured in to Lost Creek and those early days when he first met Reagan.

In the past couple of weeks, he'd written five songs. Not all of them were about her, but he hoped they would be. Country music was about a lot of things, but mostly it was about falling and being in love. His lyrics reflected that.

And that's why he was afraid to play anything for Reagan.

Josie had been his sounding board when it came to his songwriting. She would give a listen and honestly critique both music and lyrics, telling him when a phrase worked and when it didn't or shaking her head, telling him the music of the chorus sucked big time. He'd always gone back to the drawing board, wanting her approval and for the song to sound just right.

Now, he was writing rapidly, completing songs with no feedback. He thought what he had produced was good, but he wouldn't send it to Matt just yet. It was essential to have someone else listen and give him feedback. Though

Dax seemed the most likely person to do so since he was a songwriter himself, the only person Tucker could see in that role was Reagan. Tucker just hoped that what he'd written wouldn't scare the pants off her.

Or maybe that would be a way to start something up.

They hadn't made love yet. It wasn't that he didn't want to. He was certainly attracted to Reagan, but he was respectful of her and her feelings regarding Arch. Truth be told, Tucker wasn't certain if he could make love to another woman. He hadn't done so since Josie's death. Each kiss with Reagan, though, stirred new feelings within him, and they had certainly done their fair share of kissing. Maybe it was time to see if she might be interested in a more intimate relationship. If so, that would mean more than the physical. It would include emotional intimacy. Already, he felt incredibly close to her. Had shared things with her that no one else knew.

Resolve filled him. He would play her some of the new songs and go from there.

Tucker decided to call Ivy. While he'd enjoyed the past two Wednesday dinners with friends, he was drawn most to Dax and Ivy. Maybe because they both had the soul of an artist, whether through their music or painting.

"Hey, Tuck, what's up?" Ivy asked.

"I need a favor and was hoping you could help me out."

"Sure, whatever I can do," she responded.

"I've written some new songs, and I want Reagan to hear them."

"That's terrific news," Ivy enthused. "And I'm guessing one or more may be about Reagan herself."

It was no secret in the group that he and Reagan were seeing each other. "Yes. A few are. What I need is a quiet place with no interruptions in order to play them for her. I was hoping maybe we could use your studio tonight."

"Of course!" she exclaimed. "That would be perfect. You won't have any interruptions if you go there. Where are you now?"

"At Miss Jean's."

"I'm at the tasting room. Do you want me to drop off the key when I get off work?"

"Why don't I stop by and pick it up and save you the trip?" he asked.

"Sure. See you soon."

Tucker hung up and left his room, going next door to knock on Reagan's door. While he could have played for her in either her room or his or even the parlor downstairs, he wanted more privacy than the inn would give them.

She opened the door, giving him a smile. "Hey. What are you up to?"

"Are you free this evening?"

Her brown eyes sparkled, and he wanted to write a song about them.

"I can be."

"I've written some songs I'd like you to listen to and critique."

Reagan frowned. "You know I don't know a thing about country music. I'm not sure I'd be much help."

"I value your opinion. Will you give it to me?"

Nodding, she said, "I'll be happy to."

"How about dinner first? Lone Star Chop House?"

She laughed. "You think bribing me with a steak dinner will result in a positive approval rating, Cowboy?"

"Maybe I just feel like steak."

"Okay. You're on. What time?"

"Six," he replied. "Then after dinner, I'll play for you."

Her face grew serious. "I was teasing before. I really am honored that you want to play your new stuff for me, Tucker."

"I'm glad you agreed to hear it. See you later."

He called the steakhouse, making a reservation for six-fifteen, then drove to Lost Creek Vineyards and picked up the art studio key from Ivy.

"You know I'm dying to hear what you've written," she told him as she handed it over.

"If Reagan approves, I'll play them for you and Dax.

"I'm going to hold you to that, Tuck," Ivy said.

He returned to the B&B, making sure he put his guitar in the back seat of the truck. He didn't need his notebook but took it anyway in case Reagan wanted to study the lyrics before sharing her thoughts with him. When the time came, he changed clothes, putting on a fresh shirt and black slacks. Tucker was glad he did so when she opened her door.

Reagan stood there in a black cocktail dress that accentuated her curves. Though it wasn't low-cut, the square neckline showed just enough of the tops of her rounded breasts to cause a fire to light within him.

"You look incredible," he said. "If I owned a tie, I'd go put it on."

"You're fine as you are," she told him, her eyes sweeping approvingly up and down him. "I just haven't had a reason to dress up since I've been in Lost Creek. I figured a steak dinner was the closest I'd come to that."

"Don't forget the premiere next weekend," he reminded her. "Holden told me it won't be black tie, but I better spruce up a bit. Dax has already told me that since we're the same height and general build, I should fit into one of his old suits. He kept a few when he came to Lost Creek."

She laughed. "It's hard to think of Dax in anything but jeans. What did he do before he moved here?"

"Accounting. Investing. That kind of thing."

"He's certainly smart enough, but I would never have guessed that was his old world. I can't picture him anywhere other than Lost Creek, running Java Junction and playing for wedding receptions."

Tucker chuckled. "I think Dax would take that as a compliment. Ready to go?"

"Let me get a sweater."

She retrieved a sweater lying on the bed and draped it around her shoulders.

"You know I can keep you plenty warm," he said flirtatiously.

Blushing, she said, "Maybe after dinner, Cowboy."

They drove to the Lone Star Chop House, and Tucker gave his name at the hostess stand. They were led to a booth, which he had requested.

After they perused the wine menu, they both settled on a blend from Lost Creek Vineyards, with Reagan joking that she would feel disloyal drinking another label. Once the wine was brought and they ordered, he told her they would be going to Ivy's studio afterward.

"Why?"

Tucker shrugged. "I wanted a quiet place to play my songs for you. Miss Jean's a nice lady, but I think if she heard playing and singing, she'd be a little nosy and want to check things out."

"And opinionated," Reagan added. "She doesn't mind making her opinions known."

He reached across and took her hand. "It's *your* opinion I'm after, Caramel. No one else's."

Her blush deepened. "I hope I won't let you down."

"You couldn't if you tried," he responded, wishing they could skip dinner and go straight to the music.

And more.

The server brought their appetizers, mushrooms stuffed with crab for him and goat cheese and artichoke dip for her. He eyed hers with suspicion.

When she caught him doing so, she said, "Try a bite. Just one. If you don't like it, my feelings won't be hurt."

"I don't think I've ever eaten an artichoke before," he admitted. "I did eat Brussels sprouts once." Tucker made a face. "Never again."

She spooned some onto one of the triangular chips that came with it. Leaning over, he let her place it in his mouth.

"Let it sit a minute. Like wine," she recommended.

He did, chewing and then swallowing. "Not bad. But I think I'll stick with my app."

Soon, their steaks arrived, a New York strip for him and filet mignon for her, both prepared medium rare. They each had gotten a loaded baked potato. Conversation flowed freely, with Tucker telling her about a new spicy sauce Ry had come up with this week and Reagan telling him about sitting in with Harper as she met with clients.

"It's fascinating, seeing how Harper juggles so many balls with wedding planning. She's lucky to have Emerson taking care of the cakes and Finley doing the photography."

"And Ry and me catering," he prompted, causing her to laugh.

"Well, that goes without saying."

Their server approached them. "Are you interested in dessert this evening?" she asked.

Reagan shook her head. "None for me. I'm filled to the brim. Everything was wonderful, however."

"Just the check," Tucker said.

They finished their wine and paid the bill. He drove them back to the heart of Lost Creek and parked in front of the hardware store, which was now closed. Grabbing his guitar and notebook from the back, he escorted Reagan up the stairs and used Ivy's key to unlock the door. Turning on the lights, they entered the studio and he closed the door. His eyes were drawn to a half-finished canvas, and Tucker moved toward it.

"This may be a work in progress, but even incomplete, it touches my soul," he marveled.

"Have you been to Ivy's studio before?"

"No. Give me a minute. I want to look around."

Setting his things on a battered coffee table, Tucker wandered from one canvas to the next, seeing seven in all.

"I knew she was talented. Saw her work when we were kids. Boy, her work is remarkable."

Reagan said, "I was blown away when I first saw her paintings. I had to read all about her New York art exhibit online after that. She told me that she's preparing for another one, and demand is high from several previous buyers who want to add more of her work to their collections."

Slipping her arm through his, she continued, "But that's not why we're here. I want to hear what you've been working on, Tucker. I'm really excited to be the first person to hear these songs." Smiling shyly, she added, "I'll admit I've also Googled you. Found the names of what you've previously written. I even watched You Tube videos of Matt Hardy playing them. He's really talented."

"Matt is Josie's older brother," he explained. "He heard what I was working on and asked if he could purchase a few. He bought three songs total. They all did well," he said, pride in his voice.

"Are you going to approach Matt again about buying any of these new songs?" she asked.

He gazed at her. "It all depends upon what you think of them, Caramel."

Reagan took a seat on a worn-out sofa. "Then let's begin."

ucker had never been more nervous playing in front of someone than at this moment. He wanted Reagan to like his work. He *needed* her approval. Her respect. Without it, he doubted he would continue to pursue music. That's how much her opinion mattered to him.

He would never tell her this, however. Already, he feared he was putting too much pressure on her. She didn't need to be informed of how important these next few minutes were. Doing his best to relax, he retrieved his guitar and sat, facing her, handing the notebook to her.

"What's this?" she asked, opening the cover.

"It's the music and lyrics to my songs," he replied, watching her eyes skim over the first page. "I thought you might want to follow along as I sing. That way, you'll be sure you understand all the words I'm singing."

She laughed. "Oh, I'm sure I'll be able to decipher

them." She glanced at the page. "But I think it would be nice to follow along." Reagan paused a moment. "Do you want us to talk about each song after you play it, or should we wait until the end?"

"It's up to you."

Leaning down, she reached into her purse and pulled out a pen. A small notebook followed. "I may jot a few things down as you sing."

"Be my guest." He strummed the strings a few times. "The first number is called *Drawn to Your Light*."

Tucker began playing, closing his eyes as he sang.

Driving down a dusty road,
Heart beating like a radio,
There you were, straight and tall
Like warm sunshine in the fall.
Something about your ways
Caught my attention— couldn't look away
Like a magnet pulling, I can't resist,
I'm drawn to you; just can't resist.

He opened his eyes and found Reagan's lips slightly parted, a smile on her face. She looked up as he began to play the chorus.

I'm like a moth to your flame
You're the fire and I'm the same
You have a smile, that lights up the night
Damn it, babe— I'm drawn to your light.

Tucker continued to sing and play, their gazes connected. He finished the song, seeing the color had risen in her cheeks. The last guitar chord faded away.

"What do you think?"

She bit her lip, causing desire to roar through him. Tucker remained motionless, though. Waiting. Wondering.

"The tune is really catchy," she told him. "This second verse— *your voice, a melody in my ear, whispering words, sweet and clear*— that's beautiful. And this little bit before you went back into the chorus."

"The bridge?"

"Yes. *You're the spark in my darkest night,* That line. It really speaks to me," she said quietly. "Tucker, is this song about us?"

He knew the question had been coming. "Inevitably, every songwriter puts a little piece of himself into his lyrics. It's a combination of things." Looking at her steadily, he added, "Yes, you are a spark to me, Reagan. I'm attracted to you. That idea was the crux of the song, but it's not totally about you— or us. It's based in a grain of truth, and then I run with it."

Nodding to herself, she asked, "Did you ever write a song strictly about Josie?"

"I did. When you love someone and you're an artist, it's only natural to put a piece of them into your painting or song. The group of songs I've written since I arrived in Lost Creek still has a little of her in them. And a whole lot of you." Tucker shrugged. "I can't help it. You've inspired me. A lot of country songs are about expressing your feelings. Mine for you are really strong, Reagan. Country songs are about relationships. Falling in and out of love."

"Would you play another one for me?"

"I'd be happy to."

Strumming his guitar again, he told her, "This is *Just One More Chance*."

Tucker watched her as he sang the first verse. Reagan's gaze was fixed on the notebook. He reached the chorus.

Give me a second chance to make it right
To change my ways; to see the light
I promise not to let you down again,
Please believe in me— just give me a second chance.
I've learned my lessons, I'm ready to show
That I'm worthy of love, I can try to grow
Please just give me a second chance
To prove our love is one that will last.

When Reagan looked up, tears misted her eyes. Concern filled him.

"Are you all right?"

Slowly, she nodded. "That tore at my heart, Tucker. We've never fought, so I know this wasn't about the two of us."

"No. Actually, what started the idea for this song was the idea of a second chance. We've both shared how we shut off our feelings and ignored the world around us for the past two years. The idea that both of us are ready to live again and seek that second chance in life started my wheels turning. What came out, though, was far different from a second chance for us. I got to thinking of a man who'd wronged the woman he loved. How he was sorry and would do anything to get her back. So yes, in a way you did inspire the idea. The song, however, came out way different."

"It's very touching. I hope she does give him a second chance and that their love will last."

Tucker grinned. "See? I've got you thinking about that couple as if they're real people who exist. That's when the magic happens. Someone hears this song and takes it to heart. They can either picture this estranged couple. Or maybe they're the one who's been wronged or the one who's to blame. If you get a listener to relate, in whatever way possible, you can touch their hearts. Make them laugh or cry. That's the hallmark of a great country song."

She brushed her tears away before he could reach out and do it for her. "Play another one for me, Tucker."

"You got it."

He played *This Ain't Just a Friendship* next and followed it with *Let's Write Our Own Love Song.* Tucker finished with *Love Shines Bright.* After each song, Reagan told him the lines she liked best. She even had him play a few measures of the last song and shook her head.

"Something's not right here," she told him. "Sing these two lines again," she added, pointing to the notebook.

He did so and waited, seeing the wheels spin in her head. Then Reagan sang the same words— but with a slight variation on the tune. Her voice was rich with emotion and yet light and airy.

"Damn, girl. You can sing!"

"No, I can't," she quickly protested.

Setting the guitar on the coffee table, he placed his hands on her shoulders. "You. Can. Sing. Were you in choir?"

Vigorously, she shook her head. "No. I told you I wasn't in extracurricular activities."

"I thought maybe church choir."

A pained expression crossed her face. "My mom told me I couldn't sing. We were at church. The song was *Amazing Grace*, one I really loved. When we got in the car after the service, she told me how off-key I had sounded. That my voice was louder than anyone else's around us. That I had embarrassed her. She instructed me to never sing in church again. Just mouth the words and pretend I was singing."

Instantly, he knew what had happened. "She was jealous of you, Reagan."

A faraway look entered her eyes. She had gone to another time and place. Tucker sat patiently, waiting for her to return. When she did, tears brimmed in her eyes.

"I think you may be right," she said, her voice barely a whisper. "She was always picking at me. Tearing me down. Little by little, she wore away any confidence I possessed. Maybe that's why I pushed myself so hard. Tried to be the best academically. I wanted her attention. Her approval. Her love. And that was something she was never willing to give to me."

Reagan looked on the verge of a crying jag. "Come here, babe," he said as the dam burst and tears began to flow. She leaned into him, but he scooped her up, setting her in his lap. She buried her face against his chest, and he could feel the hot tears soaking his shirt. Tucker rubbed her back. Murmured comforting words to her. Let her cry it out.

When her sobs subsided, he kissed her hair. Her temple. Raised her chin and brushed his lips softly against hers. She clung to him, her mouth fusing to his, and need poured through him.

"I want you," she gasped, between kisses.

"I want you, too," he told her. "But this couch has seen better days. I'm afraid to get too randy on it else the legs break and we have some explaining to do to Ivy."

Laughter spilled from her. She looked at him through watery eyes. "I feel guilty doing anything at Aunt Jean's."

He shuddered. "I don't think she misses a thing under her roof. I'd be uncomfortable making love to you at the inn." Tucker paused. "What about this weekend? We're going to Austin for Holden's movie thing. What if we could manage to head up there a day early? See the town. Eat some great food. Have a hotel room where we can do whatever we'd like. To each other. With each other."

She shivered. "Ooh, I like the sound of that, Cowboy. And I'm free to leave town whenever you can."

"I'll talk to Ry tomorrow before we begin serving lunch. That would mean he'd have to do the Friday lunch run by himself. Work Friday's wedding alone, too."

"It's a small one," she piped up. "Only about forty guests are coming. I know because it's a second marriage for the couple. They wanted something intimate. Not much fuss. They're in their seventies."

"Whoa! Talk about second chances."

She smoothed his hair. "There are all kinds of second chances you can write about, Mr. Young."

"I know Ry will give me the time off." He kissed her, long and slow. "Let's plan on spending Friday and Saturday in Austin then."

"Thank you," Reagan said. "For giving me a second chance. With you."

She kissed him.

And Tucker had a feeling their relationship had just started a new chapter.

18

*R*eagan finished packing her bag and then picked up her cell phone. She sent a text to her new group of girlfriends, basking in the fact that she had a core group of women who supported her.

She had missed the Wednesday group dinner this week, which had been canceled. Holden and Finley had flown to New York and then Chicago for the beginning of a book tour. Holden's new thriller, *Inside Threat*, had released earlier in the week, and he was promoting it. He and Finley would fly back to Texas for the movie's premiere and then be back on the road, hitting seven more cities, from Seattle to Phoenix to Miami.

Braden had been the one to cancel the friends' dinner, saying that although he did the cooking, Harper was simply exhausted these days and needed to rest. Her due date was growing close, and she was putting in long hours at Weddings with Hart, trying to make certain everything was in order for her departure. Everyone had understood, and they had decided not to meet again until after the baby came.

Reagan had shared that news with Aunt Jean during one of their cooking lessons. Cooking had proven to be a wonderful outlet for her, one she truly enjoyed. Aunt Jean suggested the next time the group met, she should volunteer to prepare the meal for them. She would approach Braden and Finley with that idea, confident in her new skills. She hoped to enter their rotation of cooks.

Her text told her friends that she was leaving this morning for Austin with Tucker and that they planned to make it a romantic getaway in conjunction with the premiere. Immediately, she was flooded with responses, wishing her good luck, with everyone saying they couldn't wait to hear an update about her relationship with Tucker. It was wonderful to have a group of friends she could depend upon, something she'd never had, and they— and Tucker —were the reason Reagan had decided she would stay in Lost Creek. Though she still didn't know what she would do to earn a living, she was open to anything that allowed her to remain the small Hill Country town.

A light tap sounded upon her door, and Reagan's heart began beating in double-time, knowing it was Tucker. She had just seen him at breakfast, and yet she was eager to be in his company again. She wasn't ready to attach a name to the feelings he stirred within her and couldn't help but wonder if anything would change between them after this weekend together.

Opening her door, she greeted him.

"Are you ready to hit the road, Caramel?" he asked.

"I'm ready if you are," she replied.

"Do you mind taking your car? I thought as long we were in Austin, we could see about getting you a new vehicle and turning in the rental."

"That's a great idea."

"Let me get your bag for you," he offered.

Tucker went and claimed the suitcase she had packed, and they went downstairs, where Aunt Jean awaited them.

Her aunt embraced her, brushing her lips against Reagan's cheek. "You two have a wonderful time in Austin. Tell Holden I can't wait to see his new movie."

"Will do, Miss Jean," Tucker said.

They put their luggage in her rental and stopped to gas up before leaving Lost Creek. They would reach Austin by eleven o'clock.

"I hope you don't mind that I talked to the salesman who sold me my truck and Josie her car. He's got some new models for you to look at, as well as a few which are only a year old, if you're thinking of buying used. I say we go there first and see if we can strike a bargain. I also talked with the hotel people where Ana Ramirez had arranged for us all to stay Saturday night. They were able to let me book the same room for tonight, as well as tomorrow night."

She glanced to him and back to the highway. "My, Cowboy. You've been busy."

"Busier than you think. I told you I was going to get a song out of the other night. I went back to the B&B and wrote half of it. I finished up the other half yesterday afternoon after the lunch run."

"You amaze me, Tucker," Reagan told him.

"I have to admit I've been pretty surprised myself how quickly songs have flowed. Maybe I had a lot of this bottled up in me, and now the dam is broken, they're all spilling out. I don't always expect it'll come this fast and furious, but for now? I'm reveling in the speed of writing. I just hope the quality is there."

"Even though I'm a neophyte when it comes to music, the quality is first-class," she said reassuringly. "When do you think you might contact Matt?"

Reagan looked at him and saw the thoughtful expression on his face as he answered her.

"I'd told myself I wanted a half-dozen songs. Once I finish tweaking this latest one, I should be good to go. I'm thinking about trying them out, though, on a broader scale."

"Do you want to get our group together and play for them?"

"No. I think they would only be all too willing to tell me whatever I played for them was good. What I need is an impartial audience. Dax is willing to give me an opportunity to play at Java Junction."

She wrinkled her nose. "Music and coffee in the morning?"

Tucker laughed. "Dax keeps the coffeehouse open late on Saturday nights. He has local talent come in and play for an hour or so. I may want to take him up on his offer."

"You should," she said enthusiastically. "That would be

a terrific way to test your new songs and see the response they receive from an audience."

He didn't say anything, and Reagan wondered what he was thinking about. She knew he would open up to her, given time.

Finally, he said, "I haven't played in front of an audience since the night Josie was killed. I never played a single show where she wasn't there, cheering me on."

Reagan reached for his hand and squeezed it. "Josie will always be with you, Tucker. In spirit. You shouldn't have any qualms about playing because she's always in your heart."

He raised their joined hands and brushed a soft kiss against her knuckles. "How did I get so lucky to find you, Reagan Bradley? I don't think many women would be nearly as understanding as you are."

"Remember, I'm in your boat. The lifeboat of survivors. We both have lost loved ones. We've come through the worst emotional storm imaginable, Tucker. We've dealt with grief and survivor's guilt. Always know you can talk about Josie around me. I don't look at it as if I'm competing with a ghost. I know how much she meant to you, and I would never want you to forget about her and what the two of you had. Just like I'll always remember all that Arch was and what he meant to me."

She swallowed, emotion welling within her. "But I've finally realized I have decades left. To work. To live. To laugh. To love. I'm grateful I came to Aunt Jean and Lost Creek. Not only do I have her support, but I've gained a network of friends who are loving and giving. Besides, coming here led me to you."

He kissed her hand again, threading his fingers through hers. "I feel the same, Reagan. About you. Coming to Lost Creek. This is the place I want to stay. I want to become a part of this community. I've made a start with the group of friends we have and working with Ry at Smokin' Sweethearts.

"I could be happy here for the rest of my life. I hope that includes you."

Reagan gasped at this declaration, and Tucker quickly said, "I'm not trying to rush you. I don't even want to say those three words to you just yet, but my heart is leaning that way. I'm open to whatever happens with us today. Tonight. This weekend—and beyond."

She couldn't deny her feelings for this man. Although they hadn't known one another very long, her heart told her Tucker Young was the only person on the planet who would ever completely understand her.

And love her.

They drove the rest of the way to Austin in silence, both lost in their thoughts. When they reached the city limits, Tucker finally broke the quiet. He gave her directions on where to go, and twenty minutes later they pulled into the car dealership. Checking in at the front desk, he asked for Ray Richards, and the receptionist paged the salesman.

A nice-looking man in his mid-forties with a million-dollar smile approached them.

"Tucker Young. It's been a while." He offered his hand to Tucker, and they shook.

"This is Reagan Bradley, who I was telling you about."

"I hear you've been living in New York, Reagan. Bet you're a subway rider."

"It's the only way to get around the city," she said cheerily. "I've moved back to Texas, though, and I need to purchase reliable transportation."

"New or used?" Richards asked.

"I'm careful with my money, so I'll look at both and then make a decision."

"Sedan or SUV? Wait, don't tell me. You'll want to drive both."

Reagan laughed. "You're pretty astute, Ray."

She looked at new models first, both sedans and SUVs, and then she studied two used cars available. In the end, she decided to buy new and test drove a couple different vehicles.

Two hours later, Reagan drove off the lot in a silver SUV. She liked sitting high because it gave her a better view of the road and other cars around her. She drove to the Austin airport, with Tucker following her in the ugly puce rental car. While he removed their bags and transferred them to her new SUV, Reagan went inside and turned in the keys and signed the necessary paperwork.

She came out grinning like the Cheshire Cat.

"I'd say you're mighty pleased with your purchase," Tucker drawled.

"I am," she said. "This is a big step for me, buying a car. Planting roots."

Committing to you.

"It's after one. I'm starved," he announced. "Are you up for some Mexican food? There's a terrific place not five minutes from here."

"You're speaking my love language," she teased. "Sour cream enchiladas do it for me every time."

He directed her to the café, which was located in a strip shopping center. Tucker declared the best hidden jewels were in strip centers. After their food arrived and Reagan sampled a bite of enchiladas, she agreed with him.

They lingered over lunch, sipping their iced tea, as Tucker told her about the new smoker arriving early next week.

"Ry has really needed it at the winery because some of the wedding receptions have included a lot of guests. A second smoker will really make things easier, prep-wise."

"How are your lessons coming with him?"

"It'll still take time for everything to sink in because the art of barbequing is something you never totally perfect, but I'm confident in my meat smoking skills now."

His gaze met hers. "I'm the one who gave Ry the money for the smoker. It's part of the insurance settlement I got and never touched. I considered it blood money. Dirty money that was meant to make up for Josie losing her life and me losing her."

She placed her hand atop his. "You were right not to spend any of the money right away, Tucker, but investing in Ry's business is a good thing. Now that you're working with your cousin, this new smoker will help make things more convenient for both of you and help Smokin' Sweethearts grow."

Nodding solemnly, he said, "I agree. I haven't a clue what the rest of the money will go toward. I'll need to give it a lot of thought, but buying the smoker is a good start. One Josie would have approved of."

Reagan liked the fact that he could talk about his wife openly. It was good seeing Tucker come to terms with Josie's death. While her death would always stay with him — just as Arch's stayed with her —she could see them both moving beyond the pain and sorrow and simply remembering the good times with their lost loves.

He glanced at his watch. "It's almost time to check into the hotel. We have time to make one quick stop before we do so."

Curious, she asked, "Where?"

"You'll see when we get there."

Once more, Tucker gave her directions, and they pulled up in front of a place called Amy's Ice Cream.

"Hands down, the best place for ice cream in Austin. Amy's has some pretty interesting flavors, but they're all good."

They got out of the car and stepped up to order. Reagan perused the menu and decided upon a dip of Mexican vanilla, while Tucker got a double dip of Belgium chocolate and sweet cream. Since it was chilly, they returned to the SUV and sat inside to eat their cones.

"I need to do a little shopping while we're in town," she told him, savoring her ice cream.

"Hell, Caramel, I carried in those suitcases of yours

and lugged them up the stairs. You couldn't possibly need anything else," he teased.

"Actually, I need some jeans. Probably two or three pairs. I haven't had any in years, and Austin has plenty of places for me to shop for them."

"Well, little lady, we need to take care of that. Let's go check in and leave our bags in the room. I have a couple of places I can take you to shop."

They drove to Sixth Street in downtown Austin, where The Driskill Hotel was located. Tucker told her it was an iconic, historical hotel and a big deal to stay here. Their room was spacious and even had a private balcony with a beautiful view of the city.

Reagan glanced at the large bed, thinking of what they would be doing in it later.

Tucker slipped his arms about her. "I see you looking at that bed, Caramel. Don't worry. We're only going to do whatever you feel comfortable doing. If we just wind up kissing and cuddling before we fall asleep, I'm good with that."

"It wouldn't be fine with me. We talked about how important communication is, Tucker. I'm being honest with you now. I want you so much my teeth ache, but I'm scared to death."

"Why?" he asked, his concern obvious.

"I'm not the most experienced woman when it comes to having sex. Arch was the only man I've ever been with. I'm afraid of disappointing you."

He kissed her softly. "You could never disappoint me. Whatever we do together will be special. Because it's between us. I won't be like Arch. You aren't like Josie. We'll create something special together, something meant for the two of us."

His words reassured her, helping Reagan to push her fears away.

"Then I don't see any reason why we should wait any longer. Make love to me, Cowboy."

Surprise lit his hazel eyes, even as desire darkened them. Tucker kissed her.

And the magic began.

19

Reagan couldn't believe how boldly she had spoken to Tucker, but she was becoming a new person because of him. The look in his eyes caused her heart to speed up, and all she wanted was his hands on her. Her hands on him.

A slow smile spread across his face. "I guess shopping is going to have to wait, huh?"

"Yes," she said quietly, her own smile matching his.

"Hold on a minute," he said, walking to the door to hang the Do Not Disturb sign on the handle. When he turned and faced her again, the look he gave her brought shivers along her spine.

Suddenly, she was in his arms, his mouth hot and demanding on hers. They had spent many hours kissing, but she knew the end result would be much different this time. Reagan pushed aside her fears of being inadequate and simply went with the roller coaster of emotions rippling through her now.

She had never spent this much time kissing Arch and chastised herself. She couldn't compare the two men. They were individuals who had come into her life at different times. Her needs had been different when she first met Arch, and they had changed upon meeting Tucker. Reagan vowed to push aside any comparisons and delved deeper into this kiss.

Tucker's fingers moved to the shirt she wore, slowly unbuttoning each button and then parting it. His mouth left hers, his lips trailing down her throat to her chest. The heat in his fingers as they brushed her bare skin set Reagan afire. She pulled the shirt from her shoulders and quickly slipped from it, letting it fall to the floor.

He never missed a beat, his hands moving to her back, unfastening her bra, freeing her breasts. He cupped them, bringing delicious sensations to her. His tongue traced the curves of her breasts as she held on to him, and then his mouth was on one as he kneaded the other. He licked and teased her nipple with his teeth, his hands now flat on her bare back, holding her to him possessively. He feasted on the breast and then moved to the other, giving it ample attention.

She began unbuttoning his shirt now, slipping her hands inside it, gliding her palms along the hard planes of his chest. A low, growl came from him, letting her know he was pleased. She had never been one to initiate anything intimate, but she pulled his shirt from him and fastened her own mouth to his chest, running her lips along it, feeling him quiver.

Reagan moved to his nipple and imitated what he had done to her. Brushing her tongue back and forth across it, feeling it rise to meet her. She grazed her teeth against it and felt the shudder run through him.

They frantically removed the rest of their clothing, leaving pieces scattered along the floor as they fell onto the bed, laughing.

Then Tucker sat up, pulling her with him off the bed, saying, "If we're going to dance, let's dance in the sheets."

He pulled back the luxurious comforter and sheets. Once more, they tumbled onto the bed.

What happened next was a thorough exploration on both their parts. Tucker played her body as he would his guitar, his mouth and hands touching her all over, finding her sensitive spots, kissing and stroking everywhere. For her part, Reagan did the same, riding the high tide of passion as she touched his magnificent body, hard and lean.

His mouth found hers again, urgent need pouring through her. He realized it instinctively, and his finger slid along the seam of her sex, drawing a soft moan from her.

He broke the kiss, his lips hovering above hers. "You like that, don't you?"

"Mmm-hmm," she managed to get out, her head spinning and heart racing.

His finger glided along her again and then pushed inside her, causing Reagan to gasp. Soon, his fingers were stroking her, teasing her, causing her to beg for more.

Then the orgasm erupted violently, spilling from her, sending her soaring to heights unimaginable. She called his name as she rode the wave of pleasure, and he kissed her senseless.

One final shudder left her feeling limp as a noodle. He moved from the bed, and she was so utterly sated, she couldn't even protest. Tucker bent and shoved a hand into the pocket of his jeans, pulling out a foil packet.

Returning to the bed, he said, "I never was a Boy Scout, but I sure know how to be prepared when it comes to you."

His mouth moved on hers even as he tore the packet open and sheathed himself with the condom.

He broke the kiss. "Are you sure this is what you want, Caramel?"

"It's all I've ever wanted. *You're* all I've ever wanted. Bring it home, Cowboy."

A smile lit up his handsome face, and she felt feminine power flowing through her as he thrust inside her, bringing sheer delight.

Tucker began to move inside her, slowly at first, then desire took over.

"Wrap your legs around me," he commanded.

When she did so, his thrust went deeper. More filling. More fulfilling. Reagan clung to him as they went to the stars and beyond, both reaching the height of their pleasure at the same time, each calling out the other's name. He collapsed atop her, kissing her deeply. She was surrounded by the warmth of his body. His musky scent.

She felt like a new woman. The Reagan Bradley which had always lurked within her. The one who had been suppressed by things too numerous to count. Tucker Young had given her a gift.

The gift of herself.

He ended the kiss, resting his forehead against hers. Both of them breathed in spurts, trying to recover from the physical exertion.

"I must be crushing you, Babe," he said, rolling to his side, taking her with him.

They faced one another, and she knew in this moment one undeniable truth.

She loved Tucker Young.

"You think we can lie here a bit and cuddle?" he asked.

"I can't think of anything I'd rather do more," Reagan replied.

He eased out of her, and, using a tissue from the nightstand, removed the condom. Gathering her in his arms, he said, "I think you did me in. Mind if we take a little *siesta?*"

"Sounds good to me," she murmured, her eyelids already heavy.

As Reagan drifted off, she wondered if Tucker loved her.

Reagan awoke to Tucker's lips against her throat. Her fingers raked through his thick, dark waves. He made love to her again, this time tender and slow. The passion was still present but in a different way. She was just as satisfied as she had been before and wondered what else this man had up his sleeve.

"I don't know about you, but I've worked up an appetite. I could use some fuel."

"I guess we need to put off shopping until tomorrow," she said.

His eyes gleamed at her. "Nope. Need to get the shopping tonight."

"Why?" she asked. "Do you have something else planned for tomorrow?"

His wolfish smile caused her to tremble. "My plan is to keep you in bed all day. I just hope we don't miss the premiere."

His brazen words caused her to blush. They also made her feel desired.

"I like what you have planned for tomorrow," she told him.

They dressed quickly and returned to her SUV. Reagan inhaled the new car smell as they got in, thrilling her.

She had only driven a few blocks when he instructed her to pull over.

"Street tacos," he said. "Some of the best food you can get in Austin."

Parking the vehicle, they got tacos and Dr. Peppers, inhaling their food.

"That's just an appetizer to tide us over," he told her. "Let's go find you some jeans."

Tucker was one of those rare men who knew something about women's clothing, and he was the one who chose two pairs of jeans for her to try on. One was a dark denim, the other faded, as if she'd owned them for years. Reagan modeled each pair for him, noting the hungry look in his eyes as she did. It gave her a thrill to know he desired her as much as she wanted him.

"I guess we're ready for dinner now," she said after paying for her purchases.

"No. You still need a pair of boots. Every good Texan has one. For your first pair, we're going to go off the shelf. Down the road, we'll think about getting you a custom pair made."

"Custom sounds pricey," she said.

"Maybe they'll be my Christmas present to you."

Christmas had been a lonely time for her these past two years. A wave of hope washed over her, hoping she would still be with Tucker. That she could share the holiday with him. Aunt Jean. Their new friends.

Once again, Tucker proved the expert, asking her shoe size and pulling several pairs of boots for her to try on. One felt like coming home as she slid into them and strutted around.

"These are the ones," she declared.

"They were my choice, too. Come on, Caramel. Let's get out of here. Austin is hopping on Friday nights. It'll be harder getting into one of the nicer restaurants."

"I'm happy with a burger and fries."

"Then I've got a great place for you. We can listen to some music while we eat."

Tucker took her to a hole in the wall, where he was greeted by name.

"Hey, Tucker. Haven't seen you in forever and a day."

"I've been traveling a lot," he told the hostess. "Have finally settled down in Lost Creek now. That's become home." He squeezed Reagan's fingers as he said this.

"A booth just opened. It's got your name on it," the hostess said.

Reagan glanced down and saw several names on the waiting list. Apparently, Tucker was well-loved and able to bypass the line.

He ordered a bacon cheeseburger, while she opted for a Swiss mushroom burger. Tucker suggested they share a basket of fries because they were so large. Their food came about the time a singer took to the stage. They enjoyed their burgers while listening to him play. At one point, the singer even gave a shout-out to Tucker, calling him a great songwriter and an even better guy. For the first time, Reagan saw him blush.

They stayed and had a beer after they finished eating, listening to the rest of the singer's set.

Then he appeared at their booth. "Mind if I join you, Tucker?"

Reagan slid over, and the man sat beside her. "It's good to see you, man. You just upped and vanished." The singer paused. "I heard what happened. About Josie. I'm sorry."

"Thank you," Tucker said quietly. "I grieved for her for a long time." He glanced to Reagan. "This little lady has brought me from the dead, back to the living. Hank, this is Reagan."

Hank turned to her offering his hand. "You've got a good one here, Reagan. Tucker's salt of the earth."

"I think so, too."

Turning back to Tucker, Hank said, "I ran into Matt Hardy not long ago. Your name came up. He said he hadn't heard from you in a long time. You should give him a call."

"I'll do that," Tucker promised.

Hank slid from the booth, tipping his hat to them. "Singing works up a thirst. I'm gonna go wet my whistle. Good seeing you, Tucker. Nice meeting you, Reagan."

She took Tucker's hand. "Was that hard for you? Him bringing up Josie?"

"Surprisingly, no," he said. "I think what you've said has come to pass. The grief is gone. It almost swallowed me whole at one point, but I pushed through it. When I heard Josie's name, I just felt warm and fuzzy. I didn't think about the accident. That terrified look on her face. All I felt was a calm."

His gaze pinned hers. "That's thanks to you, Reagan. I didn't know if I would ever stop wallowing in my misery, but you've been a bright light. It's as if I moved from the darkness toward your light. You showed me the way."

Tears misted her eyes. "You didn't know it, Tucker, but your light was shining all that time, too. I moved toward it. And you."

He glanced around, clearing his throat. "I didn't know when I was going to say this to you. I sure didn't figure it would be in a loud, crowded bar."

Tucker paused, and she saw the love shining in his eyes

before he ever voiced the words. It excited her. Frightened her a bit. Yet Reagan was ready to go on the journey with this man, wherever it would take them.

"I love you, Reagan Bradley. You've moved into my heart. Into my soul. I want you to stay there.

"Forever."

20

---

*R*eagan was still glowing as they took the elevator to the suite Wolf and Ana Ramirez had booked. Tucker found her fingers and threaded his through them, causing warmth to envelop her.

They had spent all day in their room, most of it in bed. Teasing. Tantalizing. Exploring. Learning. Loving. Tucker had suggested they turn off their phones so there would be no interruptions. After they got ready and turned them on again, both had dozens of text messages. For her part, she merely texted the entire group that they were headed up to Wolf and Ana's room.

The doors opened, and Holden and Finley got on, Finley grinning at her outrageously.

"Guess you two were seeing so much of Austin that you didn't have time to reply to any texts," she said. Laughter then bubbled from her.

"We saw all we needed to see," Tucker said cryptically, which caused Holden to chuckle.

The writer said, "I think Finley and I have seen a lot of those same sites."

Then they all four roared with laughter. Finley hugged Reagan and whispered in her ear, "I want to hear all about it later. At least as much as you can tell me."

They got off the elevator and went to the suite. Holden knocked on the door, and Dax opened it.

"Come on in, guys," he said enthusiastically. Then his eyes landed on her, his grin lopsided. "Heard you came to town early, Reagan."

She felt the hot blush spill across her cheeks. "We did. I bought a new car."

"A new car?" asked Ivy, slipping her arm through Regan's. "What did you get?"

She told the group about her new SUV as Wolf handed her a glass of champagne. She saw Ry giving Tucker a wink as Emerson smiled fondly at both Tucker and her.

"Now that everyone is here, I want to toast the screen-writer of *Hill Country Homicide*," Wolf said. "Not only did you write an incredible, complex book, Holden, but you knocked it out of the park when you adapted it into a screenplay. Your tight, suspenseful writing made my job as a director and Ana's as a producer a piece of cake because we had such wonderful material to work with. To Holden!"

Wolf held his champagne flute high. The others did the same, echoing, "To Holden!"

Reagan drank the chilled drink, the bubbles tickling

her nose. She was happy to celebrate the success which had come to Holden, but she was secretly toasting the turn in her own personal life in finding love again with a very special man.

Ana asked, "How has the book tour gone so far, Holden? I know you've only hit two cities so far."

"Things have gone really great," he replied. "People are excited that *Inside Threat* is set in the world of Washington, D.C. again, especially those fans of *Capitol Crimes*, but I still got a ton of questions about the upcoming movie. Fans were pumped to hear it had the same director as *Capitol Crimes*."

Wolf laughed. "But not nearly the same budget. With a big studio, I was able to go all-in on special effects that first time. Thankfully, your second book was easier to budget for, especially with it taking place right here in the Hill Country. It was nice to be able to use local places to film, and a lot of the actors were already living here in Texas."

Ana added, "Since I was in charge of the budget, I was happy that filming one murder and solving it didn't involve nearly the planning and coordination needed when Wolf was responsible for shooting in D.C."

Her husband laughed. "All those permits. It took time and money to close down streets and get the exact shots I needed, not to mention blowing up a few things. I'm not sure if I'll be able to helm *Inside Threat*. That is, if you plan to sell the film rights, Holden, and I know your agent is chomping at the bit to do that very thing."

Ana placed a hand on Holden's arm. "WEBA Productions isn't built to take on filming a movie such as that, but once you've finished up your Mr. Hamilton book, *that* is exactly the type of film I want us to take on."

Holden nodded. "You're right about a big studio needing to make *Inside Threat*. I think *Mr. Hamilton's World* would be perfect for WEBA, though. Finley, Evan, and I have already had conversations about that very thing. I've already given Evan the go ahead to start shopping *Inside Threat* to the major studios, but even he agreed that WEBA would be the best home to place *Mr. Hamilton's World*."

"Would you write the script for Mr. Hamilton?" Dax asked.

"I'd like to give it a shot. I told Evan that Wolf and Ana would be calling him after this weekend. That was my one sticking point. The story is too personal for me. I want to be the one who tells it."

Reagan remembered what Holden had shared with her about Mr. Hamilton, the custodian who had mentored him and changed his life. She couldn't wait to read it.

"When will your Mr. Hamilton book be finished?" she asked.

Holden shrugged. "Maybe the beginning of December? If not, I'm certain I'll wrap it up by the end of the year. My publisher has it slated for release next September, just before Labor Day. A lot of schools go into session then, and I think they want to use that and tie it in to the fact this is a story about two individuals at an elementary school and how it only takes one person to change the trajectory of a life."

Wolf rubbed his hands together. "Once you've completed the edits for your editor, I'm dying to get my hands on an early copy."

"Definitely," Ana said. "If we read it— even before you start your screenplay —we'll have ideas about casting. Where to film. The size of the production. That kind of thing. Do you think once you finish the novel you can start on the script?"

"That my plan," Holden said. "I know it won't involve a lot of sets. You might even be able to contact a few elementary schools in the area and see about filming in one of them after school finishes for the day. I'm happy for this story to see the light of day. I think the sooner you can shoot it and the closer it can come out to the book's release, the better."

"Enough business," Finley declared. "We're here to celebrate."

Ry and Dax grabbed more champagne bottles and opened them, and everyone downed a second flute.

Ivy, who'd remained by Reagan's side, now pulled her away. The women in the group quickly joined them.

"Give us the scoop," Emerson said. "When you sent the text saying you and Tucker were coming a day earlier, I was hoping for fireworks."

Heat filled her cheeks, and everyone laughed.

"Okay. I'll tell you that things are really good between us. *Really* good."

"As in you're together? Maybe in love?" asked Ivy.

"We are a couple," Reagan confirmed. "And in love."

Squeals sounded from those surrounding her. As

different friends hugged her, she glanced over and saw Tucker's friends slapping him on the back, and Reagan knew he'd also given them the good news.

"You should have told us right away," Ana chided.

"No. This is Holden's moment. Yours and Wolf's, as well. We're here to celebrate your achievements," she said.

Ana glanced at her watch. "We better get going. The limos will be downstairs soon to take us over to the Hideout Theater. It's on Congress, just a couple of minutes from here."

"We should've walked," Ivy remarked. "It's not far at all."

"No!" Ana exclaimed. "Wolf wanted us to arrive in style and let Austin know WEBA Productions is here to make its mark on Texas filmmaking. We plan to take the industry by storm, starting tonight."

"I'm all for that," Finley said. "I'm ready for my man to shine tonight."

"You will, too, Finley," Ana told her. "Your posters of the film and billboards are breathtaking. Excuse me. Mama is entertaining Eva and Bear. I need to tell them it's time to go."

Soon, their entire party was downstairs, loading into two different limousines. The Ramirez family, accompanied by Holden and Finley, climbed into the second one. The rest of them got into the first one.

"Shouldn't we let them go first?" Reagan asked Tucker.

"My guess is they want to give us the pleasure of seeing them pull up, as well as them being the last in a limo *to* arrive. Movies and music are all about optics," he explained.

"That makes sense."

"This makes more sense." He leaned over and kissed her, causing a burst of tingles to spread through her.

They arrived at the theater, one which Dax said was part of the group that the Austin Film Festival used each year. Spilling from the vehicle, Reagan saw a large group of people gathered. A few flashbulbs went off.

"This way," a young man in his mid-twenties said, ushering them along an actual red carpet, stopping them about two-thirds of the way up it.

"Wait here," they were told.

The man hurried back to the curb, where the second limo was pulling up. He opened it, and Holden was the first to emerge, waving at the crowd. He leaned back and took Finley's hand, helping her out. Reagan could hear people calling Holden's name and saw many held a copy of *Hill Country Homicide* in their hands, waving it around, trying to attract his attention.

Wolf Ramirez was the next to appear. Apparently, the director had his own group of fans, because Reagan heard several shout his name. Ana appeared, looking chic, then her mother and their two children were helped from the vehicle. Reagan watched as Holden signed copies of his novel, and Wolf and Ana chatted with the crowd. Eva and Bear waved at the crowd and even posed for a few pictures.

Finally, Holden and Finley caught up to them, and Holden said, "Let's move inside."

The man who'd greeted them guided them along the remaining red carpet and to prime seats in the theater. Reagan found herself seated next to Tucker on one side and Ry on the other.

Ry leaned over and said, "I couldn't be happier for you and Tuck."

She smiled and said, "Honestly, I don't think I've ever been happier."

And it was true. She had loved Arch. She would always love him. But so much had changed in her life. Tucker was the right man for this time and place.

Reagan couldn't wait to see what their future held.

21

The day after the premiere, Reagan and Tucker attended a brunch hosted by Holden and Finley. The couple thanked their friends for turning out to see *Hill Country Homicide*'s opening. Already online and in the Austin morning paper, the buzz was excellent regarding Wolf's direction and Holden's ability to turn a complicated novel into a taut thriller.

Reagan had enjoyed reading *Hill Country Homicide*, and she was thoroughly impressed at the job Holden had done in reshaping the novel for the screen. While she could think of a few scenes he had omitted and a few of the townspeople which had become composite characters, the movie version of the crime novel blew her away. She pulled Holden aside just before she and Tucker left brunch and told him how much she had liked the film.

"Thank you, Reagan," he said. "I know we haven't

known each other long, but I truly value your opinion. It was great that you and Tucker were able to come last night and support us." He grinned. "And even better to hear that you're a couple now."

"We appreciated your invitation, and I look forward to many more Wednesday dinners with you and Finley and the rest of the gang."

They returned to the hotel and checked out. She asked Tucker if he would drive back to Lost Creek so she could test out the passenger seat. He agreed to do so.

On the way home, he said, "We're going to need to talk with Miss Jean. I know both of us feel a little odd making love under her roof. It's still early days between us, Reagan, and I don't want to rush you into anything. Especially marriage. I would like for us to get to know each other better. Whether that means we try living together or you stay at your aunt's and I find a small place of my own, I'll leave that up to you."

"Can I say I'm still a little overwhelmed, thinking that I have a future with you? I never thought I would find love again, Tucker. I expected to spend the rest of my life alone. Coming to Lost Creek and finding you has been a truly unexpected experience. I'm not sure what I want to do yet. Living together is a big commitment, as is marriage. I do know that I want to spend the rest of my life with you, however."

"It's early days yet," he told her. "We don't have to make any decisions right away. I'll give you all the time you need, Caramel."

The remainder of the way, they talked about a variety of topics, getting to know each other's likes and dislikes. She learned that his favorite movie was *The Sting*, and his favorite color was green. He hated English peas but couldn't get enough of black-eyed peas. Tucker preferred watching football over baseball and had decided he might pick up running. Dax ran almost every morning, and Tucker was hoping he could do the same.

For her part, Reagan let him know she was drawn to screwball comedies, such as *It Happened One Night* or *My Man Godfrey* and liked to read biographies and anything dealing with crime, fictional or real life. She let him know her favorite food was pasta, she liked cold weather over hot, and she'd hated wearing heels to work every day.

"Whatever I decide to do in Lost Creek, I'm relegating heels to the back of my closet. They'll be designated for special occasions only. In fact, I plan to give away most of my wardrobe of suits to a women's shelter, one which takes in women who have been victims of domestic violence. I'll keep a couple, but there's no use to hang on to things I'll never wear again when other women in need could get good use out of it."

By the time they pulled into The Inn at Lost Creek, Reagan was satisfied, knowing her relationship with Tucker was on solid ground, eager to learn more about the things they had in common and just as excited to learn about their differences.

He brought in their luggage and took it upstairs while she went to find her aunt. She followed her nose, inhaling the aroma of cinnamon, and found Aunt Jean pulling a coffee cake from the oven.

When her aunt caught sight of Reagan, she broke out in a smile. "Oh, it's good to have you back, honey." Aunt Jean paused a moment, studying her carefully. "I reckon you and Tucker had a wonderful weekend by the happiness you're radiating."

Nodding, Reagan said, "It was the best weekend ever. I'm in love with him, Aunt Jean."

"Saints be praised!" her aunt proclaimed, wrapping Reagan in a tight embrace.

Pulling back, Aunt Jean said, "I knew that boy was for you. He's solid. Dependable. You couldn't do better for yourself, and he's a lucky man to have you in his life."

Tucker entered the kitchen and said, "I couldn't agree more, Miss Jean. We do need to talk with you, however."

"Then I say let's do it over warm coffee cake and a hot drink," the old woman told them.

Reagan opted for hot tea and made it herself while Aunt Jean brewed coffee for Tucker and her. They sat at the kitchen table, and she bit into the cinnamon coffee cake, memories exploding within her.

"You used to bake one of these every time we came to visit you. I remember how much I looked forward to seeing you and being in Lost Creek. This coffee cake is a tangible reminder of all the good times I had in this house."

Aunt Jean smiled. "I was always glad to have you come and visit me. We've got some important things to discuss, though. I'll bet it has to do with your living arrangements here."

"Yes, ma'am," Tucker said. "I want to be respectful of you, Miss Jean. At the same time, Reagan and I need some privacy. We need to spend quality time together."

"I think I have a solution that might fit you both," Aunt Jean began. "I have two cottages. While one is booked for this coming weekend and another weekend in December, the other isn't scheduled for customers anytime soon. I go through a bit of a dry spell around Thanksgiving and Christmas and into January. Things usually pick up around Valentine's Day, but for now, I have that one cottage available. If you'd like to give up your room in the house and move out to the cottage, Tucker, you can for the next two or three months. Hopefully, that'll give you a quiet place to get your songwriting done, as well as romancing my niece here."

Tucker's gaze met Reagan's. "Does that sound agreeable to you?"

She thought it would be the best of both worlds. They wouldn't have to commit to living with one another right away and could continue exploring their relationship, making certain they wanted a lifetime commitment between them. It would still give them a place to make love without interruption, while she could keep the room she had and spend more time with her aunt.

"I think it's a terrific idea," she voiced.

"Then it's settled," Aunt Jean said. "You can move your things over tomorrow morning. I'll need to tidy up the place a bit. Put fresh sheets on the bed. Dust. That kind of thing. While I normally don't include breakfast and supper with those who rent one of the cottages, we can continue that arrangement if you'd like, Tucker. You'll be happy to know, though, that it does contain a small kitchenette. Just in case you want to stock the fridge with a few drinks and snacks."

"Reagan and I will handle getting things ready, Miss Jean," Tucker assured her aunt. "We'll do that this afternoon, and I can transfer my things over. No need to put yourself out. I insist."

"Ah, young love," Aunt Jean said, a sparkle in her eyes. "Then let's finish our cake, and I'll get you a set of sheets and some fresh towels."

An hour later, the cottage was ready for Tucker to inhabit. He told her aunt not to count on them for dinner, telling Reagan, "I think I'll run into town and pick up a pizza and a bottle of wine for us. We can have a cozy night and break in the new place."

Aunt Jean said, "I've got a nice bottle of Lost Creek Vineyards chilling in the fridge now. You're welcomed to it."

Reagan said, "You head into town for the pizza. I'll grab the wine and see you soon."

She accompanied her aunt back to the main house, where Aunt Jean said, "Don't waste too much time, Honey. If you love him— and I know you do —you need to marry him as soon as possible."

"I'm not sure about that, Aunt Jean. We haven't known each other long."

"When it's right, it's right," her aunt said, a stubborn set to her mouth. "Don't mess around, Reagan. Grab that bull by the horns and climb on the for the ride of your life."

Aunt Jean smiled fondly at her. "I'm expecting babies sooner rather than later. I'm not going to live forever, you know."

"Babies! We haven't even talked about children yet," she protested.

"Then put that on your to-do list because I think the two of you will make for terrific parents."

Reagan took the bottle of wine her aunt offered and returned to Tucker's cottage. She sat on the sofa, contemplating children. Both she and Tucker had been only children. His childhood had been unconventional, while hers had been lonely. Would they make good parents?

Tucker returned with their pizza, and she opened the wine, pouring each of them a healthy amount since neither of them would be driving.

As Tucker bit into his first slice, she asked, "Do you want kids with me?"

He chewed a moment and swallowed. "Boy, you're getting right to the heart of the matter, aren't you? Actually, I want them very much. In so many ways, my growing up years were a mess, but despite all that? I think I'll be a good dad. No, a great one. Because I will love our kids unconditionally. I'll support them in whatever they wanted to pursue, be it soccer, playing the piano, or becoming the spelling bee champion of Lost Creek."

She chuckled. "I have always thought about having kids in vague terms. I just assumed Arch would want them someday, but we really never talked about it much. I figured we'd enjoy being married a few years before that came up."

He nodded thoughtfully. "That was what Josie and I had planned. Have three or four years to ourselves, then we'd have a couple of babies." He grinned sheepishly. "After a year, Josie asked if we could alter the plan, and I was more than happy to do so."

For a moment, Regan saw pain fill his eyes. She took his hand.

"I know you didn't just lose Josie. You also lost your child that night."

"Sometimes, that does get lost in the pain of it all," he admitted. "My dad passed, then I lost Josie and the baby just a short time later. I don't know if I told you, but we'd already decided to name the baby Travis after my dad. We knew it was going to be a boy."

Bringing his hand up, she kissed it tenderly. "Baby Travis is real to you, Tucker. If we're blessed enough to have children, I promise that we won't use that name for one of them."

Tucker looked at her in wonder. "How did I luck out?" he asked. "You always seem to understand me, Reagan, sometimes better than I understand myself."

His hand cradled her nape, pulling her close for a sweet kiss.

"Pizza's getting cold he said. Let's eat while we talk."

She enjoyed their dinner, listening to stories of him on the road with his dad. For her part, Reagan told him a few things about her childhood, including the fact that she had actually been her elementary school's spelling bee champion three years running, which he got a kick out of. She realized that her mom wasn't the kind of person who should have had children, and she resolved things would be different for her own children. While it was inevitable that she and Tucker would make mistakes as all parents did, she knew the abundant love they would have for their children would outshine any mistakes. Giving their kids time and attention, something she had never received much of herself, would make them a solid family, and she knew their kids would flourish.

"Would you like to hear how I've tinkered with one of the songs I've already played for you?" he asked out of the blue.

"Of course."

He claimed his guitar. "I talked about how you were a shining light I was drawn to. I changed a few lines from before This is *Love Shines Bright*. Version two."

Reagan settled back, closing her eyes as the man she loved sang.

Holding hands, dancing under a moonlit sky,
With you, I feel I can fly.
You awakened a love I never knew,
Girl, I'm grateful that I've found you.

When he finished, she said, "I want you to play at Java Junction as soon as possible. Your songs are too good for the world not to hear them, Tucker. Call Matt and tell him you've got some winners on your hands."

She saw hesitation fill him. "It's going to be hard

enough to get up and play in front of a roomful of people again. It's been a long time since I've done that." He frowned. "I'm not sure if I'm ready. I don't know if the songs are ready for Matt to hear."

Reagan's heart told her that Matt Hardy would snatch up every song Tucker had penned. She also thought it would be good for Tucker to throw himself back out there and help build his confidence.

"Check with Dax now. See when the next opening is," she encouraged.

"If you insist."

Tucker called Dax, putting him on speaker, asking if he had any free spots in his Saturday lineup.

"You must be psychic," Dax said. "I just hung up from a gal who was scheduled for this coming Saturday night. She had to cancel because she's got mono. I can pencil you in for that slot."

"Let me check," Tucker said, pulling up his phone's calendar app. She still saw doubt in his eyes, but he said, "Actually, that works. Ry and I are catering a wedding Friday night, but our Saturday is open."

"Perfect," Dax declared. I'll put you on the schedule and see how many of the gang can come hear you play. Talk to you soon."

Tucker ended the connection and set down his phone. "Thanks for pushing me to do that, Reagan. It's hard to get out of my comfort zone sometimes, but with you in my corner, I feel as if I can conquer the world."

She slid toward him, wrapping her arms about his

neck. "Well, Cowboy, you've conquered my heart. That's a good start."

He sprang to his feet, bringing her with him, then sweeping Reagan off her feet.

Giving her a slow, lazy smile, Tucker said, "How about we check out the new bed and break it in?"

"I was hoping you'd say that very thing."

22

Reagan mulled over the action she was about to take. It might totally blow up her entire relationship with Tucker.

Or it might help make it stronger.

She had never been someone to meddle in anyone else's business, but Tucker wasn't just anyone. He was the man she loved. She wanted the best for him. He still had lingering doubts about his songwriting ability, which she believed in wholeheartedly, and was now balking about playing at Java Junction on Saturday. Reagan had told him it was a small venue and would help give him the feedback he sought. But she was going to take it a step further.

She was going to try and contact Matt Hardy— and see if Matt could be there.

First, she had Googled the country singer, trying to learn a little about him. He was thirty. Married with two small children, a boy who was three and girl who'd just turned one. He'd been nominated for but never won a CMA, one of the most prestigious awards given in country music. His songs had done well on the charts, but he hadn't had a truly big hit since the ones Tucker had written for him a few years ago. He lived on a ranch in Bandera, which was less than half an hour from Lost Creek.

Reagan's heart told her if Matt released any of the new songs Tucker had written since he'd come to Lost Creek, it would help push his career to new heights. While she was no song expert, Tucker's lyrics had touched her heart when she'd heard them. The accompanying music only added to the experience of the song. She believed they could be hits and should be heard, starting with Matt Hardy.

He had a Facebook page which was strictly for business. It posted his touring schedule. Made fans aware of new releases. It didn't look as if he interacted on the page and probably never saw it, letting some social media person manage the page. She struck out again when she found that he didn't have accounts on Threads or X. Turning to Instagram, hope sparked within her. While Matt did post occasionally, the posts were not related to his career. It was more a glimpse into his personal life. A picture with his wife on a date night. Playing with his dog and son. Reagan had no idea how often Matt checked the account, but she sent a direct message to him.

Matt—I'm Tucker Young's girlfriend & know you've tried to reach him. He took your sister's death hard &

hit the road, trying to find who he was without Josie. He's come to Lost Creek & is writing songs again. His confidence has been shaken, but I think you'd be interested in the songs he's been writing lately. He's going to play the new stuff at Java Junction, a coffeehouse in town, this coming Saturday at 7. If you can come, message me. I think it would be a good surprise for Tucker.

Hitting send, Reagan only hoped she had done the right thing. According to Matt's online fan page, he had finished a short tour in October and wouldn't be going out on the road again until late January. She prayed he'd see her message and decide to come hear his brother-in-law play.

Going down to breakfast, she heard Tucker and Aunt Jean talking in the dining room and joined them.

"What's on your agenda today?" Tucker asked brightly, as if she hadn't spent the night with him and slipped from his bed only an hour ago.

As she poured herself some orange juice and placed scrambled eggs and bacon on her plate from the buffet, she said, "I'm going into town to have coffee with the girls, which is why I'm passing on coffee now."

"Oh, who'll be there?" her aunt asked.

"Harper, for one. Since she wasn't able to go to Austin this past weekend, we promised we'd get together this morning and spill all the details of the weekend. I'm also going to share with them about Tucker playing Saturday night at Dax's coffeehouse."

"That sounds like fun," Aunt Jean said. "Remember to talk to Harper about that dinner."

Since she'd been taking cooking lessons almost daily with her aunt, they had talked about how it might be nice if the two of them cooked Thanksgiving dinner for their entire group. She didn't know what plans the others had and was going to bring it up today over coffee, hoping they could prepare the holiday meal at Harper's house for anyone who wanted to come.

An hour later, Reagan walked into Java Junction. She waved to Emerson and Finley, who were already seated and placed her order with the barista before joining them. She saw Harper and Ivy enter together, Ivy holding her sister's arm, leading her to their table and helping Harper into a seat.

"I'll place our order," Ivy said. "You sit. Doesn't she look ready to pop any moment?"

"Quit saying that," Harper said. "You're going to be in my shoes, with a belly like a basketball, sooner than you think." As Ivy left, Harper added, "She's right. I can only take baby steps on feet I haven't seen in two months. Every breath seems short. I'm so glad Braden made me take off this week before my due date. I just hope I don't go past it." She rubbed her belly. "I'm ready to meet this little fellow."

When Ivy returned, she said, "I haven't told Harper a word about the weekend." She looked at Reagan. "I think Reagan should start us off."

Laughing, Reagan deliberately avoided what she knew Ivy wanted to talk about.

"The movie was incredible. It had me on the edge of my seat. And we rode in limousines to the premiere, just like real Hollywood people. There was an actual red carpet to walk. Fans cheering. And a huge party after. Then we—"

"Come on, Reagan," Ivy said. "You know what I meant."

She arched her eyebrows innocently. "Oh, do you mean the stuff about Tucker and I getting together?"

"You're really together?" asked Harper, looking excited. "Like, together-together."

She grinned. "About as together as a couple can be."

"I knew it!" Harper declared. "Braden and I called it. You two just look right together. Anyone could see how you clicked. I'll bet you're already finishing each other's sentences." She paused. "Is it awkward, being at your aunt's B&B?"

"Tucker moved from the house into one of the guest cottages. In fact, Aunt Jean said it's the one Holden rented when he first came to Lost Creek."

Finley's face brightened. "Oh, that's perfect. It'll give you a place to be alone, with no worries about who's in the next room or anyone watching you sneak to and from each other's room." She gave Reagan a knowing smile.

"That's what we thought. Tucker wanted to be respectful of Aunt Jean. It will allow him to have some privacy for his songwriting, and it'll give us a place to get away without being self-conscious of others inside the inn."

"Ry and I are really happy for you," Emerson said. "Being in love suits you, Reagan. You look so happy."

"I feel happy," she shared. "I've had a rough couple of years. Tucker has changed everything for me. I may not know exactly what the future holds for me work-wise, but my personal life is secure."

"Well, you'll be working for Weddings with Hart for a short while," Harper said matter-of-factly. "As the business grows, I may need to hire on more help. Since you'll be staying in Lost Creek, that might be an option."

"I know I'm working that huge wedding on Friday," she said. "Paula, Dayna, and I are meeting tomorrow morning to make certain we all have our designated responsibilities lined up. For Saturday, Paula said she wouldn't need me."

"No, that's a small birthday party for a gentleman turning ninety," Harper said. "They only wanted to rent the facility. Family is taking care of bringing in the food, all of his favorites. One of his grandsons is a DJ. He'll be providing the music. Paula and Dayna will dress the tables for the occasion and will clear when they finish eating and clean up. You wouldn't be needed for that."

"It's a good thing because Reagan has somewhere to be Saturday night," Ivy revealed. "Tucker is playing Java Junction."

"Really?" Finley asked. "Why am I just hearing about this?"

"I told Tucker I'd tell everyone in person this morning. I doubt Harper can make it, but I hope some of the rest of you can."

"Absolutely, we'll be there," Emerson guaranteed.

"If I haven't had the baby, I'll have Braden roll me in.

Probably in a wheelbarrow," joked Harper. "I didn't know Tucker sang. I just thought he wrote a few songs for his brother-in-law. And I didn't know he was writing songs again."

"He's written several since he's come to Lost Creek," Reagan said proudly. "He took a break from songwriting after he lost his wife, but he's interested in making it his full-time career."

"And here I thought he was going to be a barbeque man," Emerson quipped.

"He does enjoy working with Ry," she insisted. "I think he wants to do both. He's a little worried that his new batch of songs won't live up to the previous ones he wrote for Matt. I don't know squat about country music, but Tucker has played several for me. They all sound terrific. I'm hoping he'll get a good reception at Java Junction Saturday night."

Reagan kept to herself that she was also hoping Matt Hardy might be there in person.

They returned to the movie premiere, giving Harper details on all she missed. Their friend wanted to know what everyone wore and what food they had eaten. After they had finished discussing their weekend in Austin, Ivy said it was time for her to get to the tasting room. Emerson said she had a cake consultation. Finley mentioned she needed to pack again because she and Holden were leaving in the morning for the remainder of his book tour.

"Oh, before you all go, Aunt Jean and I have something to ask." She swallowed, working up her courage. "I've been taking cooking lessons from her, and eventually, I'd like to be added to the Wednesday night rotation, once Harper's had Beau and we get back into scheduling dinners for the group."

Finley smiled. "Braden and I would like that. Holden actually has helped me prepare the last two meals I've cooked for the group. He's really learning his way around the kitchen."

"I'm happy you want to do this, Reagan. Let me have this baby, and then we'll need to get back on track for Wednesdays. Maybe that first Wednesday in December?"

"Thanksgiving is late this year," Reagan said. "Aunt Jean and I were hoping we could come over that day and cook the holiday meal for you, Braden, and Beau. And if anyone else would like to come, you'd be welcome. That is, if you agree to it, Harper."

"Agree? I'm happy for you and Miss Jean to do so," Harper said. "Usually, Mom does all the cooking, but this Thanksgiving, she and Dad are taking a trip to New York City. She's always wanted to see the Macy's parade in person, so Dad said this year was as good as any. You know our kitchen and dining room are large. The more, the merrier!"

"We'll be there," Ivy promised.

"The book tour is definitely done by then, so expect Holden and me to show," Finley added. "Usually, my brother and sister-in-law do Thanksgiving for the family since Mom and Dad put on Christmas. This year, though, they're splurging and going to a resort in Mexico. They never get fun in the sun and time to themselves because they operate Hill Country Water Sports during the warmer months. Mom and Dad thought that sounded like fun, so they're going with them."

"Let me check with Ry," Emerson said. "We'd planned to eat at his parents' house, but we can always drop by and visit with everyone before or after we eat."

"Perfect," Reagan declared. "I'll let Aunt Jean know. Maybe Harper and I can stay since you all need to run off. We'll work on the menu."

They said their goodbyes and then Harper said, "This is a sweet offer, Reagan. Especially since it'll be our first holiday with a new baby, I wasn't expecting much as far as a meal went. What do you have in mind?"

They talked about a traditional turkey and dressing, along with sweet potatoes, green bean casserole, and a fruit salad.

"Those sound great," Harper said, "but Braden simply has to have mac and cheese. The man could live on that."

"Got it," Reagan said, making a note on her phone. "We'll also have a couple of side surprises. What about desserts? Aunt Jean was thinking pumpkin and pecan pies."

"Those are perfect. Thank you so much for doing this, Reagan. And I'm so happy for you and Tucker. You make a great couple."

"We've decided we're in it for the long run. We've both lost loved ones. Tucker lost his wife, and I lost my fiancé shortly before our wedding. This second time around, I'm finding love a little richer. Different, too, because I'm in love with a new man. We still have a ways to go, but I can't imagine my life without Tucker in it."

As Harper started to get to her feet, Reagan saw she needed help and assisted her.

"Thanks. I really…" Harper's voice faded. Then her eyes grew large. "Oh… oh!"

A loud whoosh occurred, and she saw a sudden puddle at her friend's feet. Understanding dawned on Reagan.

"Your water's broken!"

"My water's broken!" Harper echoed. "Yes!"

"Dax!" Reagan waved at him, and he came rushing over.

"Harper's water broke. Someone will need to clean this up," she explained.

"My water broke," Harper repeated, her face beaming. "It's time. I need to call Braden."

"Should I call an ambulance?" Dax asked worriedly.

"No," Harper assured him, suddenly back into practical Harper mode. "First babies take hours and hours to come. My labor pains will be far apart. Plenty of time to get to the hospital in Boerne."

"Should you sit?" Dax asked worriedly.

"It's better if I walk some now. If you can stay, Reagan, I'll get you to walk up and down the sidewalk with me. It's sunny and not terribly cold today."

"Happy to stay with you," she assured her friend.

Harper dug her cell from her purse and called Braden. "It's time. My water broke!"

Reagan could hear Braden's excitement coming through the phone.

"Reagan is with me now. We were about to leave Java Junction. Dax has a terrible mess to clean up." More water began dribbling from Harper. "I'm going to be outside, walking along the pavement. Yes, I'm fine. Get my overnight case, the one sitting by the dresser. Yes, I'm fine. See you soon."

Harper ended the call. "Men. I think he's more nervous than I am." She slid her arm through Reagan's. "Shall we?"

They left the coffeehouse, more than a few interested customers watching them, and Reagan knew the small-town gossip network would now light up, letting the residents of Lost Creek know that Harper Hart Clark had gone into labor into the middle of Java Junction.

They strolled up and down the sidewalk of the square, not bothering to cross to the other side. Harper was content to walk at a leisurely pace and talk. She told Reagan a little about the brother their baby would be named for, as well as Braden's other brother, whom they would call once the baby had arrived.

"You're so calm," Reagan said.

Harper grimaced. "A little pain. Not bad. And you'll be calm, too, Reagan. We're a lot alike. I think when things around us fall apart, we're women who keep our heads screwed on straight."

Braden arrived twenty minutes later, bounding from the car, rushing to his wife.

"Are you okay? Hurting?"

"It's not too bad," Harper replied easily. "Just ready to get this show on the road."

"I had to leave the vineyard. Go to the house. Get your

bag. I got here as quick as I could." The words spilled from him.

"I know, Braden. Let's say goodbye to Reagan. Do you know she and Tucker are together? We can talk about that on the way to the hospital."

"Thank you, Reagan," Braden said fervently. "We'll let you know when Beau makes his appearance."

She hugged Harper. "You'll do great, Mama. Love you."

The words came easily from Reagan. She had never had a friend to love— and now she had an entire group whom she did, feeling free to express that love aloud. She loved these friends who already were becoming sisters of her heart, as well as the amazing men they had married. Reagan also loved her new life in Lost Creek.

And she loved Tucker Young with all her heart.

Driving back to the B&B, her heart soared with a happiness unlike any she had ever experienced before. She found Aunt Jean and shared the news that Harper had gone into labor and how they had been granted permission to prepare a Thanksgiving feast.

Aunt Jean's practical nature came out. "Then we better start planning. Think about what needs to be bought. How many will attend. Come have a seat at the kitchen table. I'll get a notepad and pen."

As they seated themselves, Reagan counted aloud. "You, me, and Tucker make three. Braden, Harper, Ivy, and Dax seven. Finley and Holden nine."

"What about Harper and Ivy's parents?"

She explained about their absence, thanks to their

New York trip. "Emerson is checking with Ry. They were supposed to eat with his parents."

Just then, her cell dinged. Reagan read the message.

"It's from Emerson. She said she talked to Shelly, and if Shelly and Shy can come, they'd be happy to bring some barbequed ribs and brisket, in addition to the turkey we'll make." Reagan smiled. "Shelly said that let her off the hook."

"Oh, no, it doesn't," Aunt Jean fired back. "That gal makes the best rolls in the Hill Country. If she's coming, she's gotta bring those yeasty rolls."

Grinning, Reagan said, "I'll let Emerson know."

She typed a quick message to her friend, saying the four of them were welcome, as was the barbeque, but Aunt Jean insisted on Shelly's famous rolls. Emerson texted back that she'd make sure that happened, leaving several emojis that caused Reagan to laugh.

Closing her texts, she opened the list she and Harper had come up with and shared it with her aunt.

"So, looks like thirteen of us then," Aunt Jean said. "We should plan for fifteen or so. Never know if someone'll drop in or not, unexpected. Even with the barbeque Shy's bringing, I think it'll take two turkeys to feed that crowd."

They fiddled with the menu. Aunt Jean mentioned preparing her roasted butternut squash, which contained onions, spinach, and cranberries. They debated on whether or not they would only serve sweet potatoes and finally decided they better add mashed potatoes to the mix, as well. The last thing her aunt said was needed were some glazed carrots and cranberry sauce.

"It isn't Thanksgiving unless you put cranberry sauce on the table," Aunt Jean insisted.

"This is a lot of food," Reagan said. "I hope we haven't bitten off more than we can chew."

"Piece of cake," her aunt declared. Pies'll be baked the day before. I may ask Emerson to do those, so she feels like she's contributing something. Bakers always want to be helpful, and that gal is a sweetheart." Her aunt looked over the menu again. "We can do some prep work the night before. I'll talk to Braden early next week, after the baby's home and settled. I'm sure he'll let us into his kitchen then and the next day.

"But I'm telling him it's hands off, as far as he's concerned. The feast will be our contribution to their first Thanksgiving at home as a family."

Reagan hugged her aunt. "Thank you for taking me in. Teaching me to cook. For always being here for me, no matter what."

Tears filled her aunt's eyes. "Baby, you've always meant the world to me. I'm just thrilled you're back in Lost Creek and have found a good man to love. And I mean it. Marry him soon. Don't waste time."

She laughed. "I'll think about it," she said, putting her aunt off. Marriage to Tucker still seemed down the line a ways, in her mind.

"We'll do the shopping together," Aunt Jean announced. "Saturday morning, so be ready. Next week, it'll be a zoo, no matter where you go. I'd already put in my turkey order, but I'll call now and change it to two."

Reagan excused herself, going to her room. Tucker

would be finishing up his lunch shift soon. She was eager to tell him about Harper and how Thanksgiving was shaping up.

She couldn't help it. She opened her phone to Instagram, knowing it was too early to have heard from Matt Hardy, yet she couldn't help herself.

To her shock, a message awaited her.

She read it once. Squealed. Read it again.

And then dialed the cell number Matt had left for her.

$\mathcal{T}$ucker slid behind the wheel of his truck and started the engine.

"Wasn't that incredible?" Reagan asked, clearly on a natural high.

"You're the one who's incredible," he said, stealing a swift kiss before he backed the truck from its parking spot and headed back to the B&B.

She babbled happily the entire way home, and he couldn't blame her. She had just pulled off the biggest wedding of the year at the event center. Harper's assistant, Paula, a petite, athletic woman in her late forties, who was very organized and slated to head up Weddings with Hart during her boss' maternity leave, had come down with a nasty stomach flu and couldn't be there to run things. Harper's other assistant, Dayna, was in her mid-twenties, and what Tucker considered a great soldier. Dayna was no leader, though. Give her a task, and she'd follow it to the letter.

That meant Reagan had to step up, and she'd led the workers with military precision.

It had been the largest wedding, by far, that he had helped Ry to cater. Because of the sheer number of guests, Ry had called in his parents to help, as well as Carlos and José, two workers from Blackwood BBQ.

Everything had gone seamlessly, and he knew it was in large part due to Reagan's direction of the evening and the many people involved.

"And the bride was so grateful for how smoothly everything came together," Reagan said, as they turned into the drive of the B&B.

He parked the truck and cut the engine. Taking her hand, he kissed it. "You did yourself proud, Caramel. Harper herself couldn't have done a better job."

"I'm not sure we should tell her that Paula couldn't make it tonight. Harper already has enough on her plate as it is."

They had gone to see mother and baby yesterday afternoon. Harper had delivered a healthy Beau late Tuesday afternoon and had gone home the next day. Since she had the baby's nursery organized and already had a schedule in mind for Beau, she had welcomed company to come and meet the newest little Clark.

The gang had texted back and forth, arranging when couples could drop in at different times so that Harper wouldn't be overwhelmed. He and Reagan had brought food and flowers, as well as a stuffed Teddy bear and copy of *Goodnight Moon* for Beau.

When Harper had passed the baby to Reagan, Tucker knew he'd grinned from ear-to-ear. Seeing a child in Reagan's arms only made him that much more eager to marry her and begin a family of their own. Because of the childhoods they had experienced, he knew they'd do many things differently as they raised their own brood of children.

"Want to come in?" he asked, squeezing her fingers.

"Now you're talking, Cowboy," she said, smiling flirtatiously.

Soon, they were inside the cottage and having boisterous, all-out sex. He loved making love with this woman. She seemed to become free from all obstacles in his arms, which made all his own troubles melt away, making her his sole focus. It was nice, too, having the cottage to come to. It offered them not only privacy but the chance to be uninhibited with one another. Or, as Miss Jean might call it, noisy.

Reagan now fell against his chest, breathing heavily after having ridden him hard.

"Are you sure you haven't ridden horses before, Caramel?" he teased. "Because you just rode me to perfection."

She stacked her hands on top of one another, resting her chin atop them. "I'll bet you say that to all the cowgirls, handsome."

Reagan looked innocent and yet seductive at the same time, and Tucker couldn't resist her.

"Come here, you," he growled, grabbing her elbows and moving her. Their mouths fused together hungrily, and he wondered if he would ever get enough of this woman.

They made love a second time, slow and sweet, her soft cries just as appealing as her shouts of exultation. They cuddled together. Soon, Reagan dropped off to sleep, her breathing slow and deep, a satisfied smile on her face.

On the other hand, Tucker stared at the ceiling in the dark. His body was exhausted from all the physical labor he had put in today, but his mind raced like a thoroughbred running a derby, something he couldn't seem to turn off.

Tomorrow night, he would debut the new songs he had written at Java Junction. He had decided to start off with one of the hits he'd written for Matt, *Another Beer, Dear*, to get the crowd going with a familiar tune. Then he would launch into some of his new material. Two, maybe three songs, before sneaking in another hit he'd penned for Matt. He would do a few more original numbers and then close with *Give Love Another Dance*. It was one Tucker had written this past week, in-between shifts at Smokin' Sweethearts. Reagan hadn't heard it yet, and he wanted to surprise her, closing his set with the love song.

He worried the new songs weren't good enough. His dream was to make a living at songwriting, but doubts continued to plague him. If it didn't happen, it didn't happen. He was already enjoying the time spent working with his cousin. The operation was growing so quickly that Tucker was happy he'd offered to invest in a second smoker at the winery. It had come in mighty handy for tonight's reception. It wouldn't hurt to add another smoker at Ry and Emerson's house though Tucker had no idea where it might go. Emerson had rented the small house and lived there with Finley before she'd married Holden. Once she and Ry had wed, he'd moved in, but even Tucker could see they were outgrowing the space.

The food truck did more than a steady business during the week and on weekends when they took it out to the city ball parks. He could see investing in another food truck and hiring a crew of two to run it. Now that he was beginning to know enough about smoking meats, maybe he could take one truck out and Ry the other. It would be something he'd run by his cousin.

Despite the thoughts swirling in his head, Tucker finally dropped off to sleep, a smile on his lips.

He awoke to Reagan nibbling on his nape and quickly turned, pinning her playfully to the bed.

"You thought you'd have your way with me, huh? What's good for the goose is good for the gander."

His lips went to her throat, his teeth grazing her pulse point, which fluttered out of control. Tucker made love to her with abandon, living in the moment, happy love had come unexpectedly into his life a second time.

They lay in bed together a few minutes before Reagan pulled away and climbed from the bed.

"I've got to go home and shower," she told him. "Aunt Jean and I are going on our grocery shopping spree today. We're buying everything for the Thanksgiving meal we'll be cooking for everyone."

She had shared the menu with him, and his mouth had watered hearing it.

"I guess that'll tie up your morning."

"What will you be up to?"

"Ry told me not to come in today. He's taking the food truck to the ball fields for a couple of hours, but he said I needed to take the time and practice for tonight."

She stopped dressing and leaned down, her palm caressing his cheek. "Do you feel ready?"

"I am ready," he said with determination. "I know I don't have the best voice. I would never make it as a country singer."

"But you played some places around Austin before," she protested.

"That was more for fun— and a little stroking of my ego," he admitted. "But I would need better pipes and range if I wanted to make it as a professional singer. I'm fine for local get-togethers like tonight, but my heart is in songwriting."

He clasped her nape, bringing her lips to his for a sweet kiss.

"Besides, country singers are constantly on the road. I know that from having traveled that road with my dad and his acts all those years. They're never home, always going town to town, playing the same songs, trying to eke out a living." His gaze met hers. "That's not what I want for us. For the family we'll grow. I want to be home with you. With the kids. I want to take little Billy to baseball practice and little Sally to soccer. I want to go to little Cindy's piano concerts and little George's karate tournaments."

Reagan chuckled softly. "I'm all about going to games and concerts, but we're going to have to negotiate better names. As in I didn't like one name you just used."

He laughed. "I figure you'll be the one doing the heavy lifting those nine months, not to mention giving birth, so you'll have earned the right to name all our kids whatever you want. With a little input from me, of course."

"You just keep thinking about those future kids to come. Or rather, think about your set list for tonight. Practice some, but not too much, Tucker. You don't want your voice to be worn and thin by the time tonight rolls around."

"You're right," he said. "I'll take it easy. You and Miss Jean go have some fun at the grocery store."

She kissed him soundly. "We will."

Tucker got in the shower after Reagan left, changing into a worn flannel shirt and even more worn faded jeans. He wasn't a dress up kind of guy, not even when debuting new songs. He wanted to be wearing comfortable clothes and boots he knew and trusted.

He had already told Miss Jean he wouldn't be eating dinner with them tonight. He didn't want to try to sing and play with a full belly. Instead, he snacked on some peanut butter and crackers and drank a tall, cold glass of milk. Somehow, the small meal comforted him.

Tucker brushed his teeth and grabbed the guitar case, thankful Dax had loaned him his own guitar to practice on and play tonight. It sounded far better than the one Dax had gifted to him earlier, and Tucker knew he would buy something similar soon.

If tonight worked out, that is.

He drove to the town square and parked, going inside Java Junction, where Dax greeted him.

"Hey, Tucker. You ready for this evening's performance?"

"Is it too late to back out?" he joked, half-meaning it.

"Definitely too late," Dax teased back. "When I put your name on the website and told my customers all week that you'd be here tonight, I aim to please them. They're expecting Tucker Young. They'll be getting Tucker Young."

He glanced about the coffeehouse, which was already about half-full, waving to a few people he knew. Working on the food truck with Ry, Tucker had met a good number of the residents of Lost Creek and was happy to see several familiar faces already in the crowd.

"I have a couple of tables in the center reserved for Reagan and Miss Jean and Ivy. Ry and Emerson are also coming, along with Ana and Wolf. Naturally, Braden and Harper are staying home with Beau tonight, but Harper said you can stop by and sing a lullaby to Beau anytime you want."

He was pleased that his friends were here to support

him and pleasantly surprised that Wolf and Ana Ramirez had also showed up. The only ones who couldn't make it tonight were Holden and Finley, who would wrap up his book tour Monday night and be back in Lost Creek by Tuesday. They'd be at the Thanksgiving meal on Thursday with the rest of the group.

"Let's go upstairs," Dax suggesting, and they headed toward the staircase. "If you want to go through a song or two, you can. There's a restroom if you need it. I'll have a second stool sitting on stage with a couple of bottles of water on it in case you get thirsty while you're up there. I forgot to ask if you'd prefer a stool as you perform or if you'd rather stand in front of the mic."

"I've done a little of both in the past," he said. "I guess I'll figure it out when I get up in front of everyone. It's been a while since I've done this kind of thing, Dax. I'm a little skittish right now."

"Then I'll send Reagan up when she gets here." Dax squeezed Tucker's shoulder. "Knock 'em dead, Tuck."

He set down his guitar case and paced. The nerves sizzled through him now, almost paralyzing him. Suddenly, he wondered if he even knew the lyrics to the songs he'd be singing tonight and quickly opened the guitar case. Glancing at the set list, he closed his eyes.

"Breathe. Just breathe," he told himself.

Suddenly, a warm body pressed against his back. Reagan wrapped her arms about him, her cheek resting against his back.

"You are an incredible man, Tucker Young. You have a God-given talent. You're going to share that talent and what it's produced with a handful of very supportive people who've gathered downstairs."

She released him, turning him so that their gazes met. "Sing from your heart, Tucker. Sing to me. I know you can do this."

He nodded. "I can. I will. I love you, Reagan. More than I'll ever be able to say or show."

"Ditto," she declared, her fingers bunching on his shirt-front, pulling him down to her for a slow, very satisfying kiss.

When she released him, a calm descended over him. Reagan was right. He could do this.

For her. For him. For them.

"I'm heading downstairs now," she told him. "Dax will come get you in a few minutes. Love you."

"Love you more," he said, watching her leave.

Then Tucker closed his eyes. "Josie, I think you were an angel in real life, and I know you're one now, watching over me every day. You brought Reagan Bradley into my life. I know you did, and I feel your approval of our match. Be with me tonight, my darling sweetheart. Help me get through this and shine."

He went to the guitar case again, folding the set list and slipping it into his pocket before lifting the guitar. He sat on the coffee table, strumming a few chords, making an adjustment and strumming again, liking the sound he heard.

A light knock sounded on the door, and Dax entered. "It's time."

The trepidation had vanished. Confidence brimmed

through him now. He'd known the love of one terrific woman and now had the love of another one. Their support bolstered him, and he would not only make it through his set tonight.

He would kill it.

24

$\mathcal{T}$ucker followed Dax down the stairs, his pulse jumping a bit. Nerves were medium. Confidence level high.

He knew he was going to be fine.

Dax stopped. "Wait here. I want to give you a little introduction. I'll leave the mic in standing position. You can adjust how you see fit."

"I'll leave it up for the first number. It's a lively one," he shared. "Then I'm going to go softer. Much softer. That's better suited for sitting."

"You know best. I tend to favor sitting when the song is more intimate myself." Dax gave him a thumbs up. "Be right back."

Tucker watched Dax move to the front of a makeshift stage and saw the two stools and microphone stand waiting for him. He glanced out at the crowd, which appeared blurry, until Reagan came into to focus. She blew him a kiss, and he pretended to catch it, delighting her. Miss Jean and Ivy sat at her table. To their right, were Ry, Emerson, Ana, and Wolf. He nodded to his friends and swung his attention back to Dax, who'd begun his introduction.

"Tucker Young is a new friend to me but an old friend to some of you. He spent summers here with his uncle Shy and aunt Shelly, who are seated right over there."

That surprised Tucker, and his eyes went to their table. Aunt Shelly waved enthusiastically at him. He grinned at her, waving back. As for Uncle Shy, he gave his nephew a brusque nod.

"Tucker's planning to stay in Lost Creek and make it his permanent home. He's a songwriter, and he's written a few new ones he wants to try out on you. So, let's give it up and show Tucker Young some Lost Creek love."

As Dax headed toward him, Tucker heard the room fill with applause.

Dax passed him, patting him on the back. "You've got this."

He went to the mic and kept his eyes on Reagan, saying, "I don't know if I deserve such an enthusiastic introduction, much less all that applause you've already given me. Yes, I'm Tucker Young, and I'm happy to be back in Lost Creek. Serving up barbeque with my cousin Ry at Smokin' Sweethearts. And writing some songs. I'll start with an oldie but goodie. One I think you'll know. I wrote it— but Matt Hardy made it famous. It's called *Another Beer, Dear*."

As he strummed his guitar and burst into the song, all

he saw was love shining in Reagan's eyes. Love for him. That freed him, and Tucker sang the fast-paced song with gusto.

When he finished playing, the crowd erupted in cheers, bolstering his spirits.

"Now, I know Matt made that famous, and I'm hoping he might be willing to buy a couple of these songs I sing for you tonight. Just remember, folks. You heard 'em hear first. From me. This one's called *Drawn to Your Light*."

Tucker launched into the country ballad, singing part of it with his eyes closed, while the rest of the time with eyes on Reagan. She gave him strength. Hope. Joy. A man couldn't ask for much else in life.

He ended the song, surprised that the crowd's response was more enthusiastic to it than the better-known song he'd opened with.

"Well, I'm glad you liked that one. I call this one *This Ain't Just a Friendship*."

He sang his second new song, knowing it was about Reagan. He was secure in his love for her and hers for him. They had traveled through separate storms, but fate had brought them together. As he sang this love song to her, Tucker felt in his bones it was as good as anything he'd previously written. Good enough for Matt to buy and sing. Good enough to become a hit.

More applause greeted him as the last note sounded, and Tucker felt pleased. Instead of launching into another hit of Matt's as he'd planned, he told those present, "I've got another one for you now. *Let's Write Our Own Love*

Song. I think some of you know I'm seeing Reagan Bradley. She's right over there."

He pointed her out. "I think it's pretty darn obvious all these songs are about her."

Reagan blushed as all eyes in the coffeehouse turned to her. Still, she beamed at him, blowing him a second kiss as everyone cheered.

Tucker began the next number, not bothering to share its name until he finished playing. After that, he did play a second song he'd written for Matt, one which had cracked the Top Ten and was a personal favorite of his. It had also been one Josie adored. It was important to him to keep a little of Josie in mind with him tonight, knowing that she had supported his songwriting and he wouldn't be here tonight if she hadn't pushed him.

He got a decent response for it, not as good as for the newer songs, making his confidence soar even higher, and he switched to another of those.

"I'm going to sing *Love Shines Bright* for you now," he told the crowd.

He played it and another song back-to-back, feeling brave enough now for his gaze to slowly roam Java Junction. He saw men wrap an arm around their sweetheart or take their hands. One couple in the corner cuddled and kissed as he played. Tucker didn't mind that in the least. He hoped these songs would be well received. That Matt would buy more than a couple. Whatever Matt wasn't interested in, Tucker decided he would approach a few other country artists and see if they might be willing to buy the rights instead.

He finally opened one of the water bottles Dax had left for him, guzzling down the entire contents, wiping his mouth with the back of his sleeve.

"I was having so much fun up here, I forgot to drink as I went," he told the crowd, causing scattered chuckles. "I only have one more song to play for you this evening, and then I'll let you get back to your coffee or tea or spiced cider. Whatever you enjoy drinking here at Java Junction."

He strummed the guitar a few times, once again making a slight adjustment. Then Tucker's gaze caught Reagan's, and he spoke straight to her.

"You haven't heard this one yet, babe, but your finger-prints are all over it. Here's *Give Love Another Dance.*"

As Tucker sang, he saw how the lyrics affected Reagan. He put his heart and soul into the song, breathing new life into it as he poured out his feelings to the woman who had captured his heart and helped him to heal.

I've been cautious and guarded, keeping my heart under lock and key,
But your love has shown me a different reality,
You've wiped away my tears, healed every old scar,
Now I believe in love again, no matter how far.

I know it's hard to trust, after being hurt so bad,
But when I hear your voice, I'm no longer sad,

'Cause I'm falling in love, trusting once more,
You've proven yourself worthy, I'm opening my door,
I'm taking a leap, hoping it's worth the chance,

Falling in love with you, giving love another dance.

He finished, and a hush fell over the coffeehouse. His gaze never wavered from Reagan's, and he saw her mouth, "I love you." He mouthed it back to her.

Then Java Junction's patrons jumped to their feet, the applause deafening. Tucker stood there, grinning like a fool, as Reagan rushed to him. She threw her arms around him. He gave her a long kiss and heard the laughter surrounding them.

Breaking the kiss, he threw an arm around her waist and drew her close.

"I hope you enjoyed the songs I played and sang for you tonight. Fingers crossed, you'll hear some of them on the radio."

"Bet you pick up a CMA for Song of the Year award, Tucker," shouted a man from the crowd, and several people nodded, applauding the remark.

"Thanks again to Dax Tennyson for allowing me to play tonight. You've been a great audience. See you soon at the Smokin' Sweethearts food truck."

Everyone laughed good-naturedly, and Tucker took the opportunity to kiss Reagan again while they did.

"You were magnificent," she said, her eyes misting with tears. "And that last song. The newest one. When did you write it?"

"Oh, the melody whispered in my ear a while ago, but the words just came to me this week. I paired the two together, and that's what I came up with."

"It was the best one of the night, Tucker. And it was for *me*," she said in wonder.

"They're all for you now, Reagan. Everything I say. Everything I do. Everything I sing. Everything I am. It's all because of you."

He kissed her again, eager to get her home and in bed. Sliding his lips to her ear, he whispered, "Want to go home and make some more music in bed?"

"You need to talk to someone before we leave," she told him. "He's a real fan of yours and wants to say hello."

Tucker gazed about the room and then saw exactly who Regan referred to.

"Matt," he said as his brother-in-law reached him.

"Tuck!" the country star called, throwing his arms around Tucker. "You blew me away tonight, man. Each song. They just got better and better."

Puzzled, he asked, "How are you even here, Matt?"

Matt motioned to Reagan. "You can thank your better half here. Reagan contacted me and told me you'd be playing Java Junction tonight."

"I hope you're not mad," she said, her voice small. "I was afraid you might be upset. That's why I didn't tell you Matt would be here."

"How can I be mad at the woman I love?" he asked, giving her a hard, swift thank you kiss.

"I liked them all, Tuck," Matt said. "Every damn one. I'm known for more upbeat songs, with a few ballads thrown in, but maybe the next album I cut might be nothing but ballads."

"You aren't upset, Matt?"

His brother-in-law looked at him quizzically. "Well, I've been mad as hell that you ignored every text and phone call from me the last couple of years, but I'm over it now. We're back in touch. That won't change."

"I thought… I thought you'd be upset. Because I've found someone new."

Matt shook his head. "Get that crazy idea out of your head, Tucker Young. You know how Josie was full of life. Laughter. Love. She'd be the last person on the planet to want you to mope around and be miserable. From what Reagan and I talked about, you did that for a couple of years. Well, the time of mourning is over. The Bible says there's a time to mourn, and a time to dance. And brother, I'm ready to make some music with you again."

Matt pulled Reagan into his arms, giving her a warm hug. "Thank you for reaching out to me, Reagan. For putting me back in touch with this guy. I've missed him, and I can't wait to get to know you."

"I know you're not touring now. That you live down the road in Bandera. Do you have plans for Thanksgiving?" she asked.

"It's just going to be the four of us this year," Matt said. "Sophie, me, and the kids. Why? Would you like to come to the ranch?"

"Actually, my aunt Jean and I will be cooking for a whole group of our friends. We'd be thrilled if you and Sophie could join us. The kids, too."

"Let me run it by the wife and see what she thinks, but Sophie's not much of a cook. I think she'd be happy to come and see Tuck again and meet you."

"I'll text you the address. We're going to eat at two Thanksgiving afternoon. It's at our friends' house, Braden and Harper Clark. She just had a baby a few days ago, which is why Aunt Jean and I are helping out."

Matt grinned. "Oh, Sophie will be all over that baby. My woman is baby mad. We've got two, and we have no plans of stopping anytime soon." He offered Tucker his hand. "Promise me we're going to stay in touch. You'll always be my brother-in-law. We'll always have that bond of Josie between us."

"I'm sorry I dropped off the face of the earth, Matt. I needed time to lick my wounds. Time to reconcile what had happened. Josie's death was the death of a lot of my dreams."

He glanced to Reagan, slipping his arm about her. "But this little lady has shown me the way. A new way. She also lost someone she loved. We've agreed we could still love our previous partners and still make room in our hearts for each other."

"You're a wise woman, Regan Bradley," Matt complimented. "I'll text you no later than tomorrow morning about Thanksgiving, but I think you can count us in." He grinned. "I also appreciate the fact we're eating at two."

"Because the Cowboys are playing around three-thirty?" Reagan asked, her eyes sparkling. "Yes, Aunt Jean insisted on the time. She's a huge Dallas Cowboys fan. She said she'd cook. She would eat. Then others will have to clean up because she wants a prime spot in front of the TV."

Matt died laughing. "I think I'm going to like your

aunt, Jean, a lot. I'll say my goodnights, and I'll see you both soon."

As Matt Hardy left Java Junction, the sea of people parted. No one stopped him for selfies or autographs, respecting his space, and he exited the coffeehouse.

Tucker turned from watching Matt to find all of his friends in front of him. They fist bumped. Hugged. Laughed. All of them praised the new songs he had written.

Ivy said, "I hope you don't mind, Tucker, but I used my cell to record every song tonight. I sent the recording to Braden and Harper so they could feel as if they had been here with you."

"Not a problem, Ivy. In fact, send it to me, too. Reagan and I can watch it, and I'll critique my own performance."

"You really moved me," Ana said. She glanced to her husband, and Wolf nodded. "We want to meet with you, Tucker."

"Meet with *me*?" he asked. "What for?"

"We're shooting a movie now, and I think it needs a theme song. I'm thinking you might be the man to write it for us."

He was blown away by the producer's request. "Ana, I'd be honored, but I'd have to know a little more about the project before committing."

She handed him a card as Wolf said, "Let's see if we can get together after Thanksgiving. Ana and I can fill you in on the storyline. Let you look at some of the footage already in the can. See if it's a project you might be interested in partnering with us."

Ana's eyes gleamed at him as she asked, "Have you ever writing strictly instrumental music?"

"No. Never gave that a thought."

"Holden had never written a script until we asked him to write the screenplay for *Hill Country Homicide*. Maybe it's time you thought about scoring a movie," she said. "Or at least contributing a theme song."

He knew absolutely nothing about scoring a movie.

But the idea intrigued him.

"I'll give you a call," he said. "We can meet and talk about the single song." He grinned. "And the score."

"Yes!" Ana exclaimed.

Wolf said, "We better get home to the kids. It was a pleasure hearing you perform tonight, Tucker."

His friends all said they needed to get home, as well, and Tucker spoke with a few others who'd lingered in Java Junction, wishing to say a few words to him. Reagan said she would retrieve the guitar case from upstairs while he finished up.

When she brought it back down, he placed the guitar inside it and then returned it to Dax.

"Thanks for the loan tonight. I'm going to buy one exactly like it," he announced. "I think that kind of guitar is my new good luck charm."

"I still have the paperwork from where I bought it," Dax shared. "I could pick one up for you next week since I'm going into San Antonio."

"That would be terrific. Let me know how much it is, and thank you again, Dax, for working me into your Saturday night lineup."

He walked Reagan and Miss Jean to the older woman's SUV, and she said, "Why don't you ride home with Tucker? I think he would appreciate that."

"Thank you, Aunt Jean." Reagan kissed her aunt's cheek.

Miss Jean looked at Tucker. "You're a hell of a songwriter, Tucker Young. You better talk my niece into marrying you soon. Got it?"

"I'll do my best, Miss Jean," he promised.

They waited until the old woman backed her vehicle from the parking space and drove down the square, then he walked hand-in-hand with his lady love to his truck.

Before he could open her door, Reagan wrapped her arms around him, drawing him in for an intimate kiss.

"I love you so much, Tucker. I'm so glad tonight was such a success."

"We've got more to celebrate, babe. Let's go home and get started."

25

Reagan awoke early Thanksgiving morning in her own bed inside the B&B. She had deliberately chosen not to spend the night with Tucker, knowing so much needed to be done today. He had helped her and her aunt cart a ton of groceries to Braden and Harper's yesterday, where she and Aunt Jean had done a good amount of prep work for today's feast. Tucker had stayed the entire time in case he was needed, mostly hanging out with Braden. Harper was in and out, sometimes Beau with her. She had let Reagan hold the baby again. Having a little one in her arms brought sweet yearnings within her, and she knew she was ready to make a lasting commitment to Tucker soon. After all, Aunt Jean was continuing to pressure them to get married. While she knew others might question the speed with which they would do so, she knew in her heart it was the right thing to do. Something told Reagan it would be the final step in healing both of them from their grief of having lost their previous loved ones.

She showered and dressed and went downstairs for a quick cup of coffee and piece of toast, something to tide her over before the big meal this afternoon. Thank goodness they had no guests in the inn to make breakfast for this morning. Aunt Jean had had a full house last Friday night, thanks to the large wedding which had taken place at the event center. Two of those couples had stayed on through Saturday night, as well.

When she had asked Aunt Jean about who would be staying over the holiday weekend, her aunt told her no one ever did. That she always marked The Inn at Lost Creek full on the website around holiday times, taking some time for herself. She and Tucker were the only guests at the moment. Even Sid Allen, who had been with Aunt Jean for months, had come to her a week ago, saying he and his wife were going to try and make another go of their marriage. He'd spoken to his foreman and had been placed on the day shift. Aunt Jean had sent Sid off with her blessings, telling him he would always have a room with her if he needed it, but she hoped that he would find success in his marriage.

Entering the kitchen, Reagan saw Aunt Jean and Tucker already sitting at the table.

"We just sat," Tucker told her. "Let me pour you a cup of coffee."

While he did so, she popped a slice of bread into the toaster. "Ready for our big day, Aunt Jean?"

"I'm glad we planned for a few extras," her aunt replied.

Reagan had been pleased that Matt Hardy and his wife and children were going to join them, as would Ry's aunt and uncle. Shelly Blackwood had agreed to bring her famous yeast rolls, which would be one less thing for them to have to worry about today.

"It's a good thing Braden said he'd put the turkeys on for us this morning,' Aunt Jean continued. "He's saved us a trip to their place and back, but we'll need to head over there soon. There's lots to do to put on a meal for this large a group."

"I'm ready. Once we finish breakfast, all I'll do is brush my teeth, and we can be out the door."

"No need for you to go as early as we do, Tucker," Aunt Jean said. "Why, it'll give you time to work on a new song."

He smiled at the old woman. "Do you have any ideas for me, Miss Jean?"

"I'd say you're doing pretty well with love songs these days. Why don't you write another one?"

"I'll take it under consideration," he said, rising from the table. He leaned down and kissed Reagan's cheek. "I'll head over about noon. If you need any help in the kitchen before that, just holler."

"Will do," she replied.

Fifteen minutes later, she and her aunt were on the way to the Clarks' house. Reagan texted ahead to let Braden know they would arrive soon.

Harper greeted them at the door, looking maternal and competent at the same time, as only Harper could.

"I just put Beau down after feeding him. Is there anything I can help to do in the kitchen? Chop? Dice?" she grinned. "Supervise?"

"I know you do that supervising best, Harper, but you are worthless in the kitchen," her husband said affectionately. "Now, if you want to sit and keep your friends company as they cook, that's another thing. Or if you want to go and grab a little nap while Beau's down, I'll keep an ear out for him."

"You know, I'm going to do that very thing," Harper said. "I've read when a baby naps, the mom should try to do the same. With so many people coming today, it would be nice to have a little extra energy to greet them after being up so much last night. See you ladies in an hour."

They went to the large kitchen, where Aunt Jean actually allowed Braden to help with some prep since no guests had arrived early.

"The minute the first people come, this becomes my kitchen, Braden Clark," Aunt Jean warned. "You need to play host and entertain your friends and look out for your wife and baby." Her face softened. "Little Beau is simply an angel."

Braden grinned. "I'm sure every new father feels like this, but I think he's the best baby in the entire world. He'll change a lot of things for us, but we're so glad to finally have him here."

"As long as I don't catch wine in his bottle, I think you'll be a great daddy," Aunt Jean declared, causing both Braden and Reagan to chuckle.

Reagan had thought cooking for such a large group would be chaos— or at least controlled chaos —but her aunt was unflappable. She had a list posted on the fridge which detailed every dish being served. Beside each were times to start them on the stovetop or oven and when they would be finished, along with oven temperatures. Braden, being the chef he was, had a dream kitchen, with double ovens and warming trays galore, making their job easy.

Guests floated in and out of the kitchen, murmuring oohs and ahhs as they saw the various dishes. A few gave a little food advice, which tickled Reagan. Aunt Jean had predicted that very thing would happen and had told her niece to smile graciously and say thank you —and then ignore everything someone had recommended.

"The only people I might give a listen to would be Braden or Finley," Aunt Jean had shared. "They both know their way around a kitchen. And notice they're the only two who haven't had advice for us."

The men gathered in the den, watching the Detroit Lions, playing in the first NFL broadcast of the day. The women sat around the kitchen table for a time, taking turns holding an agreeable Beau. Eventually, Aunt Jean shooed them all out, and Reagan supposed they found a new spot to relocate, away from the football game.

Sophie Hardy returned to the kitchen now, holding her daughter, who had just turned one the week before. Her son came with her.

"Miss Jean, if you don't mind, I'm going to feed the kids something. Waiting until two o'clock is too long for them to have lunch. I like keeping them on a schedule. Makes it easier for them and me, too."

"I can give them some sliced turkey if you think they'll eat that," her aunt said.

"On a piece of bread would be great for my boy. He likes sandwiches. I'll dice a little turkey for the baby. She's just working on solids now. I did bring a few things for them to eat, as well."

Sophie went to a cooler sitting in the corner and opened it. Since they were in a lull, Reagan and Aunt Jean joined the three at the table.

"Matt came home so excited the other night," Sophie shared. "Not just for the wonderful songs he had heard, but the fact that he'd reconnected with Tucker."

"I thought he might resent me since I wasn't his sister," Reagan admitted.

"Good heavens, no! Matt adored Josie, same as Tucker, but he knew Tucker was young and would need to move on with his life eventually. He's just glad it's with you, Reagan. That was a pretty bold move, contacting Matt out of the blue. He gets messages from his fans all the time. I'm the one who actually scrolls through his Instagram each day. I delete almost all of them. When I read your message mentioning Tucker by name, though, I knew it was the real deal."

"Thank you for passing the message along to him," she said. "It meant the world to Tucker that Matt was at the coffeehouse to hear him play."

"I wish I could've been there, too, but the baby had an ear infection. I wasn't going to leave her in the care of a sitter. All she wanted was for her mama to hold her. Matt did let me watch the recording your friend made, though. While I think Tucker's written some great songs in the past, I can hear a greater level of maturity in his songwriting now."

Once Ivy had sent what she had recorded to Tucker and the two of them had watched it together, she had encouraged him to forward it to Matt before they met again.

"Is Matt leaning toward any certain song?" she asked.

Sophie chuckled. "He loves them all. Actually, that's usually a decision my husband allows me to make. I listen to all the demos he receives and give him advice on which ones I think will be hits and which ones he can use to fill an album, as well as the ones I think he should pass on. Matt has trusted my judgment over the years."

"How long have you been married?"

"Going on eight years," Sophie replied. "We knew we wanted kids, but Matt's career hadn't caught on when we first got married. We also didn't want to be apart, especially since he was traveling so much then. He still has to, but the kids are young and flexible enough that we can take them along. That won't last forever, though. Matt has just finished building a recording studio at the ranch, so he won't have to go to Nashville to record any longer. He'll still tour some, but as they get older, I'll stay home with the kids when he does. We figure we have another couple of years where we can all be on the road together before it's time to allow the kids to stay at home. They'll have school and friends and sports by then."

"Routine is important for kids," Aunt Jean agreed. "Now, if you'll excuse me, I need to get busy again. You keep Sophie company another few minutes, Reagan. I'll let you know when you're back on duty again."

A few minutes before two, Aunt Jean summoned Braden, telling him they were ready to eat. Braden called everyone into the den, and they stood in a large circle, holding hands, as their host offered up a prayer of thanksgiving, grateful for the friends and family who had gathered with them today, and especially for the miracle of Beau being a part of it.

Because they were such a large group, the guests had to split up. Some ate in the dining room, while others took their meal in the kitchen. Aunt Jean had told everyone they would eat their main meal where she assigned them. They would switch and have dessert afterward, so each would get to spend time with their hosts.

"You're welcome to come back for seconds. Even thirds," Aunt Jean declared. "Once the game starts, though, I'm off the clock and you're on your own."

Everyone laughed, and Braden told Aunt Jean she could have the seat of her choice at game time.

Tucker hung back, waiting for others to go through the buffet line, and then pulled Reagan along with him.

"Boy, you and Miss Jean outdid yourself. Everything looks and smells fabulous."

They loaded their plates and joined their hosts in the dining room. She was proud of her contributions to this meal. For a moment, Reagan thought back to last Thanksgiving, where she had sat in her apartment, loneliness gnawing at her as she ate a meal of Chinese takeout from a carton. It was hard to believe the changes which had occurred in her life this past year, but none were as great as her relationship with the man sitting next to her.

Reagan reached under the table and clasped Tucker's fingers. He turned to her and simply said, "I love you."

"I love you, too, Tucker. I was thinking about last Thanksgiving and how sad and alone I was."

"I don't even remember where I was a year ago," he admitted. "To me, one day blended into another. Until I found my way to you, love."

They finished the meal, and Aunt Jean asked for her help in getting out the desserts for round two.

Tucker stood. "No, ma'am, I'm going to take charge now. You and Reagan just stay put." He looked to Braden. "Come help."

"With pleasure," their host said, following Tucker into the kitchen.

Emerson stood, saying, "I'm the dessert gal. I think those two could use some supervision."

Emerson had baked two pies each of pumpkin, pecan, and coconut, but she had also contributed a chocolate cake and chocolate chip cookies to the gathering.

Soon, the guests switched tables, with Reagan and Tucker remaining with Braden and Harper in the dining room. Harper had awakened Beau from his latest nap. She held the baby in her arms as she took a bit of pecan pie, proclaiming it the best she had ever eaten.

When it was time for the game to start, Reagan wasn't allowed in the kitchen for cleanup. Even though she wasn't a huge football fan yet, she was beginning to understand and like the game, so she joined the others in the den to watch the first quarter. It was nice to have participated in cooking a meal for this large a group, but it was even nicer not having to scrub pots and pans.

At halftime, Aunt Jean said she was worn out and going to watch the rest of the game at home.

Tucker and Reagan volunteered to go home with her. A few others also left, close enough to make it back to their homes before the second half kicked off. Braden and Harper thanked them profusely, with Harper saying, "If you ever need a job beyond running your B&B, Miss Jean, I'll always have a place for you at Weddings with Hart."

"Hey, wait a minute," Ry interjected. "Smokin' Sweethearts is the business that's booming. I may want to hire Miss Jean for the second food truck Tucker and I are purchasing."

Reagan was pleased to hear Ry mention the truck. Tucker had told her of his idea to fund a second food truck with the money he had received from the accident. Ry had been more than agreeable, insisting Tucker become his partner and not merely an employee. The food truck had been ordered, and it would be ready in a couple of weeks.

"I'm seventy-five," Aunt Jean told them. "Running this B&B is about all I can handle at my age. Maybe you can recruit Reagan here."

They said their goodbyes and drove home, Reagan accompanying her aunt, Tucker following in his truck.

"It was a good day," Aunt Jean said, satisfaction in her voice.

"A very good day," Reagan seconded. "I may not need to eat until this time tomorrow because I'm so full."

At the stoplight, her aunt turned to her. "I hope your life is full now, my darling girl. I see you with good friends who'll be there for you in the years to come. I see you with a good man, one who is your perfect match. I'm so glad you left New York behind and came home to Texas."

"I'm glad I had you to come home to, Aunt Jean. It's been your love and support throughout the years which has meant the most to me."

They reached the B&B, and her aunt said she was going to watch the rest of the game curled up in bed.

"All that cooking has worn me out. See you two tomorrow."

She kissed her aunt's cheek. "See you tomorrow."

Reagan and Tucker settled in on the couch in the parlor, watching some of the game, which turned into a blowout. By the time the fourth quarter started and the Cowboys had a twenty-four-point lead, Tucker asked, "Want to turn off the game and go fool around?"

She smiled at him. "I thought you'd never ask."

26

*T*ucker felt Reagan slip from the bed. She came around to his side and bent, planting a soft kiss on his lips. He grabbed her wrist, pulling her back for another one.

"You're up early."

"Lots to do today," she told him. "We have a wedding tonight at the event center. Only about eighty in attendance, so it won't be too complicated. Paula is over her stomach bug, thank goodness, and she'll be back, so that's a relief. Then tomorrow night, there's a fiftieth anniversary party for a retired banker and his wife."

He knew about the first since he and Ry were catering the wedding this evening. He assumed the anniversary party had made other arrangements regarding food, though it wouldn't surprise him if Emerson had baked the cakes for the occasion.

"Are you going to the house to have breakfast with Miss Jean?" he asked as she began pulling on her clothes.

"No, Dayna said she would stop at The Bake House and bring some Danish for us to nibble on at this morning's meeting. Harper's got a fantastic coffee machine at the office, so I'll grab a cup once I get there."

She kissed him again. "What's on your agenda today?"

"Matt and I didn't want to talk business yesterday with everyone around, so he's meeting me this morning at Aunt Shelly's diner."

"Sophie told me yesterday how much she really liked your new songs, Tucker. I think Matt may buy everything you've written since you've returned to Lost Creek."

"We'll see," he said. "In the meantime, I'll work the lunch shift with Ry, and then I'll see you at the wedding this evening."

"Talk to you later," she said, waving goodbye and exiting the cottage.

Tucker got up and showered, picking up his notebook of song ideas he'd been dabbling with. He walked across to the main house to let Miss Jean know he wouldn't be eating breakfast with her this morning. The kitchen stood empty, though. He thought maybe she was taking it easy and sleeping in today, having worked so hard yesterday preparing yesterday's meal and having no guests at the inn. He opened a couple of drawers before finding a notepad and pen and wrote her a note that he was grabbing breakfast at Lone Star Diner with Matt and that neither he nor Reagan would be home for dinner since they were working a wedding later this evening.

Tearing off the page, he left it on the counter where Miss Jean could easily find it and then drove into town, finding a parking place directly in front of the diner. He was meeting Matt at eight, which was ten minutes from now.

He entered and was immediately greeted by his aunt. She gave him a big hug.

"Yesterday went so well, didn't it?" she said cheerfully. "I like the friends you and Ry have made in Lost Creek, Tucker." Her eyes gleamed at him. "And I especially like Reagan Bradley for *you*."

"Reagan is everything I could ever want in a woman, Aunt Shelly. In a wife, actually."

She threw her arms about him again. "Oh, Tucker, I'm so happy for you. I know how much you loved Josie and how hard you took her death. You have a second chance at life and love now with Reagan. Have you asked you to marry you yet?"

"Not officially," he revealed. "We've just talked in general terms. She knows what's in my heart and that we have a future together. We haven't formalized anything yet."

"Don't wait," she advised. "Marry that girl soon. Don't risk losing her."

Changing the subject, he said, "I'm meeting Matt, Josie's brother, for breakfast." He glanced around, seeing the diner was about half-full. "I thought there'd be more of a crowd this morning."

"I think a lot of folks are still in a food coma," Aunt Shelly joked. "I'll send Matt your way the minute he gets here. Go take that back booth against the windows. That'll give you two a little privacy. I'll try not to seat anyone near you since you'll probably be talking business."

"We plan to," he told her.

"Well, after hearing those songs you wrote and sang the other night? Matt Hardy would be a fool if he didn't snatch up each and every one of them."

"It's nice having you in my corner, Aunt Shelly," Tucker said, moving to the back booth.

One of the longtime servers brought him a cup of coffee with a tall ice water and asked if might be ready to order.

"I'm waiting on a friend, Gloria. In fact, I see him coming in the door now." Tucker raised a hand and caught Matt's attention, waving him over.

"That's Matt Hardy," the server proclaimed in awe.

Matt arrived at the table and gave the woman his winning smile. "I'd love a cup of coffee, darlin'," if you have a minute," he said, his easy charm evident.

Starstruck, Gloria merely nodded and walked off, returning with a cup and saucer and pouring the coffee.

As Matt stirred sugar into it, he asked, "What's good here?"

"Everything is good here, Mr. Hardy. Tucker leans to the Sunrise Special when he comes to breakfast. Is that what you'd like, Tuck?" she asked.

He nodded and looked back to Matt. "You can't go wrong. It's got a little of everything."

Matt Smiled. "Make it two Sunrise Specials."

Gloria whipped out her pad, all business now. "Eggs?"

"Scrambled."

"Ham, bacon, or sausage?"

"Sausage," Matt replied.

"Hash browns and fruit okay with you?"

"You bet."

"Pancake or French toast?" Gloria asked.

Matt grinned. "How 'bout both?"

"You got it, Mr. Hardy," the server said, sashaying away from them.

Tucker laughed easily. "Gloria has been here at least thirty years. Maybe more. She's close to sixty. You know how to suck 'em in at any age, don't you, Matt?"

"That I do," his brother-in-law agreed. "Now, let's get down to business. I want to buy every song you sang at Java Junction the other night, Tucker. You know I run everything by Sophie. She's my sounding board and guiding light. She went wild over every song and even agreed that it might be a nice surprise for my fans and a good change of pace if I put out a CD strictly featuring country love songs. But do you have anything else in the pipe? Something a little more upbeat. More me."

"I'm glad you mentioned that because I have a few ideas."

Tucker opened the spiral notebook he'd brought along, telling Matt a few of the topics he was thinking about writing. Matt gave him the go-ahead on all of them.

"I also had time yesterday morning to start something new. I've got the chorus and almost an entire verse down. Here, take a listen."

He picked up his phone and hit play, watching Matt's

face carefully as his brother-in-law listened to the beginnings of his latest song.

Matt burst out in a big smile when the music ended. "That's what I'm talking about. That's a real boot scooter in my book. I want to hear it the minute it's finished. Send me the file. I've just completed building a recording studio on the ranch. I was taking too much time away from home, with all the touring and then following up with recording new music in Nashville. Having the studio on my property is going to let me enjoy being home more often."

"I'll work on this song and a couple of the other ideas we talked about," Tucker promised as Gloria delivered their plates of food and freshened their coffee.

"You need to get yourself a lawyer, Tucker," Matt advised. I don't expect you'll write exclusively for me. There'll be other singers who're going to want your songs. It's not wise for us to share an attorney, but I can ask mine for a few recommendations of people who specialize in entertainment law and pass those names along to you. We'll also need to talk numbers, too. I'd rather that be between our attorneys and my agent. Hell, you're probably going to need one of those, too."

"I'd appreciate any recommendations you can give me," he said, biting into his ham, which was sweet and tender.

They spent the rest of breakfast catching up with each other. Matt also asked what Tucker's intentions were toward Reagan.

"We're heading for marriage," he assured his friend. "We haven't set a date yet. We're both pretty darn busy.

Reagan is pinch hitting while Harper is out on maternity leave. I've just been made a partner in my cousin's food business, Smokin' Sweethearts. We're about to add a second food truck to the operation, and we also cater events held at Lost Creek Vineyards."

"Sophie and I drink their wines. They're really good, especially the blends."

"That's all Braden. He's the chief winemaker for the label. Harper's the one who built the event center on the winery's property. They are a dynamic duo, with strong ties to the Lost Creek business community, and they're a great couple to be around."

"Sophie was really taking with little Beau," Matt said. "She's already hinting around that it's time to begin baby making again." He grinned. "You need to slip a ring on Reagan's finger so you can catch up with us. I look at you as family, Tucker. Reagan, too. You always will be both family and friend to me."

A lump formed in his throat, and Tucker said, "I appreciate that. More than you could ever know, Matt. I know this might sound like crazy talk, but I feel as if Josie's been watching over me. That somehow, she brought Reagan and me together."

He paused. "Reagan's fiancé was killed a week before their wedding took place, so she's known her share of heartbreak, too. I kind of think of Josie as the angel who swept her wings along, bringing us together."

"I hear you," Matt said. "And I don't think that sounds crazy at all. Josie was the happiest person I ever knew. If

God is letting her dabble in matchmaking as an angel, she's probably the happiest person in heaven, too."

They finished up breakfast, with Matt insisting upon picking up the check.

"I know this is the start of a lucrative partnership, Tucker. I'll get those attorneys' names to you as soon as I can, and we can draw up formal papers regarding the sale of the songs you played last weekend. Then I want first dibs on the one I heard this morning once it's done."

"You got it," he said, feeling confident about his songwriting and Matt's ability to bring a story to life through his voice and guitar playing.

Tucker went straight to Ry's house afterward, where his cousin was turning some meat on the smoker.

"It's got another hour before it's ready for us to box up and take on the road," Ry said. "Come on in so we can catch up."

The cousins talked for an hour, mostly about ways to expand the reach of Smokin' Sweethearts and the need to hire some new help to work the food trucks.

"Last time, I found my food truck close by. I'm sorry we had to order one from Dallas this time, but it had all the bells and whistles we needed. I got a text this morning from our salesman. It'll be ready late next week, but I don't know when either of has the time to get up there and drive it home. Maybe they can deliver it to us."

"What about seeing if Uncle Shy would like to pick it up?" he suggested. "I was talking to him before lunch yesterday, and he told me he's starting to cut back a little on his hours at Blackwood BBQ. He might like to hit the road for a little trip and take Aunt Shelly along with him."

"You know, that's a great idea. Let me check with him now."

Ry called his dad and told him about needing someone to go to Dallas to pick up the newest food truck, saying it might be a nice getaway for his parents. He'd left the phone on speaker, and so Tucker heard his uncle's response.

"Just the thing your mother and I need, Ry. We could head up there and take a couple of days to do a little Christmas shopping. Maybe even see if the Cowboys are playing at home and go see the game. Then I could drive the truck down, and Shelly could follow. Thanks for the opportunity, son."

"I'll know more specifics early next week. My salesman will be getting in touch with me and let me know the exact date the truck will be outfitted and ready. Talk to you soon."

Ry grinned at Tucker. "Well, that was easy. Let's go clear the smokers."

They emptied the smokers, filling their pans with brisket and ribs, today's features, and drove to the town's square, setting up on the far end. Soon, a line formed, which surprised Tucker. He didn't think people would be wanting something such as barbeque after a big meal yesterday, but he was glad he was proven wrong. Though the city offices were closed today, many people were out on the square, starting their Christmas shopping, taking time to stop by the food truck and grab a sandwich.

By one o'clock, they had sold out. Ry drove the truck back to his house.

"We need to be at the winery no later than four," his cousin told Tucker. "Tonight's menu is easy. We should be through fairly early."

"I'll see you at the event center in a few hours then," Tucker said, heading back to the B&B.

He didn't think Reagan would be home but decided to stop inside the house anyway, using the key Miss Jean had let him keep. The house was quiet as he went upstairs and knocked on Reagan's door. No one answered, so he assumed she was at the winery, either at the Weddings with Hart office or the event center itself.

Going back downstairs, he decided he would tell Miss Jean he'd decided to propose to Reagan tonight. She was nowhere to be found, though. He knew she had to be home because he'd seen her SUV in front of the house. He wandered through the rooms downstairs again, finding them all empty.

Then a sense of dread filled him as he made his way to her bedroom door. It was closed, and he lightly tapped on it, hearing the TV playing within.

"Miss Jean? Are you in there?"

No response.

Tucker was concerned enough now that he turned the knob and slowly pushed open the door, seeing a small lamp on the nightstand lit. As he crossed the room, he saw Jean Bradley propped against the pillows, a contented smile upon her lips.

"Miss Jean?" he asked softly, touching and shaking her shoulder gently.

She didn't move. His gut clenched.

Raising his hand, Tucker touched the back of his fingers to her cheek and felt no warmth. He slipped them to the pulse point in her throat. Still nothing.

Lifting her wrist, he gently placed his fingers along her pulse.

Jean Bradley was gone.

How in the world would he break this news to Reagan?

27

$\mathcal{T}$ucker's first call was to Ry.

When his cousin picked up, he said, "I won't be able to cater the wedding with you tonight. I just found Miss Jean. She's dead, Ry."

Ry whistled low. "Oh, this is going to kill Reagan."

"I know. She's at the event center now. I need to go get her and share the bad news, then bring her home so she can say her last goodbyes."

"Mom and Dad have always told me they'll help out in a pinch. Since tonight's wedding is on the small side, I'm going to call them to take over for us. Emerson and I will come be with you. Help you get through this."

Emotion swelled within him. "You don't know how much I appreciate that, Ry."

"I'll call Emerson now and give her a heads up. She'll be waiting in the wings whenever you need her."

"I don't know the first thing about what needs to be

done," Tucker admitted. "Who to call. What Miss Jean might've wanted."

"We'll get that all figured out, Tucker. Together."

He ended the call and looked down at the sweet, feisty lady who had so warmly welcomed and accepted him upon his arrival in Lost Creek. Tucker bent and brushed a kiss upon her brow and then turned off the TV. Gently, he closed the door, wondering what her death would mean for Reagan.

Tucker drove to Lost Creek Vineyards, heading straight to the event center, where he saw Reagan's car parked in back. Most likely, she would be in no shape to drive. Emerson could follow them home in Reagan's car.

He cut through the kitchen door, seeing Emerson pacing.

She came to Tucker, enfolding him in an embrace. "I just talked with Ry. I'm so sorry for your loss, Tucker. Miss Jean was the best." She released him. "I'll be in my office. Ready for whenever you need me."

Stepping from the kitchen, Tucker looked over the event center, seeing Regan in conversation with Paula. She spied him and waved, excusing herself and heading his way. He drank in her beauty, thinking how happy she looked.

And how he was about to crush her spirits.

"You're certainly here early," she said. "Emerson told me Ry wouldn't get here until around four. Is something up?"

He threaded his fingers through hers. "Let's go talk. In private."

Tucker led her back into the deserted kitchen and faced her.

Alarm filled her eyes. "Tucker, you're scaring me. What's wrong?"

Swallowing, he placed his hands on her shoulders. "There's no easy way to say this, Reagan, so I'm just going to say it. Miss Jean… is gone."

Confusion clouded her eyes. "Gone? She didn't tell me she was…" Her voice trailed off. Her body stiffened beneath his fingers.

She had figured out her aunt was dead.

"No," she wailed, the cry of anguish like a knife to his heart.

Tucker wrapped her tightly in his arms, her own going around him, clinging to him.

"She was fine," Reagan insisted. "Fine. She cooked for all those people yesterday."

Then the sobs came, harrowing ones which racked her body and his. He let her cry it out, kissing her hair, making soothing noises.

She lifted her tear-stained face. "How?"

"I wanted to talk to her about something," he began. "When I couldn't find her downstairs, I tapped on her bedroom door. The TV was playing, and I thought she might not have heard me, so I slowly opened the door."

He paused, smoothing her hair. "She was in bed, Reagan. Propped up on her pillows. A sweet smile on her face. It's obvious she didn't suffer."

Tears slid down her cheeks. "I don't know what to do. There's so much to do," she said, sounding lost.

"I'm here for you." He glanced over her shoulder and saw Emerson had emerged from her office. "Emerson and Ry are going to help us get through this."

"The wedding," she said dully. "Harper. I can't let her down."

Emerson came toward them and slipped her hand around Reagan's. "You know tonight's wedding is a small one. Paula and Dayna can easily handle it. Same for the anniversary party tomorrow. It's a low-key affair. Let me go tell Paula and Dayna that you won't be able to participate this weekend. Give me your keys, and I'll drive your car back to the B&B. You go with Tucker now."

Reagan went to her purse and handed over her car key to Emerson. Tucker guided her from the kitchen to his truck as if she were a sleepwalker. They said nothing to one another on the drive home, but she never let go of his hand the entire ride.

By the time they reached The Inn at Lost Creek, Ry's truck was sitting out front. He opened the passenger door and helped Reagan out, hugging her to him.

"I'm so sorry for your loss, Reagan," he said gently. "Miss Jean was a stalwart in the community and one of the finest women I've ever known."

She brushed the tears from her cheeks. "Thank you, Ry. Thanks for coming. For being here."

They entered the house, and Reagan stood in the foyer, frozen.

"Do you want me to go with you to see her?" Tucker asked quietly.

Nodding, she found his fingers, and they went hand-in-hand back to Miss Jean's bedroom. He opened the door and guided her inside. Reagan broke away from him and headed toward the bed, where Tucker joined her, standing a few feet away.

"You're right," she said. "She looks… so peaceful. As if she hasn't a care in the world."

Turning, she looked at him, tears misting her eyes. "I feel so guilty, Tucker. She worked so hard the last few days, feeding an army of people. What if that's what did her in?"

He slipped his arm about her waist. "I don't think preparing one meal is what ended her, babe. Miss Jean was a giver. A lover of others. She loved every minute of preparing that Thanksgiving meal for friends and family. I think it was just her time to go. On her terms. She wouldn't have been one who would have wanted to linger in a sickbed for years. Jean Bradley did things her way, even in death."

"I wish I could've talked with her one more time. She was so wise, Tucker. She's been the one constant in my life all these years. I don't know what I'm going to do without her."

Reagan began crying softly again, and he pulled her to him, comforting her the best he could.

Finally, she pulled away, placing her palm against her aunt's cheek. "You were a shining example, Aunt Jean. The way you lived your life, you led with your heart. Thank you for loving me always."

She brushed her lips against her aunt's brow. Turning to face Tucker, she said, "I've said my goodbyes. Now, we need to figure out what needs to be done. I know where she kept her important papers. She showed me once before. Any final wishes she has should be located in a manila folder."

They left the room and returned downstairs. By now, Emerson had arrived and returned Regan's keys to her.

"I've made some coffee," Emerson told them. "Water for tea is also on to boil."

"Thank you," Reagan said, embracing her friend. "Thank you and Ry for being here for us."

"Whatever you need," Emerson said. "We want to help however we can."

Ry said, "I talked to the sheriff to find out what should happen next. He said when you were ready, Reagan, give him a call. He'll set the wheels in motion."

"Let's hold off on that for a couple of minutes," Tucker said. "Reagan knows where Miss Jean kept her final wishes. We'll look at those first."

He followed Reagan into the small nook off the kitchen, which had a built-in desk. This was where Miss Jean had kept her business records and did her accounting. Reagan pulled out a folder. Labeled on the front it said, "*When I Kick the Bucket.*" Both of them chuckled, and Tucker said, "Feisty until the end."

They opened the folder and skimmed through its contents. Miss Jean had already paid for her own funeral services and plot. She had picked out the music to be played and said she wanted the service to be short and sweet, with a nice party after at Blackwood BBQ.

Attached was a copy of her will, which she said had been filed with Merilee Swan.

"I can't look at this now," Reagan said, anguish filling her face. "I can only take things one step at a time. Right now, that means having Aunt Jean taken care of."

Tucker closed the folder but took it with him as they returned to Ry and Emerson.

"You can call the sheriff now." He shared with Ry the name of the funeral home where Miss Jean was to be taken to.

"I'll get on it," Ry reassured them.

"Come sit, Reagan," Emerson said. "Have something hot to drink. I also found some cookies Miss Jean had baked. You need to eat something to keep up your strength."

Through watery eyes, Reagan said, "Those were the last cookies we baked together."

Emerson nodded calmly. "Then we're going to freeze two of them. Just like a couple does a slice of their wedding cake. On the anniversary of Miss Jean's death next year, you and Tucker are going to thaw and eat them to celebrate her life and your treasured memories of her."

The baker wrapped the two cookies tightly in plastic wrap and then added a layer of foil around them. She slipped them into a freezer bag and sealed it tightly, finding a permanent marker and labeling the date on it.

Reagan and Emerson drank tea while Tucker poured coffee for him and Ry. By then, the county coroner had shown up, along with an ambulance. He gave his condolences to Reagan, calling Miss Jean the finest first citizen of Lost Creek.

Several minutes later, he returned downstairs as her body was being moved to the ambulance, saying, "Looks like natural causes to me. I don't think I've ever seen a more contented soul in death."

"Do you think she had a heart attack?" Reagan asked. "A stroke?"

"I think Miss Jean simply passed peacefully in her sleep," the coroner assured her. "People who suffer don't have that kind of smile on their face. Miss Jean was able to let go *because* she was happy. Because she knew you were happy."

A single tear cascaded down Reagan's cheek, and she wiped it away. "Thank you."

Once they left, Ry said, "The funeral home would like to meet with you at your convenience, Reagan. Do you feel up to it now, or would you rather put it off until tomorrow morning?"

"Now. I want to get this part over with."

Tucker said, "I'll go with you."

Emerson pulled her aside, "Would you like me to start contacting friends, Reagan?"

"Yes. That's a good idea. I'll know more once I've met with the funeral director and decided about the service, but you can let people know she's passed."

He opened the manila folder and pulled out a neatly penned list. "These are the people Miss Jean wanted to know."

"I love how organized she was," Reagan said, smiling

through her tears.

It took less than an hour at the funeral home to confirm all of Jean Bradley's final wishes. The funeral director looked over the calendar with Reagan, and they decided to hold the service at two o'clock on Tuesday afternoon in the chapel at the funeral home.

Tucker texted that information to Emerson so she could get the word out. By the time they reached the B&B, it was filled with their friends. Dax and Ivy. Holden and Finley. Wolf and Ana. Even Braden and Harper turned out, bringing a sleeping Beau.

Reagan went straight for the baby, lifting Beau in her arms, resting her cheek against his.

Harper slipped her hand through Tucker's arm. "Life and death. They go hand in hand," she said. "If ever there was a woman full of life, it was Miss Jean." She gazed up at Tucker. "How is Reagan really doing?"

"As good as can be expected. I think part of her is a bit numb. It's a lot to take in. Miss Jean was her only living relative."

"You're her family now, Tucker," Harper said fiercely. "You— and all of us. We'll make sure we take care of you both."

Reagan's gaze met Harper's. "Thank you for saying that." She glanced across the room. "Thank you all for being here. For me. For Tucker. For Aunt Jean."

Handing Beau back to Harper, Reagan told those gathered, "Aunt Jean loved preparing Thanksgiving for us. It was her last act of kindness, one I'm sure we'll all remember for years to come." She paused, swallowing, and then said, "I will only mourn my aunt's death for a short while because she was so full of life. I'm going to take all the wonderful memories I have of her and dedicate myself to being the kind of woman she was. The kind of woman I aspire to be on my journey through life."

She looked to Tucker and held out her hand. He joined her, taking it, squeezing her fingers.

"This may sound crazy. Then again, I see a lot of love in this room, so I think you'll understand. Aunt Jean had been on my case. Tucker's, too. She was eager for us to get married, the sooner the better.

"And that's what we're going to do."

Her words shocked him. "Reagan, we don't have to rush things."

"I lost Arch. You lost Josie. Both of us suffered tremendous pain and grieved deeply when they left our lives. If Aunt Jean taught me anything, it was to live in the now. Don't waste precious time."

Her gaze met his, her love for him pouring from her. "You are my light, Tucker. My home. You are the one I turn to in good times and bad. I need your love and support to get through this dark time, but Aunt Jean predicted many happy times ahead for the two of us. We're going to praise her. Mourn her. Bury her. And then we'll step into the next chapter of our lives. Together."

Tucker drew Reagan into his arms, knowing their love would see them through this latest tragedy— and into a bright tomorrow.

28

*R*eagan took a last look at The Inn at Lost Creek before starting her car to drive to her wedding at the winery. The B&B was now hers. She and Tucker had met with Merilee Stone, and the attorney had said that everything Jean Bradford owned had gone to her niece.

After talking over things with Tucker, she decided she would keep the inn open. Her new role in Lost Creek would have her stepping into her aunt's shoes. She would fill them her own way, something she knew Aunt Jean would approve of.

The B&B only had two bookings between Thanksgiving and Christmas and none in January. Reagan called both couples who had made reservations, explaining how the innkeeper had passed away suddenly, and that they would be closed for the next month. She offered to book both for a weekend in February when she was reopening, and they were happy to take her up on the offer of a free weekend to make up for the cancellation.

She was giving the place a new lease on life and had already had all the floors sanded, bringing out the beauty of the original wood. Finley and Ivy both had great eyes for design and had walked through each room with her, helping make notes on the changes Reagan wanted to implement, from hanging different curtains to choosing new comforters and pillows for the beds.

For now, Tucker was keeping the cottage as a writing retreat. Its first booking wasn't until the beginning of March, so he had a bit of time to decide if he wanted to write music from the main house after that time or find somewhere in town, as Ivy had for her art. Ivy was also overseeing the construction crew who would come in and work during the next two weeks on the updates. Modernizing the bathrooms. Painting the entire inside and outside. Placing the antiques Reagan had found in the attic in various rooms. All that would occur while she and Tucker were on their honeymoon.

Aunt Jean's funeral had gone smoothly. Not a dry eye had been found in the house by the time Tucker finished with his touching, humorous eulogy. She was grateful her groom had gotten to know Aunt Jean and that her aunt had approved of their match. They had celebrated her life with a grand party at Blackwood BBQ after the burial. Dax and Tucker had brought along their guitars, playing music for the crowd to dance to. There had been food, fun, and laughter as they had danced the night away.

Another celebration now lay ahead. Her wedding. The

first one had been pushed aside by Arch's death. She hadn't been able to even look at her wedding dress and put it on consignment. Reagan chose to sell her engagement and their wedding rings, marriage being the last thing she thought she would ever consider.

But a different man waited for her now. One who was kind. Strong. Caring. Talented. Tucker wasn't anything like Arch, and she supposed she wasn't much like Josie. Still, they had learned they made magic together. They still held their first loves dear in their hearts, but their everlasting love for one another would be the foundation for what they built in the years ahead.

Reagan pulled into the winery, not as a worker, but as the bride. Quickly, she was swept up into getting ready in the bridal suite. Paula brought in a tray of champagne flutes, and Harper lifted a glass high. Her mother was keeping Beau today so she could kick up her heels at Reagan and Tucker's wedding.

"To Reagan. Our wonderful friend whom we all feel as if we've known forever," Harper declared. "Here's to a happy life with Tucker!"

"Hear, hear," the others called, and she drank the fizzy liquid, which lifted her spirits even higher.

How her friends had thrown together a wedding in such a short amount of time amazed her, but Harper had said it was what Weddings with Hart did. Finley was photographing the event. Emerson had baked the wedding and groom's cakes. Harper had personally chosen the flowers and dressed the tables herself. Ry and his parents were catering the reception. Dax was serving as their DJ.

Her only attendant would be Emerson, and Ry would stand beside Tucker as his best man. Judge Grady, who married many of the couples at the event center, was waiting at the front, ready to begin. Reagan felt herself floating along, seeing a sea of happy faces, her heart light and filled with gratitude for those who had turned out to see her and Tucker speak their vows to one another.

She walked to him now, wishing that Aunt Jean had been on her arm. That was the only shadow on this happy day, but Reagan knew her aunt watched from heaven and cheered her on as she took Tucker's hand.

They spoke their vows to one another, their eyes never wavering. Tucker had told her he wrote a love song for their wedding, but he was afraid he would become a blubbering fool if he tried to sing it to her. He promised he would play it for her when they reached their honeymoon, a destination she had planned, based upon a remark he had made to her when they first met. She had even packed for him since he still didn't know where they were headed. Easy-going as ever, her groom had gone along with her plans without question.

"I now pronounce you husband and wife," Judge Grady declared to the cheers of those gathered.

Bride and groom walked up the makeshift aisle, Finley snapping away, capturing every moment for them. They gathered different groups, taking more pictures, with Finley handing off her camera to get in a few photographs herself, then the party truly started. A wonderful meal of savory Hill Country barbeque. Luscious cakes to die for. Dancing until sheer exhaustion overwhelmed her.

"Time to go change," Harper said in Reagan's ear as she finished a slow dance with Tucker.

"You might have to undress and redress me," she murmured. "I can barely move."

With Harper's help, she was soon in her going away outfit, winter white pants and a bright red blouse. Ivy assured her she would send only a few texts regarding the updates so that the honeymoon could be enjoyed. Finley said she would send wedding pictures soon.

Then she and Tucker were leaving the event center, people lined on both sides, waving sparklers at them in the dark of night. Laughing, they climbed into Holden's car, their driver to San Antonio.

"That was a fun night," Holden said, looking over his shoulder as they cuddled in the back. "And with that, just pretend I'm not here for the rest of the way."

An hour later, Holden helped them with their luggage, and they checked into their hotel. Champagne awaited them in their room, and Tucker opened it, pouring them each a glass, before offering a toast.

"Here's to the life we've led which brought us here. The life we have this very moment. And the life which will unfold and play out in the years ahead."

Reagan tapped her glass against his. "To us. To our lives. To our family and our future."

They finished the champagne and undressed one another slowly, savoring each kiss. Each touch. The feel of bare skin. The caresses and whispers of love.

As they lay together in the afterglow of making sweet love, Tucker asked, "Are you going to tell me now where we'll be tomorrow at this time?"

"Hawaii," she said. "You once told me you'd visited forty-nine of the fifty states, but you had yet to visit Hawaii. We're going to Maui and Oahu."

"Hot damn," he said, nuzzling her neck. "I hope you packed one of those string bikinis."

"I did. Why?"

His wolfish grin said it all. "Because I look forward to untying those strings. With my *teeth*, Mrs. Young."

Her skin grew hot at his words. "Why, Mr. Young. You are a devil in disguise."

He slipped his arms around her. "I'm your devil, Reagan Young. For years and years to come."

Tucker kissed her again.

And they went, once more, to the stars.

EPILOGUE

THANKSGIVING—A YEAR LATER...

*T*ucker helped a heavily pregnant Reagan from his truck. He didn't think she would make her due date, which was ten days away. His wife glowed, though, and he couldn't help but stop and kiss her before they headed up the sidewalk to the Clarks' front door.

"Mmm. What was that for?" she asked.

His thumb caressed her cheek. "A just because kiss."

"Give me another one."

"With pleasure."

He took his time, the kiss lengthy. And very satisfying.

"I better get the sides you brought," he said. "Let me get you in the door first."

By now, Dax and Ivy had pulled up. Dax unbuckled Kristina from her car seat and handed the eight-month-old baby, named for Ivy's birth mom, to his wife.

"Kissing is contagious," Dax called cheerfully. "I think I

might catch it." He leaned in and gave Ivy a kiss, following it with a sweet kiss to Kristina's head.

The two men escorted their wives to the porch, where Harper answered the door. Beau stood beside her. He had just started walking last week, and Harper joked keeping up with him was the greatest challenge she'd ever faced, said with a smile, of course.

"Take the women off our hands," Tucker said. "We're going back for the food."

By the time he and Dax had made two trips from their vehicles to the kitchen, Holden and Finley had arrived. They brought in an additional turkey, along with sweet potato casserole, ladened with a thick layer of marsh-mallows.

Ry and Emerson followed, Ry pushing a stroller with twins Hayley and Mark inside it. Emerson had given birth to the twins in late September after being in labor thirty-six hours. She said labor had been harder than creating a nine-tiered wedding cake— but worth every minute.

"Go back and grab the desserts, Ry," Emerson encour-aged. "I baked apple, pumpkin, and pecan this year and also brought a chocolate ganache cake and peanut butter cookies."

"I think I'll go straight for the desserts and skip the rest," Holden teased.

The doorbell rang again, and soon Wolf and Ana, along with Eva and Bear, had joined them in the kitchen.

"What did you bring?" Harper asked.

"Acorn squash slices," Ana replied. "They've got some

maple syrup and pecans mixed in. Also, some creamed pearl onions. Wolf can't seem to get enough of those."

"Sounds heavenly," Harper said.

Braden got everyone organized, placing dishes in warming trays and others in the oven to finish baking. He shooed everyone but Finley from the kitchen, saying the two of them would make certain food went on the table at the right time.

Just before two that afternoon, Braden asked for everyone to gather in the den. They joined hands and formed a circle, and Tucker couldn't help but recall doing the same last Thanksgiving, when Miss Jean had been with them.

Braden offered a prayer of thanksgiving, saying how grateful he was for family and friends who had become family. Then he concluded with, "And today we remember Miss Jean Bradley, who was with us this time last year. Feeding us. Loving us. Inspiring us. She's with us in spirit today."

He squeezed Reagan's hand. She squeezed back.

"Let's eat!" Braden proclaimed.

Finley and Braden had lined up all the dishes along the counters, using the island as a spillover zone. Tucker held Reagan's plate for her, not wanting her to carry anything too heavy.

"I won't break," she said.

"I know. I just like spoiling you."

She brushed a kiss along his jaw. "I like being spoiled."

At the table, Braden said, "I think we should reflect on what's gone well for us all this past year as we chow down.

Maybe think on what's to come in the next year. I'll start." He paused. "I have a new blend I've tweaked over the last two months. I think it's going to be a big seller for Lost Creek Vineyards. And the past year has been the best of my life, seeing Beau move through so many different stages. Harper?"

"Weddings with Hart was totally booked this year, and only a few slots remain open for next year. But work is secondary to me now. Beau is the focus. Promoting Paula and hiring another assistant is the smartest decision I've made in years. Next to marrying Mr. Handsome over there, that is." She turned to her sister. "Ivy?"

"I'd say Kristina tops our list." She smiled down at the infant, asleep in her arms. "But I was thrilled to complete my second art exhibition for Clive. And Harmony & Hues has really taken off."

Ivy referred to a fusion night of music and art, a summer festival she and Dax had started.

Dax said, "We're going to try to take Harmony & Hues to another town beyond Lost Creek this coming summer." He grinned. "Naturally, it's going to be where we just opened our second Java Junction. The coffeehouse will help support the fusion nights, and we'll continue to give local talent the mike on Saturday nights once summer is over."

Turning to Holden, Dax said, "You're on, Writer Man."

Holden touched the bridge of his nose, pushing his glasses up. "Well, my win for best first screenplay at the Independent Spirit Awards started off a great year for me.

Then *Mr. Hamilton's World*, the book and movie, came out. Both are doing well."

He took Finley's hand and nodded encouragingly. She looked at the group. "What Holden is letting me share with everyone is that we're pregnant. Eight weeks now. Due in June."

The occupants at the table offered the couple warm congratulations, then Holden said, "Ball's in your court, Wolf."

The film director nodded sagely. "WEBA Productions continues to thrive. Ana and I work well as a team. We couldn't be prouder of the films we've released, especially *Mr. Hamilton's Story*." He raised his wife's hand to his lips and kissed it. *"Te amo mi querida."*

Harper looked to her husband. "You need to learn Spanish, Braden. Anytime Wolf speaks Spanish, it always sounds so romantic."

"I'll take that under consideration," he said solemnly, causing everyone at the table to laugh.

"I'll go next," Ry said. "Obviously, the twins were the highlight of this year for Emerson and me. Smokin' Sweethearts continues to thrive, thanks to the second food truck." He smiled at his wife. "You're on, honey."

"Ditto regarding the twins, but I do have some really cool news." She paused, a smile lighting her face. "I've been asked to write a wedding cake cookbook. I'll include classic, traditional recipes, along with some more creative efforts. It'll also include grooms' cakes, too. Finley has agreed to provide the pictures. It'll be part coffee table book, part guide to those aspiring to learn how to bake the ultimate wedding or groom's cakes."

"That's fantastic, Emerson," Braden enthused. "We're becoming quite the celebrity-filled group." He eyed Tucker.

"Okay. I'll go," he said. "You all know I sold a total of ten songs to Matt, and the album of country love ballads he cut is his bestselling CD of all time. I also wrote a number one hit for him with a lot of pep in it." He inhaled a deep breath, letting it out slowly. "And last week, I signed a contract to provide Jon Jack Payne half a dozen songs for his next album."

"Seriously?" Dax enthused. "He's the top country solo act, Tuck. Way to go!"

Tucker slipped an arm around his wife's shoulder. "We're pleased. But we're happier about the coming baby."

Reagan rubbed her belly. "The Inn at Lost Creek is thriving. I have to thank Harper for continuing to recommend it to guests coming to Lost Creek for weddings."

"Not a problem," Harper said. "It's the best place to stay in town."

"Since Braden mentioned Aunt Jean, I thought we'd share with you that we're going to name our little girl Jean Marie, which was Aunt Jean's name."

"That's a lovely gesture," Emerson said. "She would love having the baby named in her honor."

They finished their meal, taking a short break before they tackled Emerson's array of desserts. The Cowboys game started. Tucker saw that Reagan looked tired.

"Ready to go home?" he asked quietly.

She nodded. "I haven't done much of anything today other than eat, but I am so tired. The heartburn is really bad right now."

"Emerson told me heartburn means the baby will be born with a head of hair. Mark and Haley are perfect examples of that."

They said their goodbyes and headed toward the truck. Reagan came to a sudden halt on the sidewalk.

"Something wrong?" he asked, trying to keep the worry from his voice.

"I feel... funny."

Then a whoosh sounded, and Tucker saw the water at her feet, dripping down her legs. Relief filled him.

"Your water broke," he said. "We need to head to the hospital."

"No, we need to go home first and get my bag."

Grinning, Tucker said, "I've put your bag in the truck every time we've gone somewhere the past week. I wanted to be *prepared*."

Her sunny smile had vanquished all the darkness in his soul. He had been drawn to her light, and Reagan had saved him in every way.

"Let's go have a baby, Mr. Young," his wife said.

Seven hours later, she cradled Jean Marie Young in her arms. Tucker sat in the bed next to them, his arm around his wife, his finger stroking the cheek of the baby.

Life with Reagan and Jean Marie in Lost Creek was all Tucker could have asked for.

PREVIEW: SHADOWS OF THE PAST

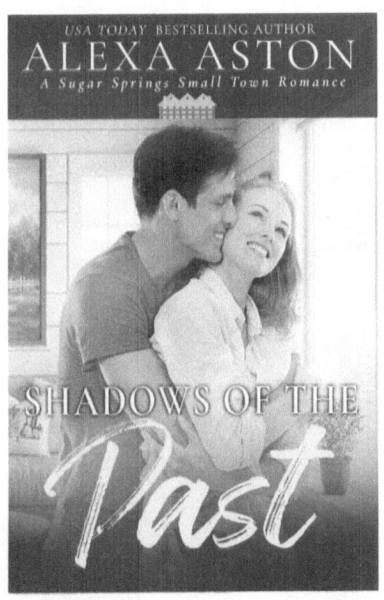

Read on for a preview of Shadows of the Past, book 1 in
the Sugar Springs series.

PROLOGUE

SUGAR SPRINGS, TEXAS—TWENTY
YEARS AGO...

*P*aige Laramie knew she had aced the spelling test. Nana had practiced the entire list of words with her last night. Not that Paige needed her to do so. Nana just liked helping Paige with her homework while Mama pulled a double shift at the diner.

She was the smartest girl in her class. Danny Henderson was the smartest boy. They always competed against one another. Danny had the edge in science, while Paige was better with math. They were pretty much the same in everything else—writing, grammar, social studies. Danny thought he was better, though, because he was rich. He always had the newest tennis shoes and the latest cell phone. His dad was president of the local bank, and his mom didn't have to work.

Her mom worked all the time. Her dad? Not so much. At least he hadn't before The Divorce. Paige didn't know where Daddy worked now or what he did or where he lived. When her parents had been married, Daddy sometimes worked as a mechanic at the local body shop. Or he drove a truck, making a run from Dallas to Houston and back a few times a week. After The Divorce last year, Mama got full custody of Paige. Daddy was supposed to pay money for her food and clothes, but he hadn't done so yet. She had only seen him once, on Christmas Day, and that was only for an hour. He'd showed up two hours late and had driven her to the local park. They sat on a picnic bench and she watched him drink a six-pack.

When he drank, three things happened. After the first two beers, he became funny and charming. After two more, he grew loud and belligerent. That was when she had to be careful around him. One wrong word would set him off—and when he was mean, he would yell and sometimes hit her. Another two beers in him, and Daddy grew sappy and sleepy. He'd cry a little and then say he was sorry. Then he'd fall asleep.

On Christmas, he'd actually asked her a few questions about school at first. She'd told him about winning the school spelling bee and how she'd done more push-ups and sit-ups in the fitness challenge than any other girl in her entire elementary school. He'd listened in that distracted way and then apologized, saying he didn't have a present for her because things had been tight. When he finished the third beer, she put some distance between them, going to sit on the swings and staying there even as he yelled at her and told her she was just as worthless as her mother. By the time he opened the last beer in the six-pack, he was blubbering and telling her how sorry he was.

Paige doubted things would ever change.

She waited until he put his head down on his forearms before she left the swings and came closer. His loud snores let her know it was time to leave. Mama had told her even before The Divorce never to get in the car with Daddy when he was drunk. She walked the two miles home, thankful it was just cold and not windy. Cold, she could take. Cold and windy, and she was miserable. When she grew up, she was going to be a famous writer and travel the world. She would have a house on the beach and another one in the mountains, two places she'd never seen in person, but she liked the looks of them on TV.

Mama had taken one look at Paige when she got home and wrapped her arms about her daughter. They might not have much, but they had each other. And Nana. After The Divorce, they had moved from their trailer into Nana's small house, a few blocks off the Sugar Springs town square. Paige and Mama shared a bed and room, but it was so peaceful at her grandmother's house. No one yelled. No one hit. The house was just full of love—and the good smells from Nana's baking.

The teacher asked Paige to collect the spelling tests and she did so, each student passing them to the front of the row so she could come by and gather them. Miss Biggs then told everyone to take out their books for thirty minutes of free reading time. The class went once a week to the library and checked out a book for free read. Paige always finished hers by the next day. Because of that, she got to help Miss Biggs while the other students in the class read. Not even Danny Henderson got to be a helper like Paige because Miss Biggs had told Danny he was fast but careless, and accuracy was important.

Handing Miss Biggs the stack of papers, the teacher said, "Would you like to grade these for me, Paige?"

"Yes, ma'am," she said with enthusiasm.

"Let's pull yours out first and see how you did."

Miss Biggs located it and skimmed a finger along the twenty-five words. Smiling, she said, "Perfect, as always." She marked *100* on the top of the page. "You may use yours as the key, Paige. Remember, no half-offs. Each word must be legible and the entire word spelled correctly to receive full credit."

"Yes, ma'am."

She'd done this before, many times. Miss Biggs didn't even need to give her a points chart. Paige just did the math in her head and took four points off for each misspelled word, placing the score at the top of the paper. If someone had a perfect score, she would draw smiley faces inside the two zeroes of the *100*.

Glancing up after she finished grading the stack of spelling tests, she saw Danny Henderson glaring at her. She narrowed her eyes and glared right back. He rolled his eyes and mouthed a dirty word and went back to his book. She didn't tattle on him. Mama had told her not to, saying Danny was a bully and that Paige should ignore him.

She brought the papers to Miss Biggs, who gave her a

note to take to the office. Paige loved being in the halls when no one else was in them. It was as if the entire school belonged to her. She loved school. Mama said that was a good thing because if Paige wanted to go to college, she would need to do well in school and earn a scholarship. Mama had gone a year to community college and said she always regretted not having more education. But Daddy had come along and charmed her into marriage.

She wondered what Daddy had been like before the drinking. She had looked at pictures of her parents in those early years. They looked so young and happy. Mama was thirty now, but Paige thought she looked much older than that. And Daddy had looked terrible on Christmas, with his bloodshot eyes and uncombed hair and stubble on his face. Paige swore she would never get married and if she did, her husband would never drink and he would shave every day.

After she returned from her trip to the office and reading time ended, they broke into groups for a half-hour to work on a Social Studies project, then it was time for lunch and then recess. She had her usual peanut butter and grape jelly sandwich, along with a banana. It was the lunch she had started making for herself so that Mama didn't have to. Paige had learned to do lots of things for herself when she was young. Mama had worked in a restaurant before The Divorce and she always said customers at night tipped better. Daddy was supposed to stay with Paige when Mama waited tables nights, but he rarely did. She had learned to take a bath and brush her teeth and hair and put herself to bed, even saying her prayers, while Daddy was out doing whatever he did with whomever he did it.

It was okay. They were okay. The Divorce had been good for them. It let her and Mama live with Nana and she didn't have to worry about Daddy yelling at her or slapping her or punching Mama. Paige didn't realize how tense everything at home was until after The Divorce and they moved to Nana's. Nana baked banana bread, cakes, and pies, and she cooked a heavenly goulash. She hummed when she did her housework and let Paige watch TV. She and Paige worked in the vegetable garden together. Life was blissful, one of this week's spelling words.

At recess, her stomach dropped to her knees when she saw Daddy standing at the far end of the schoolyard. He was on the other side of the fence and beckoned her— another spelling word last week—to come over. She did so. Reluctantly.

"Hi, baby girl," he said.

She ran her eyes up and down him. He was dressed decently, his clothes clean, a flannel shirt and a pair of jeans. His eyes were clear. He smiled, all his attention on her, and suddenly Paige could see how Mama might have fallen in love with a younger version of him.

"Hey, Daddy," she said cautiously. "Why're you here? I haven't seen you in four months. Not since Christmas."

"I wanted to apologize about Christmas," he began. "I was in a bad place back then. I want to make it up to you. What about after school I take you to get some ice cream?"

Her belly did a flip-flop, her guard still up. Daddy had never taken her for ice cream, not once in her life. Her body tingled in a funny way, and she knew she shouldn't trust him.

"I've got newspaper club today," she told him, hoping he would understand. "We're turning in our stories and deciding what'll be in the newspaper we put out next week. It's our April edition. It'll be published before Easter."

"I'll bet you have a great story for them," he praised.

"I do. Two, in fact."

He looked pleadingly at her. "Could you turn your stories in and then go for ice cream with me? Please?"

Against her better judgment, Paige heard herself say, "Okay. But just for a little while. And you'll need to drop me off a block from home."

Anger suddenly sparked in his eyes. "Why? Does that old woman still talk bad about me?"

"Nana never talks bad about you," she said, defending her grandmother. "She never talks about you at all."

"Hmm."

Glancing over her shoulder, Paige said, "I need to go. Recess is over."

"All right, baby girl."

"I'm not a baby anymore, Daddy. I'm in fourth grade. I'm nine—almost ten."

He grinned. "Whatever you say. See you soon."

Paige ran and fell in at the back of the line of students entering the building. She focused on the math worksheet waiting on her desk, not wanting to think about Daddy or The Divorce or what Mama might say about her skipping newspaper club to go eat a treat with Daddy.

When the bell rang, Miss Biggs dismissed them, reminding them newspaper club would start in ten minutes.

She let the class file out before she approached Miss Biggs, her two stories in hand.

"Miss Biggs? I can't stay today—but here are my stories. One is on the Sugar Springs farmers' market starting back up. The other is the interview I did with the fire chief."

Her teacher accepted them. "Oh, I'll bet they are wonderful, Paige. You are such a strong writer. It is a delight to read your work."

"I want to be a writer when I grow up."

Miss Biggs smiled approvingly. "I think you'll make for a terrific writer. I'm sorry you can't stay today."

She thought Miss Biggs would have asked her why she couldn't stay after school, but she didn't. Paige said goodbye and returned to her desk, collecting her backpack and heading out the front door of the school. She glanced up and down the street, not seeing Daddy. A tiny part of her felt disappointed. He'd probably already forgotten he promised to take her for ice cream. It sure would've tasted good, now that spring had arrived.

Dejected, she turned east and began walking home, not in the mood to go back to newspaper club. She hadn't gone two blocks when a horn honked beside her. Turning, she saw a black pickup truck, Daddy behind the wheel.

"Get in," he called cheerfully.

She did so, asking, "When did you get a new truck?"

"Oh, I borrowed it from a friend. I did a few favors for him, and he's letting me use it for a while."

"Oh."

She buckled her seatbelt and locked her door, always conscious about safety, especially with her father behind the wheel. But she hadn't smelled any beer on his breath. His eyes still looked bright and clear. Relaxing, she began answering his questions about school.

Then Paige realized they were leaving town. Panic filled her.

"Where are we going?"

"Oh, just the next town over from Sugar Springs. They've got a new ice cream place. I think you'll like it."

Uneasiness filled her. She tamped it down, wanting to trust him, wanting desperately for him to be a dad like all the other dads.

He pointed to the cup holder. "Hey, I got you a drink. You still like lemonade, right?"

"Yes. Thank you."

Paige was thirsty and drank the cold, refreshing lemonade quickly. Lemonade was a treat she didn't get very often.

They were on the highway now. She sighed, feeling sleepy. Her eyelids grew heavy and she leaned her head against the window.

When she woke up, it was dark.

And they were still driving.

"Daddy? Where are we? Where are we going?" she demanded, keeping her tone even though panic swelled within her, causing her heart to race.

He turned, his face no longer affable—a spelling word from two weeks ago.

"We're going away for a bit," he informed her, his voice harder now.

"Where? Why?"

"Because I need to punish that bitch," he spat out.

She sensed the waves of anger rolling off him and wanted to make herself small. Then she noticed the open beer can in the cup holder next to him.

And three others crushed and in the floorboard beneath her feet.

"She ruined everything," he railed. "She couldn't like me for who I am. She was always complaining. She said I couldn't see you."

"That was the court, Daddy. And they did say you could—"

"Shut your trap!" he roared, slamming his fist into her belly.

Pain filled her, followed by terror when she couldn't breathe. He hadn't hit her in a long time. She was out of practice. The air would come. It just took a minute. Her brain told her not to worry, that her insides were paralyzed, but they would unfreeze.

When they did, she gasped air into her lungs, breathing quick and hard. She realized now he had drugged her. The dashboard clock said eight forty-eight. She had no idea where they were or how far away from Sugar Springs they'd gone. Mama would be getting home soon. Nana would be worried. They would call the police. They would look for her. They had to. Please, God, let them find her.

Daddy continuing cursing and badmouthing Mama. What Paige got out of his rant—a last year spelling word that fit Daddy's words to perfection---was that he didn't really want her. He just didn't want Mama and Nana to have her. She worried he might kill her and dump her body somewhere. She had to pretend to like him. Pretend to like what he was doing.

It just might save her life.

"Thank you, Daddy."

His head whipped toward her. "For what?" he asked, suspicion in his eyes.

"For coming for me. I always liked you better than Mama. I'm glad we can live together. I know you said you don't want me, but I can be good, Daddy. I can help you. I'll clean and cook for you. I'll take care of you. You'll be so happy you came and got me."

"Huh."

They drove on into the night.

"You'll need a new name. We both will."

Smiling brightly, hoping he bought into her act, Paige asked, "Can I pick it, Daddy? My new name?"

"Sure," he said agreeably, surprising her.

"I think I'll be Nancy," she said. "After Nancy Drew. She's a girl detective. Nana bought me some of the books at a garage sale, three for a quarter, and I—"

"Don't talk about her again," Daddy warned.

Paige played dumb. "Nancy Drew?"

"No, that woman. Or your mama."

"Oh, okay." Her mind raced, knowing she walked a tightrope. "But I can still be Nancy, right?"

"Sure. Be whoever the hell you want to be. Doesn't matter to me."

That worried Paige. It still sounded as if he were going to do something to her.

Well, she would do something first. She would get away. She would be smart like Nancy Drew always was.

And when she got back to Sugar Springs, she would never leave it. Ever again.

TANNER HADDOCK WASHED DOWN HIS BURGER AND FRIES with a Coke, enjoying the burn in his throat from the soft drink. Summertime was meant for drinking a cold Coke over crushed ice, and on this hot, late summer evening, the soft drink had hit the spot.

"Ready for dessert?" his mom asked.

"Really?"

"Whatever you want," his dad added. "Pie. Ice cream. Call it an early birthday celebration."

Annie, who owned the diner, came over. "Any dessert tonight, folks?"

He grinned. "I'd like a chocolate soda. Vanilla ice cream with chocolate syrup. About half the glass filled with the soda water."

Annie smiled. "Three scoops good enough, Tanner?"

"Yes, ma'am!"

"Pie for Helen and me," Dad said. "Apple for both of us, Annie. Hold the ice cream."

"You got it." Annie jotted their orders onto her notepad and moved toward the counter.

"Thanks again, Dad," Tanner said.

"You pitched a good game today, son. I thought a little treat would be nice."

His parents started talking about a cow whose milk had dried up. Bored, he stared out the window, watching a truck pull into the parking lot. A man got out and motioned. A girl climbed out from the driver's side. Tanner thought that odd, wondering why she didn't get out on her side of the truck. Maybe the door was broken. But the truck looked pretty new.

As they moved across the parking lot, the man placed his hand on the girl's neck. She winced, keeping her head down.

Something didn't seem right.

His dad had always told him to pay attention to details. Not that Tanner wanted to go into police work, a job where you had to really look at the nitty-gritty. He wanted to either be a famous baseball player or an actor. Maybe both. Either way, he knew he wanted to leave Owens, Oklahoma. Living in a small town, everyone knew who he was, especially with Dad being the chief of police. He wanted to go somewhere that had a million people or more, not the two thousand plus in Owens. He wanted to see the world. Make money. Discover new things about himself.

The door to the diner opened and the man moved the

girl through the opening. They had to be father and daughter. At least he thought they must be. Then he decided that he shouldn't assume anything.

"Sit anywhere you'd like," Annie called from behind the counter.

His family were the only customers in the diner since it was almost nine and closing time. Most people had eaten dinner long ago. They'd come from a baseball tournament two towns over, and Mom had suggested grabbing a quick dinner after his dad had stopped and changed a flat tire for the Baptist preacher's wife on their way home. His little sister, Alana, was spending the night with a friend, so they didn't have to worry about getting home to relieve a babysitter.

Now, he watched the man pick a table in the corner, his eyes searching the place. The girl sat, her head still bowed.

Tanner got a bad feeling. He continued watching them as Annie delivered dessert to the Haddocks, his father digging into the pie with gusto, his mother taking dainty bites. Tanner sipped some of the soda and then spooned ice cream into his mouth.

Annie took the newcomers' orders and then the girl said something to the man. He nodded and they both stood up, Again, he put his hand on her neck, guiding her past their table.

Tanner's gaze connected with the girl's for a brief moment, and then they passed. He glanced down and saw she held her left hand out, palm facing him.

Help.

That was the word dug into her palm.

Cold fear puddled in his belly. Quickly, he swung his head around and watched them continue toward the restrooms. He turned and looked at his dad, who was talking and laughing.

"Gotta go to the restroom. Be right back," he said, sliding from the booth and following the pair through the door.

The girl went into the ladies' restroom. The man stayed in the tight space that led to both restrooms.

"Uh, excuse me," Tanner said, brushing past the man and entering the men's restroom.

Inside, his brain was spinning in fast-forward. The man lingering outside the door, waiting for the girl, was weird enough. She had to be at least nine or ten and should've been able to go to the restroom herself. But the fact that she'd carved *HELP* into her hand told him she was in trouble. Big trouble.

He washed his hands and left, the man still hovering outside, waiting for the girl. Squeezing past the man again, he looked up. What he saw in the guy's eyes frightened him.

Tanner hurried back to the table and interrupted his mother's story. "Dad."

Mom frowned. "Tanner, you know not to—"

"There's a girl in trouble in the restroom," he hissed. "I watched her and maybe a guy who's her dad come in. He keeps his hand on her neck. He guided her into the diner and then to the restroom. He didn't even go himself. He's just waiting for her."

"Well, some fathers are a little overprotective," Dad said, frowning slightly.

"No," he insisted. "I saw her hand. She held it out to me when she passed our booth." He swallowed. "Dad, it said *HELP*."

Immediately, his father's demeanor changed. "You saw that word?"

"Yes," he said, nodding vigorously. "Like she'd carved it there. She needs us, Dad."

His father's eyes glanced to the back and then returned to Tanner. "They're coming," he said quietly, taking a bite of pie.

As the two moved passed their table, Tanner noticed the girl kept her hands by her side this time. The hand with her cry for help was on the far side and couldn't be easily seen anyway. She was smart not to try again a second time.

Once the pair returned to their table, Dad said, "Stay right here. I'll be back. Don't look at them. He might spook."

Dad scooted from the booth and called to Annie, "Left my wallet in the car. Be right back."

Keeping his eyes on Mom, Tanner asked, "Is Dad calling for back-up?"

Mom had her back to the man and girl. She nodded. "He will. He'll also run the plates. See if the vehicle is stolen and who it's registered to." She reached out a hand and he gave her his. "That was very brave of you, Tanner. And very observant. Let's just hope this girl isn't in trouble. That it's all a misunderstanding."

"She is, Mom," he said earnestly. "I can tell. She doesn't look up. She's not talking. Girls are always talking, all the time."

He remembered the look in her green eyes in that brief moment when their gazes had connected. Something told him he would always remember those eyes.

Dad reentered the diner and slid into the booth. "Let's get the two of you out of here now," he said quietly. "Helen, take Tanner. Go to the car and lock the doors."

Tanner had barely touched his chocolate soda but it didn't matter. He couldn't eat it. Not when that girl was in trouble.

"Check, Annie," Dad said, standing to let Mom out of the booth.

"Right away, Chief. Let me get this order out." She scooped up two baskets from where the cook had pushed them through the pass-through window and headed across the diner.

As he pushed out of the booth, Tanner watched the man react to hearing Annie call her dad that. His eyes narrowed. He frowned. Tanner looked away and could sense the stranger's gaze boring into his family.

"Changed my mind. We need these to go," he told Annie as she set the food on their table.

"Okay. Give me a minute to box them up for you, sir." Annie took out her pad from her apron's pocket and tore off the ticket, placing it on the table. "Here's your check."

She turned to leave, baskets in hand again. Tanner's heart raced as he glanced up. His gaze met that of the girl's once more. In it, he saw both sadness and fear.

The stranger jerked her to her feet and moved them toward the door.

"Dad, he's leaving with her. Stop him," he begged.

Dad slipped his gun from its holster. "You two get under the table. Now," he urged, and Mom slipped into the booth again, both of them immediately sliding beneath the table.

His dad raised his gun. "Stop right there!" he said, his voice calm and firm and full of authority.

Tanner could still see from his vantage point and watched the man whirl, his left hand tightening on the girl's neck as his right jerked a pistol free, swinging it up, pointing it at Tanner's dad.

Annie screamed. He heard two shots fired almost simultaneously, the noise deafening. His father grunted and fell back two steps, giving Tanner a good view of the blood that stained his dad's shoulder.

"Dad!" he cried, scrambling out.

"I'm okay, son."

"You're shot!" Mom cried, bursting from the floor.

Tanner did the same, except he looked to the other side of the diner. The stranger had collapsed on the floor, his body still. Blood pooled around his head. Tanner knew the man was dead.

He was drawn, though, to the girl. She stood stock-still, gazing down at the body. Her own started trembling as she looked up. Tanner moved to her and stopped in front of her.

"Thank you," she said, tears welling in her eyes and then spilling down her cheeks. "You saw my message."

He reached for her hand and lifted it, her palm facing up. The four letters were etched into the smooth skin, an angry red in contrast to the white of her skin. He searched her face.

"I did it and didn't know if anyone would ever see it. I tried showing it a few times."

Tanner said, "You are very brave."

"Thank you," she whispered, tears pooling in her emerald eyes.

Sirens sounded in the distance, and he supposed Annie or someone had called for help.

"Come meet my dad."

He took her wrist, afraid to hold her hand because it might hurt her, and led her toward his parents. Mom had called for clean dish towels and had wrapped them around Dad's shoulder.

"Dad? This is—"

He stopped because he hadn't even asked the girl her name.

"I'm Paige," she said, her head held high, her voice strong. "And I want to go home."

Dad smiled. "We'll get you home, Paige. I promise you that."

"Thank you," she said softly. "He . . . He was my daddy. But he was a bad man. Can I call Mama and Nana now? I know they're worried about me."

Mom produced her cell phone and stepped to the girl, wrapping a protective arm about her. "You can use mine, honey. Let's go outside and sit in the car."

"Good idea," Dad said.

As Mom led Paige away, she turned over her shoulder and mouthed, "Thank you," to Tanner.

He smiled and gave a wave.

With his good arm, Dad drew Tanner into a bear hug. "You did something wonderful tonight, son. You saved that girl's life."

Tanner knew he would never forget this night.

Or Paige.

ALSO BY ALEXA ASTON

Hollywood Flirt

Hollywood Player

Hollywood Double

Hollywood Enigma

LAWMEN OF THE WEST

Runaway Hearts

Blind Faith

Love and the Lawman

Ballad Beauty

SAGEBRUSH BRIDES

A Game of Chance

Written in the Cards

Outlaw Muse

KNIGHTS OF REDEMPTION

A Bit of Heaven on Earth

A Knight for Kallen

SUDDENLY A DUKE

Portrait of the Duke

Music for the Duke

Polishing the Duke

Designs on the Duke

Fashioning the Duke

Love Blooms with the Duke

Training the Duke

Investigating the Duke

SECOND SONS OF LONDON

Educated by the Earl

Debating with the Duke

Empowered by the Earl

Made for the Marquess

Dubious about the Duke

Valued by the Viscount

Meant for the Marquess

DUKES DONE WRONG

Discouraging the Duke

Deflecting the Duke

Disrupting the Duke

Delighting the Duke

Destiny with a Duke

DUKES OF DISTINCTION

Duke of Renown

Duke of Charm

Duke of Disrepute

Duke of Arrogance

Duke of Honor

SOLDIERS AND SOULMATES

To Heal an Earl

To Tame a Rogue

To Trust a Duke

To Save a Love

To Win a Widow

THE ST. CLAIRS

Devoted to the Duke

Midnight with the Marquess

Embracing the Earl

Defending the Duke

Suddenly a St. Clair

STANDALONE ROMANTIC THRILLERS

Leave Yesterday Behind

Illusions of Death

ABOUT THE AUTHOR

USA Today and Amazon Top 100 bestselling author Alexa Aston lives with her husband in a Dallas suburb, where she eats her fair share of dark chocolate and plots out stories while she walks every morning. She enjoys travel, sports, and binge-watching—and never misses an episode of *Survivor*.

Alexa brings her characters to life in steamy historicals, contemporary romances, and romantic suspense novels that resonate with passion, intensity, and heart.

KEEP UP WITH ALEXA
Visit her website
Newsletter Sign-Up

MORE WAYS TO CONNECT WITH ALEXA

www.ingramcontent.com/pod-product-compliance
Lightning Source LLC
Chambersburg PA
CBHW050505110726
47899CB00005B/1337